THE CAMPFIRE
COLLECTION

THRILLING, CHILLING
TALES OF
ALIEN ENCOUNTERS

THE CAMPFIRE COLLECTION
THRILLING, CHILLING TALES OF
ALIEN ENCOUNTERS

Edited by Gina Hyams

Introduction by Michael Berry

CHRONICLE BOOKS
SAN FRANCISCO

Cover photographs copyright ©
Antonio M. Rosario/The Image Bank,
Ben Stockley/Stone.

Pages 252–253 constitute a continuation of
the copyright page.

Library of Congress Cataloging-in-
Publication Data:

The campfire collection : thrilling, chilling
tales of alien encounters / edited by Gina
Hyams ; introduction by Michael Berry.

p. cm.

ISBN 0-8118-4514-1

1. Science fiction, American. 2. Human-
alien encounters—Fiction. I. Hyams, Gina.

PS648.S3C36 2005

813'.0876208—dc22

2004022554

Manufactured in Canada

Designed by Jacob T. Gardner
Typeset in Trade Gothic and Joanna MT

Distributed in Canada by
Raincoast Books
9050 Shaughnessy Street
Vancouver, British Columbia V6P 6E5

10 9 8 7 6 5 4 3 2 1

Chronicle Books LLC
85 Second Street
San Francisco, California 94105

www.chroniclebooks.com

PART III ALIEN ABDUCTIONS

INTRODUCTION

I have never been abducted. There are no ominous gaps of "lost time" in my memory. Beyond the minor indignities of an annual physical, no probes have ever been jammed into my nostrils or other orifices. I bear no mysterious scars. The Men in Black have never knocked upon my front door.

And yet, I have seen a UFO. I'm sure of it. I have witnesses who will back me up.

When I was growing up in Portsmouth, New Hampshire, northern New England was reputed to be a hotbed of extraterrestrial activity. Few of us sensible Yankees gave much thought to this matter. Residents of a city whose main industry was building nuclear submarines, we were more concerned about being invaded by the Soviets than by any Martians.

One warm night in the early eighties, my friends Tom, Ken, and I were riding along the beach road in my parents' big, red Plymouth Satellite, staving off boredom with banter and beer. We stopped at Odiorne Point State Park, just over the town border in Rye, a favorite late-night hangout. We climbed a small hill that overlooked the parking lot and some service buildings. We sat and talked about the things that interest college students during their summer breaks.

At some point, Tom grabbed my arm and whispered, "What's that?"

"What?" I said.

"That light!"

I looked. There was a big, bright, white light just above the roof of the bathhouse. Presumably it had been placed there so no one would trip on the stairs in the dark.

I said, "That's the light over the bathhouse. What's your problem?"

And then the light suddenly dimmed to half its intensity—and moved.

We certainly knew that mysterious light at Odiorne Point was Not Right. It moved in spooky silence, without even the whisper of any motor. It dipped and weaved at angles not likely for any kind of aircraft with which I am familiar. It was not a weather balloon. It was not swamp gas.

The light hovered over the bathhouse for a few minutes, then zigged and zagged through the air until it was out over the dark water, where it was joined by two other glowing, silent objects. Ken, Tom, and I watched open-mouthed as these lights flew out to sea and then disappeared from view. We ran for the car.

From a restaurant pay phone, Ken called Pease Air Force Base in near-by Newington and asked if they had received any reports of strange lights in the sky. They claimed not to know what the hell we were talking about. (Although of course they would say that, wouldn't they?)

I have no explanation for what we saw that night. That's why I am confident in saying that it was an Unidentified Flying Object. It was definitely something that flew and that could not be recognized.

In each of the stories in this collection, there comes a moment when the characters realize that Something Is Not Right. A missile from Mars lands in a Texas pasture in Howard Waldrop's "Night of the Cooters." In Ray Nelson's "Eight O'Clock in the Morning," a man awakens from hypnosis suddenly able to see the hideous visages of Earth's alien conquerors.

It's good to be reminded occasionally that not everything can be explained, that it is still possible to witness a genuine mystery. That's part of why I've always loved science fiction, from the time I first read a "Classics Illustrated" comics version of The War of the Worlds by H. G. Wells. As my tastes matured, science fiction brought to me a galaxy of tantalizing possibilities, not merely about the existence of UFOs, but about such topics as time travel, immortality, artificial intelligence, biotechnology, and human space travel. Far more than just an entertainment for adolescents, it is a vital body of literature that keeps me captivated and astonished after nearly two decades as a professional reviewer.

Many of the genre's most influential and best-loved writers, from Stephen King to Philip K. Dick, from Kristine Kathryn Rusch to James Tiptree Jr. are represented in this volume. Take this book with you to a quiet, dark place like Odiorne Point, gather your friends, and read the words of men and women who can imagine more than what we can see right in front of us. Let the tales open your mind to the possibility that, for good or ill, we're not alone in the universe.

And keep watching the skies.

— Michael Berry

PART I CLOSE ENCOUNTERS

I AM THE DOORWAY
BY STEPHEN KING

Richard and I sat on my porch, looking out over the dunes to the Gulf. The smoke from his cigar drifted mellowly in the air, keeping the mosquitoes at a safe distance. The water was a cool aqua, the sky a deeper, truer blue. It was a pleasant combination.

"You are the doorway," Richard repeated thoughtfully. "You are sure you killed the boy—you didn't just dream it?"

"I didn't dream it. And I didn't kill him, either—I told you that. They did. I am the doorway."

Richard sighed. "You buried him?"

"Yes."

"You remember where?"

"Yes." I reached into my breast pocket and got a cigarette. My hands were awkward with their covering of bandages. They itched abominably. "If you want to see it, you'll have to get the dune buggy. You can't roll this"—I indicated my wheelchair—"through the sand." Richard's dune buggy was a 1959 VW with pillow-sized tires. He collected driftwood in it. Ever since he retired from the real estate business in Maryland he had been living on Key Caroline and building driftwood sculptures which he sold to the winter tourists at shameless prices.

He puffed his cigar and looked out at the Gulf. "Not yet. Will you tell me once more?"

I sighed and tried to light my cigarette. He took the matches away from me and did it himself. I puffed twice, dragging deep. The itch in my fingers was maddening.

"All right," I said. "Last night at seven I was out here, looking at the Gulf and smoking, just like now, and—"

"Go further back," he invited.

"Further?"

"Tell me about the flight."

I shook my head. "Richard, we've been through it and through it. There's nothing—"

The seamed and fissured face was as enigmatic as one of his own driftwood sculptures. "You may remember," he said. "Now you may remember."

"Do you think so?"

"Possibly. And when you're through, we can look for the grave."

"The grave," I said. It had a hollow, horrible ring, darker than anything, darker even than all that terrible ocean Cory and I had sailed through five years ago. Dark, dark, dark.

Beneath the bandages, my new eyes stared blindly into the darkness the bandages forced on them. They itched.

* * *

Cory and I were boosted into orbit by the Saturn 16, the one all the commentators called the Empire State Building booster. It was a big beast, all right. It made the old Saturn 1-B look like a Redstone, and it took off from a bunker two hundred feet deep—it had to, to keep from taking half of Cape Kennedy with it.

We swung around the earth, verifying all our systems, and then did our inject. Headed out for Venus. We left a Senate fighting over an appropriations bill for further deep-space exploration, and a bunch of NASA people praying that we would find something, anything.

"It don't matter what," Don Lovinger, Project Zeus's private whiz kid, was very fond of saying when he'd had a few. "You got all the gadgets, plus five souped-up TV cameras and a nifty little telescope with a zillion lenses and filters. Find some gold or platinum. Better yet, find some nice, dumb little blue men for us to study and exploit and feel superior to. Anything. Even the ghost of Howdy Doody would be a start."

Cory and I were anxious enough to oblige, if we could. Nothing had worked for the deep-space program. From Borman, Anders, and Lovell, who orbited the moon in '68 and found an empty, forbidding world that looked like dirty beach sand, to Markhan and Jacks, who touched down on Mars eleven years later to find an arid wasteland of frozen sand and a few struggling lichens, the deep-space program had been an expensive bust. And there had been casualties—Pedersen and Lederer, eternally circling the sun when all at once nothing worked on the second-to-last Apollo flight. John Davis, whose little orbiting observatory was holed by a meteoroid in a one-in-a-thousand fluke. No, the space program was hardly swinging along. The way things looked, the Venus orbit might be our last chance to say we told you so.

It was sixteen days out—we ate a lot of concentrates, played a lot of gin, and swapped a cold back and forth—and from the tech side it was a milk run. We lost an air-moisture converter on the third day out, went to backup, and that was all, except for nits and nats, until re-entry. We watched Venus grow from a star to a quarter to a milky crystal ball, swapped jokes with Huntsville Control, listened to tapes of Wagner and the Beatles, tended to automated experiments which had to do with everything from measurements of the solar wind to deep-space navigation. We did two midcourse corrections, both of them infinitesimal, and nine days into the flight Cory went outside and banged on the retractable DESA until it decided to operate. There was nothing else out of the ordinary until . . .

"DESA," Richard said. "What's that?"

"An experiment that didn't pan out. NASA-ese for Deep Space Antenna—we were broadcasting pi in high-frequency pulses for anyone who cared to listen." I rubbed my fingers against my pants, but it was no good; if anything, it made it worse. "Same idea as that radio telescope in West Virginia—you know, the one that listens to the stars. Only instead of listening, we were transmitting, primarily to the deeper space planets— Jupiter, Saturn, Uranus. If there's any intelligent life out there, it was taking a nap."

"Only Cory went out?"

"Yes. And if he brought in any interstellar plague, the telemetry didn't show it."

"Still—"

"It doesn't matter," I said crossly. "Only the here and now matters. They killed the boy last night, Richard. It wasn't a nice thing to watch—or feel. His head . . . it exploded. As if someone had scooped out his brains and put a hand grenade in his skull."

"Finish the story," he said.

I laughed hollowly. "What's to tell?"

*   *   *

We went into an eccentric orbit around the planet. It was radical and deteriorating, three twenty by seventy-six miles. That was on the first swing. The second swing our apogee was even higher, the perigee lower. We had a max of four orbits. We made all four. We got a good look at the planet. Also over six hundred stills and God knows how many feet of film.

The cloud cover is equal parts methane, ammonia, dust, and flying shit. The whole planet looks like the Grand Canyon in a wind tunnel. Cory estimated windspeed at about 600 mph near the surface. Our probe beeped all the way down and then went out with a squawk. We saw no vegetation and no sign of life. Spectroscope indicated only traces of the valuable minerals. And that was Venus. Nothing but nothing—except it scared me. It was like circling a haunted house in the middle of deep space. I know how unscientific that sounds, but I was scared gutless until we got out of there.

I think if our rockets hadn't gone off, I would have cut my throat on the way down. It's not like the moon. The moon is desolate but somehow antiseptic. That world we saw was utterly unlike anything that anyone has ever seen. Maybe it's a good thing that cloud cover is there. It was like a skull that's been picked clean—that's the closest I can get.

On the way back we heard the Senate had voted to halve space-exploration funds. Cory said something like "looks like we're back in the weather-satellite business, Artie." But I was almost glad. Maybe we don't belong out there.

Twelve days later Cory was dead and I was crippled for life. We bought all our trouble on the way down. The chute was fouled. How's that for life's little ironies? We'd been in space for over a month, gone further than any humans had ever gone, and it all ended the way it did because some guy was in a hurry for his coffee break and let a few lines get fouled.

We came down hard. A guy that was in one of the copters said it looked like a gigantic baby falling out of the sky, with the placenta trailing after it. I lost consciousness when we hit.

I came to when they were taking me across the deck of the *Portland*. They hadn't even had a chance to roll up the red carpet we were supposed to've walked on. I was bleeding. Bleeding and being hustled up to the infirmary over a red carpet that didn't look anywhere near as red as I did . . .

*   *   *

". . . I was in Bethesda for two years. They gave me the Medal of Honor and a lot of money and this wheelchair. I came down here the next year. I like to watch the rockets take off."

"I know," Richard said. He paused. "Show me your hands."

"No." It came out very quickly and sharply. "I can't let them see. I've told you that."

"It's been five years," Richard said. "Why now, Arthur? Can you tell me that?"

"I don't know. I don't know! Maybe whatever it is has a long gestation period. Or who's to say I even got it out there? Whatever it was might have entered me in Fort Lauderdale. Or right here on this porch, for all I know."

Richard sighed and looked out over the water, now reddish with the late-evening sun. "I'm trying. Arthur, I don't want to think that you are losing your mind."

"If I have to, I'll show you my hands," I said. It cost me an effort to say it. "But only if I have to."

Richard stood up and found his cane. He looked old and frail. "I'll get the dune buggy. We'll look for the boy."

"Thank you, Richard."

He walked out toward the rutted dirt track that led to his cabin—I could just see the roof of it over the Big Dune, the one that runs almost the whole length of Key Caroline. Over the water toward the Cape, the sky had gone an ugly plum color, and the sound of thunder came faintly to my ears.

*   *   *

I didn't know the boy's name but I saw him every now and again, walking along the beach at sunset, with his sieve under his arm. He was tanned almost black by the sun, and all he was ever clad in was a frayed pair of denim cutoffs. On the far side of Key Caroline there is a public beach, and an enterprising young man can make perhaps as much as five dollars on a good day, patiently sieving the sand for buried quarters or dimes. Every now and then I would wave to him and he would wave back, both of us noncommittal, strangers yet brothers, year-round dwellers set against a sea of money-spending, Cadillac-driving, loud-mouthed tourists. I imagine he lived in the small village clustered around the post office about a half mile further down.

When he passed by that evening I had already been on the porch for an hour, immobile, watching. I had taken off the bandages earlier. The itching had been intolerable, and it was always better when they could look through their eyes.

It was a feeling like no other in the world—as if I were a portal just slightly ajar through which they were peeking at a world which they hated and feared. But the worst part was that I could see, too, in a way. Imagine your mind transported into a body of a housefly, a housefly looking into your own face with a thousand eyes. Then perhaps you can begin to see why I kept my hands bandaged even when there was no one around to see them.

It began in Miami. I had business there with a man named Cresswell, an investigator from the Navy Department. He checks up on me once a year—for a while I was as close as anyone ever gets to the classified stuff our space program has. I don't know just what it is he looks for; a shifty gleam in the eye, maybe, or maybe a scarlet letter on my forehead. God knows why. My pension is large enough to be almost embarrassing.

Cresswell and I were sitting on the terrace of his hotel room, sipping drinks and discussing the future of the U.S. space program. It was about three-fifteen. My fingers began to itch. It wasn't a bit gradual. It was switched on like electric current. I mentioned it to Cresswell.

"So you picked up some poison ivy on that scrofulous little island," he said, grinning.

"The only foliage on Key Caroline is a little palmetto scrub," I said. "Maybe it's the seven-year itch." I looked down at my hands. Perfectly ordinary hands. But itchy.

Later in the afternoon I signed the same old paper ("I do solemnly swear that I have neither received nor disclosed and divulged information which would . . .") and drove myself back to the Key. I've got an old Ford, equipped with hand-operated brake and accelerator. I love it—it makes me feel self-sufficient.

It's a long drive back, down Route 1, and by the time I got off the big road and onto the Key Caroline exit ramp, I was nearly out of my mind. My hands itched maddeningly. If you have ever suffered through the healing of a deep cut or a surgical incision, you may have some idea of the kind of itch I mean. Live things seemed to be crawling and boring in my flesh.

The sun was almost down and I looked at my hands carefully in the glow of the dash lights. The tips of them were red now, red in tiny, perfect circlets, just above the pad where the fingerprint is, where you get calluses if you play guitar. There were also red circles of infection on the space between the first and second joint of each thumb and finger, and on the skin between the second joint and the knuckle. I pressed my right fingers to my lips and withdrew them quickly, with a sudden loathing. A feeling of dumb horror had risen in my throat, woolen and choking. The flesh where the red spots had appeared was hot, feverish, and the flesh was soft and gelid, like the flesh of an apple gone rotten.

I drove the rest of the way trying to persuade myself that I had indeed caught poison ivy somehow. But in the back of my mind there was another ugly thought. I had an aunt, back in my childhood, who lived the last ten years of her life closed off from the world in an upstairs room. My mother took her meals up, and her name was a forbidden topic. I found out later that she had Hansen's disease—leprosy.

When I got home I called Dr. Flanders on the mainland. I got his answering service instead. Dr. Flanders was on a fishing cruise, but if it was urgent, Dr. Ballanger—

"When will Dr. Flanders be back?"

"Tomorrow afternoon at the latest. Would that—"

"Sure."

I hung up slowly, then dialed Richard. I let it ring a dozen times before hanging up. After that I sat indecisive for a while. The itching had deepened. It seemed to emanate from the flesh itself.

I rolled my wheelchair over to the bookcase and pulled down the battered medical encyclopedia that I'd had for years. The book was maddeningly vague. It could have been anything, or nothing.

I leaned back and closed my eyes. I could hear the old ship's clock ticking on the shelf across the room. There was the high, thin drone of a jet on its way to Miami. There was the soft whisper of my own breath.

I was still looking at the book.

The realization crept on me, then sank home with a frightening rush. My eyes were closed, but I was still looking at the book. What I was seeing was smeary and monstrous, the distorted, fourth-dimensional counterpart of a book, yet unmistakable for all that.

And I was not the only one watching.

I snapped my eyes open, feeling the constriction of my heart. The sensation subsided a little, but not entirely. I was looking at the book, seeing the print and diagrams with my own eyes, perfectly normal everyday experience, and I was also seeing it from a different, lower angle and seeing it with other eyes. Seeing not a book but an alien thing, something of monstrous shape and ominous intent.

I raised my hands slowly to my face, catching an eerie vision of my living room turned into a horror house.

I screamed.

There were eyes peering up at me through slits in the flesh of my fingers. And even as I watched, the flesh was dilating, retreating, as they pushed their mindless way up to the surface.

But that was not what made me scream. I had looked into my own face and seen a monster.

* * *

The dune buggy nosed over the hill and Richard brought it to a halt next to the porch. The motor gunned and roared choppily. I rolled my wheelchair down the inclined plane to the right of the regular steps and Richard helped me in.

"All right, Arthur," he said. "It's your party. Where to?"

I pointed down toward the water, where the Big Dune finally begins to peter out. Richard nodded. The rear wheels spun sand and we were off. I usually found time to rib Richard about his driving, but I didn't bother tonight. There was too much else to think about—and to feel: they didn't want the dark, and I could feel them straining to see through the bandages, willing me to take them off.

The dune buggy bounced and roared through the sand toward the water, seeming almost to take flight from the tops of the small dunes. To the left the sun was going down in bloody glory. Straight ahead and across the water, the thunderclouds were beating their way toward us. Lightning forked at the water.

"Off to your right," I said. "By that lean-to."

Richard brought the dune buggy to a sand-spraying halt beside the rotted remains of the lean-to, reached into the back, and brought out a spade. I winced when I saw it. "Where?" Richard asked expressionlessly.

"Right there." I pointed to the place.

He got out and walked slowly through the sand to the spot, hesitated for a second, then plunged the shovel into the sand. It seemed that he dug for a very long time. The sand he was throwing back over his shoulder looked damp and moist. The thunderheads were darker, higher, and the water looked angry and implacable under their shadow and the reflected glow of the sunset.

I knew long before he stopped digging that he was not going to find the boy. They had moved him. I hadn't bandaged my hands last night, so they could see—and act. If they had been able to use me to kill the boy, they could use me to move him, even while I slept.

"There's no boy, Arthur." He threw the dirty shovel into the dune buggy and sat tiredly on the seat. The coming storm cast marching, crescent-shaped shadows along the sand. The rising breeze rattled sand against the buggy's rusted body. My fingers itched.

"They used me to move him," I said dully. "They're getting the upper hand, Richard. They're forcing their doorway open, a little at a time. A hundred times a day I find myself standing in front of some perfectly familiar object—a spatula, a picture, even a can of beans—with no idea how I got there, holding my hands out, showing it to them, seeing it as they do, as an obscenity, something twisted and grotesque —"

"Arthur," he said. "Arthur, don't. Don't." In the failing light his face was wan with compassion. "*Standing* in front of something, you said. *Moving* the boy's body, you said. *But you can't walk, Arthur.* You're dead from the waist down."

I touched the dashboard of the dune buggy. "This is dead, too. But when you enter it, you can make it go. You could make it kill. It couldn't stop you even if it wanted to." I could hear my voice rising hysterically. "I am the doorway, can't you understand that? They killed the boy, Richard! They moved the body!"

"I think you'd better see a medical man," he said quietly. "Let's go back. Let's—"

"Check! Check on the boy, then! Find out—"

"You said you didn't know his name."

"He must have been from the village. It's a small village. Ask——"

"I talked to Maud Harrington on the phone when I got the dune buggy. If anyone in the state has a longer nose, I've not come across her. I asked if she'd heard of anyone's boy not coming home last night. She said she hadn't."

"But he's a local! He has to be!"

He reached for the ignition switch, but I stopped him. He turned to look at me and I began to unwrap my hands.

From the Gulf, thunder muttered and growled.

*   *   *

I didn't go to the doctor and I didn't call Richard back. I spent three weeks with my hands bandaged every time I went out. Three weeks just blindly hoping it would go away. It wasn't a rational act; I can admit that. If I had been a whole man who didn't need a wheelchair for legs or who had spent a normal life in a normal occupation, I might have gone to Doc Flanders or to Richard. I still might have, if it hadn't been for the memory of my aunt, shunned, virtually a prisoner, being eaten alive by her own failing flesh. So I kept a desperate silence and prayed that I would wake up some morning and find it had been an evil dream.

And little by little, I felt them. Them. An anonymous intelligence. I never really wondered what they looked like or where they had come from. It was moot. I was their doorway, and their window on the world. I got enough feedback from them to feel their revulsion and horror, to know that our world was very different from theirs. Enough feedback to feel their blind hate. But still they watched. Their flesh was embedded in my own. I began to realize that they were using me, actually manipulating me.

When the boy passed, raising one hand in his usual noncommittal salute, I had just about decided to get in touch with Cresswell at his Navy Department number. Richard had been right about one thing—I was certain that whatever had gotten hold of me had done it in deep space or in that weird orbit around Venus. The Navy would study me, but they would not freakify me. I wouldn't have to wake up anymore into the creaking darkness and stifle a scream as I felt them watching, watching, watching.

My hands went out toward the boy and I realized that I had not bandaged them. I could see the eyes in the dying light, watching silently. They were huge, dilated, golden-irised. I had poked one of them against the tip of a pencil once, and had felt excruciating agony slam up my arm. The eye seemed to glare at me with a chained hatred that was worse than physical pain. I did not poke again.

And now they were watching the boy. I felt my mind sideslip. A moment later my control was gone. The door was open. I lurched across the sand toward him, legs scissoring nervelessly, so much driven deadwood. My own eyes seemed to close and I saw only with those alien eyes—saw a monstrous alabaster seascape overtopped with a sky like a great purple way, saw a leaning, eroded shack that might have been the carcass of some unknown, flesh-devouring creature, saw an abominated creature that moved and respired and carried a device of wood and wire under its arm, a device constructed of geometrically impossible right angles.

I wonder what he thought, that wretched, unnamed boy with his sieve under his arm and his pockets bulging with an odd conglomerate of sandy tourist coins, what he thought when he saw me lurching at him like a blind conductor stretching out his hands over a lunatic orchestra, what he thought as the last of the light fell across my hands, red and split and shining with their burden of eyes, what he thought when the hands made that sudden, flailing gesture in the air, just before his head burst.

I know what I thought.

I thought I had peeked over the rim of the universe and into the fires of hell itself.

The wind pulled at the bandages and made them into tiny, whipping streamers as I unwrapped them. The clouds had blotted the red remnants of the sunset, and the dunes were dark and shadow-cast. The clouds raced and boiled above us.

"You must promise me one thing, Richard," I said over the rising wind. "You must run if it seems I might try . . . to hurt you. Do you understand that?"

"Yes." His open-throated shirt whipped and rippled with the wind. His face was set, his own eyes little more than sockets in early dark.

The last of the bandages fell away.

I looked at Richard and they looked at Richard. I saw a face I had known for five years and come to love. They saw a distorted, living monolith.

"You see them," I said hoarsely. "Now you see them."

He took an involuntary step backward. His face became stained with a sudden unbelieving terror. Lightning slashed out of the sky. Thunder walked in the clouds and the water had gone black as the river Styx.

"Arthur—"

How hideous he was! How could I have lived near him, spoken with him? He was not a creature, but mute pestilence. He was—

"Run! Run, Richard!"

And he did run. He ran in huge, bounding leaps. He became a scaffold against the looming sky. My hands flew up, flew over my head in a screaming, orlesque gesture, the fingers reaching to the only familiar thing in this nightmare world—reaching to the clouds.

And the clouds answered.

There was a huge, blue-white streak of lightning that seemed like the end of the world. It struck Richard, it enveloped him. The last thing I remember is the electric stench of ozone and burnt flesh.

When I awoke I was sitting calmly on my porch, looking out toward the Big Dune. The storm had passed and the air was pleasantly cool. There was a tiny sliver of moon. The sand was virginal—no sign of Richard or of the dune buggy.

I looked down at my hands. The eyes were open but glazed. They had exhausted themselves. They dozed.

I knew well enough what had to be done. Before the door could be wedged open any further, it had to be locked. Forever. Already I could notice the first signs of structural change in the hands themselves. The fingers were beginning to shorten . . . and change.

There was a small hearth in the living room, and in season I had been in the habit of lighting a fire against the damp Florida cold. I lit one now, moving with haste. I had no idea when they might wake up to what I was doing.

When it was burning well I went out back to the kerosene drum and soaked both hands. They came awake immediately, screaming with agony. I almost didn't make it back to the living room, and to the fire.

But I did make it.

*　　*　　*

That was all seven years ago.

I'm still here, still watching the rockets take off. There have been more of them lately. This is a space-minded administration. There has even been talk of another series of manned Venus probes.

I found out the boy's name, not that it matters. He was from the village, just as I thought. But his mother had expected him to stay with a friend on the mainland that night, and the alarm was not raised until the following Monday. Richard—well, everyone thought Richard was an odd duck, anyway. They suspect he may have gone back to Maryland or taken up with some woman.

As for me, I'm tolerated, although I have quite a reputation for eccentricity myself. After all, how many ex-astronauts regularly write their elected Washington officials with the idea that space-exploration money could be better spent elsewhere?

I get along just fine with these hooks. There was terrible pain for the first year or so, but the human body can adjust to almost anything. I shave with them and even tie my own shoelaces. And as you can see, my typing is nice and even. I don't expect to have any trouble putting the shotgun into my mouth or pulling the trigger. It started again three weeks ago, you see.

There is a perfect circle of twelve golden eyes on my chest.

PROJECT: EARTH
BY PHILIP K. DICK

The sound echoed hollowly through the big frame house. It vibrated among the dishes in the kitchen, the gutters along the roof, thumping slowly and evenly like distant thunder. From time to time it ceased, but then it began again, booming through the quiet night, a relentless sound, brutal in its regularity. From the top floor of the big house.

In the bathroom the three children huddled around the chair, nervous and hushed, pushing against each other with curiosity.

"You sure he can't see us?" Tommy rasped.

"How could he see us? Just don't make any noise." Dave Grant shifted on the chair, his face to the wall. "Don't talk so loud." He went on looking, ignoring them both.

"Let me see," Joan whispered, nudging her brother with a sharp elbow. "Get out of the way."

"Shut up." Dave pushed her back. "I can see better now." He turned up the light.

"I want to see," Tommy said. He pushed Dave off the chair onto the bathroom floor. "Come on."

Dave withdrew sullenly. "It's our house."

Tommy stepped cautiously up onto the chair. He put his eye to the crack, his face against the wall. For a time he saw nothing. The crack was narrow and the light on the other side was bad. Then, gradually, he began to make out shapes, forms beyond the wall.

Edward Billings was sitting at an immense old-fashioned desk. He had stopped typing and was resting his eyes. From his vest pocket he had taken a round pocket watch. Slowly, carefully, he wound the great watch. Without his glasses his lean, withered face seemed naked and bleak, the features of some elderly bird. Then he put his glasses on again and drew his chair closer to the desk.

He began to type, working with expert fingers the towering mass of metal and parts that reared up before him. Again the ominous booming echoed through the house, resuming its insistent beat.

Mr. Billings' room was dark and littered. Books and papers lay everywhere, in piles and stacks, on the desk, on the table, in heaps on the floor. The walls were covered with charts, anatomy charts, maps, astronomy charts, signs of the zodiac. By the windows rows of dust-covered chemical bottles and packages lay stacked. A stuffed bird stood on the top of the bookcase, gray and drooping. On the desk was a huge magnifying glass, Greek and Hebrew dictionaries, a postage stamp box, a bone letter opener. Against the door a curling strip of flypaper moved with the air currents rising from the gas heater.

The remains of a magic lantern lay against one wall. A black satchel with clothes piled on it. Shirts and socks and a long frock coat, faded and threadbare. Heaps of newspapers and magazines, tied with brown cord. A great black umbrella against the table, a pool of sticky water around its metal point. A glass frame of dried butterflies, pressed into yellowing cotton.

And at the desk the huge old man hunched over his ancient typewriter and heaps of notes and papers.

"Gosh," Tommy said.

Edward Billings was working on his report. The report was open on the desk beside him, an immense book, leather-bound, bulging at its cracked seams. He was transferring material into it from his heaps of notes.

*   *   *

The steady thumping of the great typewriter made the things in the bathroom rattle and shake, the light fixture, the bottles and tubes in the medicine cabinet. Even the floor under the children's feet.

"He's some kind of Communist agent," Joan said. "He's drawing maps of the city so he can set off bombs when Moscow gives the word."

"The heck he is," Dave said angrily.

"Don't you see all the maps and pencils and papers? Why else would—"

"Be quiet," Dave snapped. "He will hear us. He is not a spy. He's too old to be a spy."

"What is he, then?"

"I don't know. But he isn't a spy. You're sure dumb. Anyhow, spies have beards."

"Maybe he's a criminal," Joan said.

"I talked to him once," Dave said. "He was coming downstairs. He spoke to me and gave me some candy out of a bag."

"What kind of candy was it?"

"I don't know. Hard candy. It wasn't any good."

"What's he do?" Tommy asked, turning from the crack.

"Sits in his room all day. Typing."

"Doesn't he work?"

Dave sneered. "That's what he does. He writes on his report. He's an official with a company."

"What company?"

"I forget."

"Doesn't he ever go out?"

"He goes out on the roof."

"On the roof?"

"He has a porch he goes out on. We fixed it. It's part of the apartment. He's got a garden. He comes downstairs and gets dirt from the backyard."

"Shhh!" Tommy warned. "He turned around."

Edward Billings had got to his feet. He was covering the typewriter with a black cloth, pushing it back and gathering up the pencils and erasers. He opened the desk drawer and dropped the pencils into it.

"He's through," Tommy said. "He's finished working."

The old man removed his glasses and put them away in a case. He dabbed at his forehead wearily, loosening his collar and necktie. His neck was long and the cords stood out from yellow, wrinkled skin. His Adam's apple bobbed up and down as he sipped some water from a glass.

His eyes were blue and faded, almost without color. For a moment he gazed directly at Tommy, his hawk-like face blank. Then abruptly he left the room, going through a door.

"He's going to bed," Tommy said.

Mr. Billings returned, a towel over his arm. At the desk he stopped and laid the towel over the back of the chair. He lifted the massive report book and carried it from the desk over to the bookcase, holding it tightly with both hands. It was heavy. He laid it down and left the room again.

The report was very close. Tommy could make out the gold letters stamped into the cracked leather binding. He gazed at the letters a long time—until Joan finally pushed him away from the crack, shoving him impatiently off the chair.

Tommy stepped down and moved away, awed and fascinated by what he had seen. The great report book, the huge volume of material on which the old man worked, day after day. In the flickering light from the lamp on the desk he had easily been able to make out the gold-stamped words on the ragged leather binding.

PROJECT B: EARTH.

"Let's go," Dave said. "He'll come in here in a couple minutes. He might catch us watching."

"You're afraid of him," Joan taunted.

"So are you. So is Mom. So is everybody." He glanced at Tommy. "You afraid of him?"

Tommy shook his head. "I'd sure like to know what's in that book," he murmured. "I'd sure like to know what that old man is doing."

*   *   *

The late afternoon sunlight shone down bright and cold. Edward Billings came slowly down the back steps, an empty pail in one hand, rolled-up newspapers under his arm. He paused a moment, shielding his eyes and gazing around him. Then he disappeared into the backyard, pushing through the thick wet grass.

Tommy stepped out from behind the garage. He raced silently up the steps two at a time. He entered the building, hurrying down the dark corridor.

A moment later he stood before the door of Edward Billings' apartment, his chest rising and falling, listening intently.

There was no sound.

Tommy tried the knob. It turned easily. He pushed. The door swung open and a musty cloud of warm air drifted past him out into the corridor.

He had little time. The old man would be coming back with his pail of dirt from the yard.

Tommy entered the room and crossed to the bookcase, his heart pounding excitedly. The huge report book lay among heaps of notes and bundles of clippings. He pushed the papers away, sliding them from the book. He opened it quickly, at random, the thick pages crackling and bending.

Denmark

Figures and facts. Endless facts, pages and columns, row after row. The lines of type danced before his eyes. He could make little out of them. He turned to another section.

New York

Facts about New York. He struggled to understand the column heads. The number of people. What they did. How they lived. What they earned. How they spent their time. Their beliefs. Religion. Politics. Philosophy. Morals. Their age. Health. Intelligence. Graphs and statistics, averages and evaluations.

Evaluations. Appraisals. He shook his head and turned to another section.

California

Population. Wealth. Activity of the state government. Ports and harbors. Facts, facts, facts—

Facts on everything. Everywhere. He thumbed through the report. On every part of the world. Every city, every state, every country. Any and all possible information.

Tommy closed the report uneasily. He wandered restlessly around the room, examining the heaps of notes and papers, the bundles of clippings and charts. The old man, typing day after day. Gathering facts, facts about the whole world. The earth. A report on the earth, the earth and everything on it. All the people. Everything they did and thought, their actions, deeds, achievements, beliefs, prejudices. A great report of all the information in the whole world.

Tommy picked up the big magnifying glass from the desk. He examined the surface of the desk with it, studying the wood. After a moment he put down the glass and picked up the bone letter knife. He put down the letter knife and examined the broken magic lantern in the corner. The frame of dead butterflies. The drooping stuffed bird. The bottles of chemicals.

He left the room, going out onto the roof porch. The late afternoon sunlight flickered fitfully; the sun was going down. In the center of the porch was a wooden frame, dirt and grass heaped around it. Along the rail were big earthen jars, sacks of fertilizer, damp packages of seeds. An over-turned spray gun. A dirty trowel. Strips of carpet and a rickety chair. A sprinkling can.

Over the wood frame was a wire netting. Tommy bent down, peering through the netting. He saw plants, small plants in rows. Some moss, growing on the ground. Tangled plants, tiny and very intricate.

At one place some dried grass was heaped up in a pile. Like some sort of cocoon.

Bugs? Insects of some sort? Animals?

He took a straw and poked it through the netting at the dried grass. The grass stirred. Something was in it. There were other cocoons, several of them, here and there among the plants.

Suddenly something scuttled out of one of the cocoons, racing across the grass. It squeaked in fright. A second followed it. Pink, running quickly. A small herd of shrilling pink things, two inches high, running and dashing among the plants.

Tommy leaned closer, squinting excitedly through the netting, trying to see what they were. Hairless. Some kind of hairless animals. But tiny, tiny as grasshoppers. Baby things? His pulse raced wildly. Baby things or maybe—

A sound. He turned quickly, rigid.

Edward Billings stood at the door, gasping for breath. He set down the pail of dirt, sighing and feeling for his handkerchief in the pocket of his dark blue coat. He mopped his forehead silently, gazing at the boy standing by the frame.

"Who are you, young man?" Billings said, after a moment. "I don't remember seeing you before."

Tommy shook his head. "No."

"What are you doing here?"

"Nothing."

"Would you like to carry this pail out onto the porch for me? It's heavier than I realized."

Tommy stood for a moment. Then he came over and picked up the pail. He carried it out onto the roof porch and put it down by the wood frame.

"Thank you," Billings said. "I appreciate that." His keen, faded-blue eyes flickered as he studied the boy, his gaunt face shrewd, yet not unkind. "You look pretty strong to me. How old are you? About eleven?"

Tommy nodded. He moved back toward the railing. Below, two or three stories down, was the street. Mr. Murphy was walking along, coming home from the office. Some kids were playing at the corner. A young woman across the street was watering her lawn, a blue sweater around her slim shoulders. He was fairly safe. If the old man tried to do anything—

"Why did you come here?" Billings asked.

Tommy said nothing. They stood looking at each other, the stooped old man, immense in his dark old-fashioned suit, the young boy in a red sweater and jeans, a beanie cap on his head, tennis shoes and freckles. Presently Tommy glanced toward the wood frame covered with netting, then up at Billings.

"That? You wanted to see that?"

"What's in there? What are they?"

"They?"

"The things. Bugs? I never saw anything like them. What are they?"

Billings walked slowly over. He bent down and unfastened the corner of the netting. "I'll show you what they are. If you're interested." He twisted the netting loose and pulled it back.

Tommy came over, his eyes wide.

"Well?" Billings said presently. "You can see what they are."

Tommy whistled softly. "I thought maybe they were." He straightened up slowly, his face pale. "I thought maybe—but I wasn't sure. Little tiny men!"

"Not exactly," Mr. Billings said. He sat down heavily in the rickety chair. From his coat he took a pipe and a worn tobacco pouch. He filled the pipe slowly, shaking tobacco into it. "Not exactly men."

Tommy continued to gaze down into the frame. The cocoons were tiny huts, put together by the little men. Some of them had come out in the open now. They gazed up at him, standing together. Tiny pink creatures, two inches high. Naked. That was why they were pink.

"Look closer," Billings murmured. "Look at their heads. What do you see?"

"They're so small—"

"Go get the glass from the desk. The big magnifying glass." He watched Tommy hurry into the study and come out quickly with the glass. "Now tell me what you see."

Tommy examined the figures through the glass. They seemed to be men, all right. Arms, legs—some were women. Their heads. He squinted.

And then recoiled.

"What's the matter?" Billings grunted.

"They're—they're queer."

"Queer?" Billings smiled. "Well, it all depends on what you're used to. They're different—from you. But they're not queer. There's nothing wrong with them. At least, I hope there's nothing wrong." His smile faded, and he sat sucking on his pipe, deep in silent thought.

"Did you make them?" Tommy asked.

"I?" Billings removed his pipe. "No, not I."

"Where did you get them?"

"They were lent to me. A trial group. In fact, the *trial* group. They're new. Very new."

"You want—you want to sell one of them?"

Billings laughed. "No, I don't. Sorry. I have to keep them."

Tommy nodded, resuming his study. Through the glass he could see their heads clearly. They were not quite men. From the front of each forehead antennae sprouted, tiny wire-like projections ending in knobs. Like the vanes of insects he had seen. They were not men, but they were similar to men. Except for the antennae they seemed normal—the antennae and their extreme minuteness.

"Did they come from another planet?" Tommy asked. "From Mars? Venus?"

"No."

"Where, then?"

"That's a hard question to answer. The question has no meaning, not in connection with them."

"What's the report for?"

"The report?"

"In there. The big book with all the facts. The thing you're doing."

"I've been working on that a long time."

"How long?"

Billings smiled. "That can't be answered, either. It has no meaning. But a long time indeed. I'm getting near the end, though."

"What are you going to do with it? When it's finished."

"Turn it over to my superiors."

"Who are they?"

"You wouldn't know them."

"Where are they? Are they here in town?"

"Yes. And no. There's no way to answer that. Maybe someday you'll—"

"The report's about us," Tommy said.

Billings turned his head. His keen eyes bored into Tommy. "Oh?"

"It's about us. The report. The book."

"How do you know?"

"I looked at it. I saw the title on the back. It's about the earth, isn't it?"

Billings nodded. "Yes. It's about the earth."

"You're not from here, are you? You're from someplace else. Outside the system."

"How—how do you know that?"

Tommy grinned with superior pride. "I can tell. I have ways."

"How much did you see in the report?"

"Not much. What's it for? Why are you making it? What are they going to do with it?"

Billings considered a long time before he answered. At last he spoke. "That," he said, "depends on *those*." He gestured toward the wood frame. "What they do with the report depends on how Project C works."

"Project C?"

"The third project. There've been only two others before. They wait a long time. Each project is planned carefully. New factors are considered at great length before any decision is reached."

"Two others?"

"Antennae for these. A complete new arrangement of the cognitive faculties. Almost no dependence on innate drives. Greater flexibility. Some decrease in over-all emotional index, but what they lose in libido energy they gain in rational control. I would expect more emphasis on individual experience, rather than dependence on traditional group learning. Less stereotyped thinking. More rapid advance in situation control."

Billings' words made little sense. Tommy was lost. "What were the others like?" he asked.

"The others? Project A was a long time ago. It's dim in my mind. Wings."

"Wings."

"They were winged, depending on mobility and possessing considerable individualistic characteristics. In the final analysis we allowed them too much self-dependence. Pride. They had concepts of pride and honor. They were fighters. Each against the others. Divided into atomized antagonistic factions and—"

"What were the rest like?"

Billings knocked his pipe against the railing. He continued, speaking more to himself than to the boy standing in front of him. "The winged type was our first attempt at high-level organisms. Project A. After it failed we went into conference. Project B was the result. We were certain of success. We eliminated many of the excessive individualistic characteristics and substituted a group orientation process. A herd method of learning and experiencing. We hoped general control over the project would be assured. Our work with the first project convinced us that greater supervision would be necessary if we were to be successful."

"What did the second kind look like?" Tommy asked, searching for a meaningful thread in Billings' dissertation.

"We removed the wings, as I said. The general physiognomy remained the same. Although control was maintained for a short time, this second type also fractured away from the pattern, splintering into self-determined groups beyond our supervision. There is no doubt that surviving members of the initial type A were instrumental in influencing them. We should have exterminated the initial type as soon—"

"Are there any left?"

"Of Project B? Of course." Billings was irritated. "You're Project B.

That's why I'm down here. As soon as my report is complete the final disposition of your type can be effected. There is no doubt my recommendation will be identical with that regarding Project A. Since your Project has moved out of jurisdiction to such a degree that for all intents and purposes you are no longer functional—"

But Tommy wasn't listening. He was bent over the wood frame, peering down at the tiny figures within. Nine little people, men and women both. Nine—and no more in all the world.

Tommy began to tremble. Excitement rushed through him. A plan was dawning, bursting alive inside him. He held his face rigid, his body tense.

"I guess I'll be going." He moved from the porch, back into the room toward the hall door.

"Going?" Billings got to his feet. "But—"

"I have to go. It's getting late. I'll see you later." He opened the hall door. "Goodbye."

"Goodbye," Mr. Billings said, surprised. "I hope I'll see you again, young man."

"You will," Tommy said.

*   *   *

He ran home as fast as he could. He raced up the porch steps and inside the house.

"Just in time for dinner," his mother said, from the kitchen.

Tommy halted on the stairs. "I have to go out again."

"No you don't! You're going to—"

"Just for awhile. I'll be right back." Tommy hurried up to his room and entered, glancing around.

The bright yellow room. Pennants on the walls. The big dresser and mirror, brush and comb, model airplanes, pictures of baseball players. The paper bag of bottle caps. The small radio with its cracked plastic cabinet. The wooden cigar boxes full of junk, odds and ends, things he had collected.

Tommy grabbed up one of the cigar boxes and dumped its contents out on the bed. He stuck the box under his jacket and headed out of the room.

"Where are you going?" his father demanded, lowering his evening newspaper and looking up.

"I'll be back."

"Your mother said it was time for dinner. Didn't you hear her?"

"I'll be back. This is important." Tommy pushed the front door open. Chill evening air blew in, cold and thin. "Honest. Real important."

"Ten minutes." Vince Jackson looked at his wristwatch. "No longer. Or you don't get any dinner."

"Ten minutes." Tommy slammed the door. He ran down the steps, out into the darkness.

* * *

A light showed, flickering under the bottom and through the key-hole of Mr. Billings' room.

Tommy hesitated a moment. Then he raised his hand and knocked. For a time there was silence. Then a stirring sound. The sound of heavy footsteps.

The door opened. Mr. Billings peered out into the hall.

"Hello," Tommy said.

"You're back!" Mr. Billings opened the door wide and Tommy walked quickly into the room. "Did you forget something?"

"No."

Billings closed the door. "Sit down. Would you like anything? An apple? Some milk?"

"No." Tommy wandered nervously around the room, touching things here and there, books and papers and bundles of clippings.

Billings watched the boy a moment. Then he returned to his desk, seating himself with a sigh. "I think I'll continue with my report. I hope to finish very soon." He tapped a pile of notes beside him. "The last of them. Then I can leave here and present the report along with my recommendations."

Billings bent over his immense typewriter, tapping steadily away. The relentless rumble of the ancient machine vibrated through the room. Tommy turned and stepped out of the room, onto the porch.

In the cold evening air the porch was pitch black. He halted, adjusting to the darkness. After a time he made out the sacks of fertilizer, the rickety chair. And in the center, the wood frame with its wire netting over it, heaps of dirt and grass piled around.

Tommy glanced back into the room. Billings was bent over the typewriter, absorbed in his work. He had taken off his dark blue coat and hung it over the chair. He was working in his vest, his sleeves rolled up.

Tommy squatted beside the frame. He slid the cigar box from under his jacket and laid it down, lid open. He grasped the netting and pried it back, loose from the row of nails.

From the frame a few faint apprehensive squeaks sounded. Nervous scuttlings among the dried grass.

Tommy reached down, feeling among the grass and plants. His fingers closed over something, a small thing that squirmed in fright, twisting in wild terror. He dropped it into the cigar box and sought another.

In a moment he had them all. Nine of them, all nine in the wood cigar box.

He closed the lid and slipped it back under his jacket. Quickly he left the porch, returning to the room.

Billings glanced up vaguely from his work, pen in one hand, papers in the other. "Did you want to talk to me?" he murmured, pushing up his glasses.

Tommy shook his head. "I have to go."

"Already? But you just came!"

"I have to go." Tommy opened the door to the hall. "Goodnight."

Billings rubbed his forehead wearily, his face lined with fatigue. "All right, boy. Perhaps I'll see you again before I leave." He resumed his work, tapping slowly away at the great typewriter, bent with fatigue.

Tommy shut the door behind him. He ran down the stairs, outside on the porch. Against his chest the cigar box shook and moved. Nine. All nine of them. He had them all. Now they were his. They belonged to him— and there weren't any more of them, anywhere in the world. His plan had worked perfectly.

He hurried down the street toward his own house, as fast as he could run.

He found an old cage out in the garage he had once kept white rats in. He cleaned it and carried it upstairs to his room. He spread papers on the floor of the cage and fixed a water dish and some sand.

When the cage was ready he emptied the contents of the cigar box into it.

The nine tiny figures huddled together in the center of the cage, a little bundle of pink. Tommy shut the door of the cage and fastened it tightly. He carried the cage to the dresser and then drew a chair up by it so he could watch.

The nine little people began to move around hesitantly, exploring the cage. Tommy's heart beat with rapid excitement as he watched them.

He had got them away from Mr. Billings. They were his, now. And Mr. Billings didn't know where he lived or even his name.

They were talking to each other. Moving their antennae rapidly, the way he had seen ants do. One of the little people came over to the side of the cage. He stood gripping the wire, peering out into the room. He was joined by another, a female. They were naked. Except for the hair on their heads they were pink and smooth.

He wondered what they ate. From the big refrigerator in the kitchen he took some cheese and some hamburger, adding crumbled up bits of bread and lettuce leaves and a little plate of milk.

They liked the milk and bread. But they left the meat alone. The lettuce leaves they used to begin the making of little huts.

Tommy was fascinated. He watched them all the next morning before school, then again at lunch time, and all afternoon until dinner.

"What you got up there?" his dad demanded, at dinner.

"Nothing."

"You haven't got a snake, have you?" his mom asked apprehensively. "If you have another snake up there, young man—"

"No." Tommy shook his head, bolting down his meal. "It's not a snake."

He finished eating and ran upstairs.

The little creatures had finished fixing their huts out of the lettuce leaves. Some were inside. Others were wandering around the cage, exploring it.

Tommy seated himself before the dresser and watched. They were smart. A lot smarter than the white rats he had owned. And cleaner. They used the sand he had put there for them. There were smart—and quite tame.

After awhile Tommy closed the door of the room. Holding his breath he unfastened the cage, opening one side wide. He reached in his hand and caught one of the little men. He drew him out of the cage and then opened his hand carefully.

The little man clung to his palm, peering over the edge and up at him, antennae waving wildly.

"Don't be afraid," Tommy said.

          *   *   *

The little man got cautiously to his feet. He walked across Tommy's palm, to his wrist. Slowly he climbed Tommy's arm, glancing over the side. He reached Tommy's shoulder and stopped, gazing up into his face.

"You're sure small," Tommy said. He got another one from the cage and put the two of them on the bed. They walked around the bed for a long time. More had come to the open side of the cage and were staring cautiously out onto the dresser. One found Tommy's comb. He inspected it, tugging at the teeth. A second joined him. The two tugged at the comb, but without success.

"What do you want?" Tommy asked. After a while they gave up. They found a nickel lying on the dresser. One of them managed to turn it up on end. He rolled it. The nickel gained speed, rushing toward the edge of the dresser. The tiny men ran after it in consternation. The nickel fell over the side.

"Be careful," Tommy warned. He didn't want anything to happen to them. He had too many plans. It would be easy to rig up things for them to do—like fleas he had seen at the circus. Little carts to pull. Swings, slides. Things they could operate. He could train them, and then charge admission.

Maybe he could take them on tour. Maybe he'd even get a write-up in the newspaper. His mind raced. All kinds of things. Endless possibilities. But he had to start out easy—and be careful.

The next day he took one to school in his pocket, inside a fruit jar. He punched holes in the lid so it could breathe.

At recess he showed it to Dave and Joan Grant. They were fascinated.

"Where did you get it?" Dave demanded.

"That's my business."

"Want to sell it?"

"It's not it. It's him."

Joan blushed. "It doesn't have anything on. You better make it put clothes on right away."

"Can you make clothes for them? I have eight more. Four men and four women."

Joan was excited. "I can—if you'll give me one of them."

"The heck I will. They're mine."

"Where did they come from? Who made them?"

"None of your business."

Joan made little clothes for the four women. Little skirts and blouses. Tommy lowered the clothing into the cage. The little people moved around the heap uncertainly, not knowing what to do.

"You better show them," Joan said.

"Show them? Nuts to you."

"I'll dress them." Joan took one of the tiny women from the cage and carefully dressed her in a blouse and skirt. She dropped the figure back in. "Now let's see what happens."

The others crowded around the dressed woman, plucking curiously at the clothing. Presently they began to divide up the remaining clothes, some taking blouses, some skirts.

Tommy laughed and laughed. "You better make pants for the men. So they'll all be dressed."

He took a couple of them out and let them run up and down his arms.

"Be careful," Joan warned. "You'll lose them. They'll get away."

"They're tame. They won't run away. I'll show you." Tommy put them down onto the floor. "We have a game. Watch."

"A game?"

"They hide and I find them."

The figures scampered off, looking for places to hide. In a moment none were in sight. Tommy got down on his hands and knees, reaching under the dresser, among the bedcovers. A shrill squeak. He had found one.

"See? They like it." He carried them back to the cage, one by one. The last one stayed hidden a long time. It had got into one of the dresser drawers, down in a bag of marbles, pulling the marbles over its head.

"They're clever," Joan said. "Wouldn't you give me even one of them?"

"No," Tommy said emphatically. "They're mine. I'm not letting them get away from me. I'm not giving any of them to *anybody*."

*   *   *

Tommy met Joan after school the next day. She had made little trousers and shirts for the men.

"Here." She gave them to him. They walked along the sidewalk. "I hope they fit."

"Thanks." Tommy took the clothes and put them in his pocket. They cut across the vacant lot. At the end of the lot Dave Grant and some kids were sitting around in a circle, playing marbles.

"Who's winning?" Tommy said, stopping.

"I am," Dave said, not looking up.

"Let me play." Tommy dropped down. "Come on." He held out his hand. "Give me your agate."

Dave shook his head. "Get away."

Tommy punched him on the arm. "Come on! Just one shot." He considered. "Tell you what—"

A shadow fell over them.

Tommy looked up. And blanched.

Edward Billings gazed down silently at the boy, leaning on his umbrella, its metal point lost in the soft ground. He said nothing. His aged face was lined and hard, his eyes like faded blue stones.

Tommy got slowly to his feet. Silence had fallen over the children. Some of them scrambled away, snatching up their marbles.

"What do you want?" Tommy demanded. His voice was dry and husky, almost inaudible.

Billings' cold eyes bored into him, two keen orbs, without warmth of any kind. "You took them. I want them back. Right away." His voice was hard, colorless. He held out his hand. "Where are they?"

"What are you talking about?" Tommy muttered. He backed away. "I don't know what you mean."

"The Project. You stole them from my room. I want them back."

"The heck I did. What do you mean?"

Billings turned toward Dave Grant. "He's the one you meant, isn't he?"

Dave nodded. "I saw them. He has them in his room. He won't let anybody near them."

"You came and stole them. *Why?*" Billings moved toward Tommy ominously. "Why did you take them? What do you want with them?"

"You're crazy," Tommy murmured, but his voice trembled. Dave Grant said nothing. He looked away sheepishly. "It's a lie," Tommy said.

Billings grabbed him. Cold, ancient hands gripped him, digging into his shoulders. "Give them back! I want them. I'm responsible for them."

"Let go." Tommy jerked loose. "I don't have them with me." He caught his breath. "I mean—"

"Then you do have them. At home. In your room. Bring them here. Go and get them. All nine."

Tommy put his hands in his pockets. Some of his courage was returning. "I don't know," he said. "What'll you give me?"

Billings' eyes flashed. "Give you?" He raised his arm threateningly. "Why, you little—"

Tommy jumped back. "You can't make me return them. You don't have any control over us." He grinned boldly. "You said so yourself. We're out of your power. I heard you say so."

Billings' face was like granite. "I'll take them. They're mine. They belong to me."

"If you try to take them I'll call the cops. And my dad'll be there. My dad and the cops."

Billings gripped his umbrella. He opened and shut his mouth, his face a dark, ugly red. Neither he nor Tommy spoke. The other kids gazed at the two of them wide-eyed, awed and subdued.

Suddenly a thought twisted across Billings' face. He looked down at the ground, the crude circle and the marbles. His cold eyes flickered. "Listen to this. I will—I will play against you for them."

"What?"

"The game. Marbles. If you win you can keep them. If I win I get them back at once. All of them."

Tommy considered, glancing from Mr. Billings down at the circle on the ground. "If I win you won't ever try to take them? You will let me keep them—for good?"

"Yes."

"All right." Tommy moved away. "It's a deal. If you win you can have them back. But if I win they belong to me. And you don't ever get them back."

"Bring them here at once."

"Sure. I'll go get them."—And my agate, too, he thought to himself. "I'll be right back."

"I'll wait here," Mr. Billings said, his huge hands gripping the umbrella.

Tommy ran down the porch steps, two at a time.

His mother came to the door. "You shouldn't be going out again so late. If you're not home in half an hour you don't get any dinner."

"Half an hour," Tommy cried, running down the dark sidewalk, his hands pressed against the bulge in his jacket. Against the wood cigar box that moved and squirmed. He ran and ran, gasping for breath.

Mr. Billings was still standing by the edge of the lot, waiting silently. The sun had set. Evening was coming. The children had gone home. As Tommy stepped onto the vacant lot a chill, hostile wind moved among the weeds and grass, flapping against his pants legs.

"Did you bring them?" Mr. Billings demanded.

"Sure." Tommy halted, his chest rising and falling. He reached slowly under his jacket and brought out the heavy wood cigar box. He slipped the rubber band off it, lifting the lid a crack. "In here."

Mr. Billings came close, breathing hoarsely. Tommy snapped the lid shut and restored the rubber band. "We have to play." He put the box down on the ground. "They're mine—unless you win them back."

Billings subsided. "All right. Let's begin, then."

Tommy searched his pockets. He brought out his agate, holding it carefully. In the fading light the big red-black marble gleamed, rings of sand and white. Like Jupiter. An immense, hard marble.

"Here we go," Tommy said. He knelt down, sketching a rough circle on the ground. He emptied out a sack of marbles into the ring. "You got any?"

"Any?"

"Marbles. What are you going to shoot with?"

"One of yours."

"Sure." Tommy took a marble from the ring and tossed it to him. "Want me to shoot first?"

Billings nodded.

"Fine." Tommy grinned. He took aim carefully, closing one eye. For a moment his body was rigid, set in an intense, hard arc. Then he shot.

Marbles rattled and clinked, rolling out of the circle and into the grass and weeds beyond. He had done well. He gathered up his winnings, collecting them back in the cloth sack.

"Is it my turn?" Billings asked.

"No. My agate's still in the ring." Tommy squatted down again. "I get another shot."

He shot. This time he collected three marbles. Again his agate was within the circle.

"Another shot," Tommy said, grinning. He had almost half. He knelt and aimed, holding his breath. Twenty-four marbles remained. If he could get four more he would have won. Four more—

He shot. Two marbles left the circle. And his agate. The agate rolled out, bouncing into the weeds.

Tommy collected the two marbles and the agate. He had nineteen in all. Twenty-two remained in the ring.

"Okay," he murmured reluctantly. "It's your shot this time. Go ahead."

Edward Billings knelt down stiffly, gasping and tottering. His face was gray. He turned his marble around in his hand uncertainly.

"Haven't you ever played before?" Tommy demanded. "You don't know how to hold it, do you?"

Billings shook his head. "No."

"You have to get it between your first finger and your thumb." Tommy watched the stiff old fingers fumble with the marble. Billings dropped it once and picked it quickly up again. "Your thumb makes it go. Like this. Here, I'll show you."

Tommy took hold of the ancient fingers and bent them around the marble. Finally he had them in place. "Go ahead." Tommy straightened up. "Let's see how you do."

The old man took a long time. He gazed at the marbles in the ring, his hand shaking. Tommy could hear his breathing, the hoarse, deep panting, in the damp evening air.

The old man glanced at the cigar box resting in the shadows. Then back at the circle. His fingers moved—

There was a flash. A blinding flash. Tommy gave a cry, wiping at his eyes. Everything spun, lashing and tilting. He stumbled and fell, sinking into the wet weeds. His head throbbed. He sat on the ground, rubbing his eyes, shaking his head, trying to see.

At last the drifting sparks cleared. He looked around him, blinking.

The circle was empty. There were no marbles in the ring. Billings had got them all.

Tommy reached out. His fingers touched something hot. He jumped. It was a fragment of glass, a glowing red fragment of molten glass. All around him, in the damp weeds and grass, fragments of glass gleamed, cooling slowly into darkness. A thousand splinters of stars, glowing and fading around him.

Edward Billings stood up slowly, rubbing his hands together. "I'm glad that's over," he gasped. "I'm too old to bend down like that."

His eyes made out the cigar box, lying on the ground.

"Now they can go back. And I can continue with my work." He picked up the wood box, putting it under his arm. He gathered up his umbrella and shuffled away, toward the sidewalk beyond the lot.

"Goodbye," Billings said, stopping for a moment. Tommy said nothing.

Billings hurried off down the sidewalk, the cigar box clutched tightly.   *   *   *

He entered his apartment, breathing rapidly. He tossed his black umbrella into the corner and sat down before the desk, laying the cigar box in front of him. For a moment he sat, breathing deeply and gazing down at the brown and white square of wood and cardboard.

He had won. He had got them back. They were his, again. And just in time. The filing date for the report was practically upon him.

Billings slid out of his coat and vest. He rolled up his sleeves, trembling a little. He had been lucky. Control over the B type was extremely limited. They were virtually out of jurisdiction. That, of course, was the problem itself. Both the A and B types had managed to escape supervision.

They had rebelled, disobeying orders and therefore putting themselves outside the limit of the plan.

But these—the new type, Project C. Everything depended on them. They had left his hands, but now they were back again. Under control, as intended, within the periphery of supervisory instruction.

Billings slid the rubber band from the box. He raised the lid, slowly and carefully.

Out they swarmed—fast. Some headed to the right, some to the left. Two columns of tiny figures racing off, head down. One reached the edge of the desk and leaped. He landed on the rug, rolling and falling. A second jumped after him, then a third.

Billings broke out of his paralysis. He grabbed frantically, wildly. Only two remained. He swiped at one and missed. The other—

He grabbed it, squeezing it tight between his clenched fingers. Its companion wheeled. It had something in its hand. A splinter. A splinter of wood, torn from the inside of the cigar box.

It ran up and stuck the end of the splinter into Billings' finger.

Billings gasped in pain. His fingers flew open. The captive tumbled out, rolling on its back. Its companion helped it up, half-dragging it to the edge of the desk. Together the two of them leaped.

Billings bent down, groping for them. They scampered rapidly, toward the door to the porch. One of them was at the lamp plug. It tugged. A second joined it and the two tiny figures pulled together. The lamp cord came out of the wall. The room plunged into darkness.

Billings found the desk drawer. He yanked it open, spilling its contents onto the floor. He found some big sulphur matches and lit one.

They were gone—out onto the porch.

Billings hurried after them. The match blew out. He lit another, shielding it with his hand.

The creatures had got to the railing. They were going over the edge, catching hold of the ivy and swinging down into the darkness.

He got to the edge too late. They were gone, all of them. All nine, over the side of the roof, into the blackness of the night.

Billings ran downstairs and out onto the back porch. He reached the ground, hurrying around the side of the house, where the ivy grew up the side.

Nothing moved. Nothing stirred. Silence. No sign of them anywhere.

They had escaped. They were gone. They had worked out a plan of escape and put it into operation. Two columns, going in opposite directions, as soon as the lid was lifted. Perfectly timed and executed.

Slowly Billings climbed the stairs to his room. He pushed the door open and stood, breathing deeply, dazed from the shock.

They were gone. Project C was already over. It had gone like the others. The same way. Rebellion and independence. Out of supervision. Beyond control. Project A had influenced Project B—and now, in the same way, the contamination had spread to C.

Billings sat down heavily at his desk. For a long time he sat immobile, silent and thoughtful, gradual comprehension coming to him. It was not his fault. It had happened before—twice before. And it would happen again. Each Project would carry the discontent to the next. It would never end, no matter how many Projects were conceived and put into operation. The rebellion and escape. The evasion of the plan.

After a time, Billings reached out and pulled his big report book to him. Slowly he opened it to the place he had left off. From the report he removed the entire last section. The summary. There was no use scrapping the current Project. One Project was as good as any other. They would all be equal—equal failures.

He had known as soon as he saw them. As soon as he had raised the lid. They had clothes on. Little suits of clothing. Like the others, a long time before.

RADIANCE
BY NINA KIRIKI HOFFMAN

You know how you object to laws in principle, distantly and without heat, until they come home to you?

I would have voted against any law that gave the Radiants rights to our corpses, but we didn't get to vote on it; Congress passed it, and that was that. It became a box you could check on the back of your driver's license. Medical donor. Alien donor. It was up to each individual.

They could have done it differently, those politicians. They could have. But they didn't.

Energy politics. Cheap power. Pollutionless fuel. A lot of the big PACs fought it, but when we saw how other countries who signed on with the Radiants earlier than we did were about to outstrip us in technology and production, I guess maybe we had to go with the new law.

I don't want the aliens playing with my body after I'm gone. Cremation, that's the death-style for Judy D'Angelo.

My sister Carla felt differently.

Once the Radiants get our bodies, they're supposed to move them to someplace on the other side of the world, where there's less chance of encountering people who knew the bodies in life. So there was no reason for me to ever run into Carla after she died. I'm not a traveler. I've spent all my life within fifty miles of where I was born.

Most of the Radiants we have in Sparrow Creek look like they come from East India, rules about relocation being what they are. They have their own enclave on the far side of the creek from the rest of town. They do some mixing, though not a whole lot. You see them in the Quick Lunch Diner and at the library and hanging around the bus station. Sometimes they're at the public pool in the summer—guess they get hot same as we do—but when they get into the pool, most regular people get out.

I don't know. There's just something creepy about swimming with corpses.

Skin goes gray after death; that's one of the systems the Radiants don't repair just right, though from rumors, I hear they get everything else in the bodies working as well as or better than it did in life. My husband, Tony, has a theory about Radiant skin color. He has a lot of theories, and he likes to tell me about them.

You can always tell a Radiant from that gray skin, and also from the light in the eyes, as though the Radiants just can't stop themselves from shining, even though they clothe themselves in flesh.

I saw some Radiants without bodies when I was a little girl.

I had hiked down the creek a ways toward where the water got pinched into a rock canyon and ran faster. There was a big flat rock out that way I used to do some dreaming on. I had to wade to it, surrounded as it was by moving water on all sides.

I was there at twilight, having left a Fourth of July picnic before we even got to the fireworks. Carla had been teasing me again about being stupid. It was true she got all the good grades, and it was true that when she teased me I just turned red and couldn't get my mouth to say anything smart back, so I felt stupider and stupider, as though she put a spell on me with every taunt.

I ran away, and waded to my dreaming rock on the underwater rocks I knew as well as anything my bare feet had ever touched, and I sat there as night crept out of all the places it hides during the day. The rock was still warm from leftover sun, and the air was summer-dusty and water-wet.

So I kept looking toward the fairgrounds, where the rest of my family was probably still scarfing homemade ice cream and chocolate chip cookies, maybe even roasting marshmallows, and where the fireworks would bloom eventually. My family wouldn't miss me. I was too stupid to bother with.

The floating lights came to me there on my dreaming rock.

I didn't hear them. I noticed flickering near my feet and turned to look over my shoulder down the canyon and there they were, drifting a few feet above the stream, flickers of light reflecting off the water below them.

One was purple as a spring violet, a cluster of dark purple lights with lighter purple streamers up and down; one was yellow as firelight, a big smudge of light like a giant reverse fingerprint hanging in the air; and one was pale pale blue as the edge of sky just after dawn, spiky with light as a porcupine is with quills.

Radiants had only been on Earth about three years then, during what people called the First Phase, in hindsight—they could come and go at will as long as they didn't hurt anybody. Not that we knew how to stop them from doing whatever they wanted. How do you cage an energy creature? How do you hurt one? That was before the Radiants made the deal for bodies with various world governments; at that point, none of us knew what they really wanted. Linguists could communicate with them, but the rest of us couldn't.

All I knew in that moment was that they were beautiful.

I swiped away the tears that blurred my vision and stared at the lights, not quite sure what they were. I had seen a few stories in the paper—Carla liked talking about the Radiants for Current Events—but I had never seen Radiants before. Fireworks that didn't burn themselves out?

They drifted closer. Over the chuckle of the creek I could hear a faint humming sound, not a human hum but more like wind going through wires.

They stared at me and I stared at them for a long time. Parts of them shifted and spun, but they stayed pretty much in the same space they had started in; no drift of disintegration.

At last the purple one stretched out a ray of light and touched my face with it. I was so lost in dreaming wonder that at first I didn't think anything about it. The light touched my cheek like my mother's fingertip, soft and warm.

The warmth seeped into my face and spread under the skin. I still dreamed, but now I dreamed that something asked me questions, and I gave answers. I thought about Carla, about Mom and Dad, about our cousins; about the cool bite of pink lemonade in the mouth on a hot afternoon, and about roasting hot dogs over a coal fire, how they sizzled, and how the first bite was too hot but wonderful, juicy and charred; about what Carla had said to me before I ran away from the picnic, and how I had felt hearing it, the fire that had burned in my face, the way my throat had closed on tears.

I liked remembering the tastes, and the good way the sun warmed me on hot summer days, but thinking about Carla calling me stupid made me cry all over again, and I didn't like that.

I woke from my dream and clapped my hand over my cheek.

The purple light stopped shining directly at me.

I was afraid of them then. I knelt on the edge of my rock and splashed water on my face, trying to wash away the alien heat. I was afraid to look up. What if they shone into my eyes and blinded me? What if they wanted more from me, the secret dreams of rage I had after I turned the lights out at night, the sick miserable feeling in the pit of my stomach after I had told a lie to Mom about who had really eaten the chocolate cake? I didn't want any more questions that I would answer before I decided whether I wanted to answer.

I lay face down on the rock, shielding my face with my hands, for a long time. When at last I looked up, the lights had disappeared.

*　　　*　　　*

My husband, Tony, is a psychologist. He says the Radiants keep their skin gray because they want us to know what they are. He says if they blended better they would scare us more. As long as we can identify them we don't have to be afraid that they're sneaking around doing things we can't understand.

So I was more than startled when I saw Carla again six months after her funeral. Her skin was the wrong color.

I was in the Quick Lunch having my usual pastrami on rye and watching the other secretary from the insurance office where I work, Arlene, eat a salad. She hates salads, but she always eats them. She was talking about her cat, Puffball, who does more cute things than you would think a cat could.

"He's learning to open doors," she said.

"Imagine," I said. Which was mostly what I said when talking to Arlene. I lifted my coffee mug off the circle of light on the table that kept it just the right temperature, and took a sip.

"Reaches up and turns the knob. It works better if he's on the side of the door he can push when he gets it open. But he can tug on the bottom of the door if he has to."

"Imagine."

"I have to tell you, it's starting to spook me," she said. "I don't want the cat to be able to open doors. I want him to stay where I put him."

I glanced over and saw that in the next booth there was a woman all in black, wearing a black broad-brimmed straw hat with a heavy black veil. But behind the veil, where her eyes should be, there were two spots of purple glow, staring at me.

I looked at her hands and they were pink. Pink fingers clutched a mug of coffee tight. Coffee steam rose past her veiled face.

How could she drink through that veil?

Radiants don't like the taste of coffee, only the smell.

Alien and not gray. Something wrong with that picture.

"What do you think I should do?" Arlene said.

"Huh?" I turned back to her, watched her eat the last bite of salad.

"The cat can open *doors*, Judy. Aren't you listening?"

"Lock them," I said, remembering a purple touch on my face and mental doors I had not been able to close. In the twenty-five years since I had met the Radiants at the creek, I had avoided them, both during Phase One, exploration, and Phase Two, corpse occupation. I never met their eyes. I didn't want to look at the light. I didn't want them seeing who I was inside.

Nobody in any of the news stories during Phase One had talked about experiences similar to what had happened to me. No lights reaching out to touch a person's face, no mind-opening. I sometimes thought I had made it up.

"I don't want to live like that," Arlene said. "I want to go from one room to the next without having to unlock doors. Maybe if I just lock the front door all the time . . . "

The woman in black touched my shoulder. "Judy," she said in a low voice.

I startled like a fly-bitten horse.

"Excuse me," said the veiled woman. "I didn't mean to frighten you." She didn't take her hand off my shoulder, though.

"Someone you know?" Arlene asked.

"No," I said. My voice came out strained. Shock seeped through me. I was staring at the hand on my shoulder, at the long pudgy fingers, the half-moon nails. Carla's capable hand, last seen in the temporary coffin the Sparrow Creek Mortuary used as though it were a hotel room: put the corpses in for viewing, take them out and hand them over to the Radiants, fluff the satin for the next corpse.

Or perhaps the Radiants were already at work inside the corpses while they were being viewed. I wasn't sure what the procedure was.

"We need to get back to work," Arlene said, lowering her salad plate into the green pool of light in the center of the table. We had both already thumbed the small pink light patches at our places that registered our thumb-prints and extracted money from our access accounts to pay for our meals.

Smart light. What the Radiants had traded us for our dead.

"I have to talk to you," said the woman.

I kept my eyes down. "I can't imagine being interested in anything you have to say," I said. I astonished myself. I would never have had the courage to talk that way to Carla while she was alive.

"She doesn't have time to talk to you," Arlene said. I felt an upwelling of gratitude toward her. The hand on my shoulder seemed to have paralyzed me. "We have to go back to work."

"I'll pay for your time," said the woman.

"Please," said Arlene, "what do you take us for? Come on, Judy!" She reached past the woman in black, grasped my hand, pulled me to my feet. The woman's hand slid from my shoulder.

Arlene and I ran out of the restaurant.

Our office was only two doors away, but we were both panting by the time we got there. "Thanks," I said to her. "Thanks, Arlene."

"Who was that? Did you know her?"

"Did you see her eyes?" I asked.

"How could I see anything through that veil?"

I hesitated. A Radiant who wasn't gray? This might be the start of a huge scandal. Or maybe not. Maybe there was no law that said the Radiants had to be gray. Maybe they just did it to keep us pacified, like Tony said.

A Radiant who used to be Carla.

My aggravating sister.

My sister.

A Radiant. No one I knew.

But still . . . Carla.

"I can't explain yet," I said.

Arlene frowned at me, then shrugged and said, "All right."

*   *   *

The Radiant was waiting for me when I got off at four-thirty. Arlene took a different light-bus home, so she wasn't there to save me this time.

"Judy," said the Radiant.

"What do you want?" I asked.

"Just to talk to you."

"My husband will be waiting for me." Actually Tony's last appointment on Thursdays ended at six, and we didn't have that much to say to each other anyway, unless he had come up with a new theory of something.

"Please," it said.

It might be the sort to wait around until I said yes. Wait across the street and watch the house while I was home. Wait at my bus stop in the morning. Wait in the restaurant while I ate lunch. Wait here, on the street near the office, when I got off.

Might as well get this over with.

It was summer in Sparrow Creek, and though the Radiants had taught us how to augment the atmosphere and tame weather into useful storms and modified sun, it was still hot in the late afternoon. I headed down the sidewalk toward the fairgrounds, thinking of the picnic tables there, neutral ground, where no one I knew was likely to see me talking to this—thing.

"Aren't you supposed to be on the other side of the world?" I asked it as it walked beside me.

"In one reality," it said.

"What, now we have more than one reality?"

"It is time for another shift."

"Phase Three? What's Phase Three going to be? Who decides stuff like that?"

"It is part of a repeating pattern of contact," it said.

"Why tell me? I'm less than nothing to you. I'm not even a donor. I don't want you . . . things inside me."

"Just making conversation," it said, which seemed very strange to me.

It followed me across the summer-browned grass to the picnic table where I had eaten twenty-five summers before, the table I had run away from because of Carla. I brushed off the bench and sat down. Nothing here had been modernized. You couldn't touch a pool of light and order food or water. Here was just stained and somewhat splintery wood with initials and cuss words carved into it.

The Radiant sat across from me and lifted off its hat and veil.

And it was Carla. Her chipmunk cheeks, sagging a little with middle age, her freckled pug nose, her expressive mouth with the full lower lip; her broad, thinker's forehead and her heavy, wavy chestnut hair, just another thing I had envied her, because my hair was too fine and never grew long, and it was a lighter color of brown called dishwater.

Her eyes had changed. A lavender swirl of light had replaced the iris in each eye.

"So talk," I said.

"Do you recognize me?" it asked.

"What are you talking about? I don't know you from . . . from starlight."

"We met not far from here." It turned and glanced at the creek through the trees, and then south, toward the canyon where my dreaming rock had been.

"What?" I touched my cheek, remembering the three wild Radiants I had seen. I had told no one about them.

"What I did to you, that was against the rules of early contact."

I squinted at the face that used to be my sister's. It didn't have any real expression, and the voice, too, was flat. I had overheard Radiants talking to people—in the market, in restaurants. They could mimic human speech perfectly if they wanted to. They could use facial muscles to communicate the emotions we expected from them, as though they had the same palette of feelings we had. I had never been sure how real it was for them, but then, I hadn't wanted to get close enough to test it. I had let Tony tell me what he thought about them. It wasn't the same as knowing.

I shrugged. "So what?" I said.

"So who are you now?" It sounded curious and worried.

It was strange to look into my sister's face and see someone else. The restless, crushing intelligence was gone, the impatience with anyone around her slower than she, the casual cruelty and constant questions. She had always been too swift to slow down for answers, as though she'd lose momentum and was afraid she would never regain it. She had died in Tasmania, researching something forest related, and her body had been brought home just long enough for us to have a memorial, and then back she went, newly inhabited, to the other side of the world.

I thought.

I said, "If you're the one who touched me, how did you end up inside my sister? That seems beyond coincidence."

It nodded. "It was planned. I broke a rule. I must make reparations."

"Really?"

It nodded again.

"What does that mean? Reparations to who? Me?"

"Yes."

I wondered if it would let me set my sister on fire and dance around her while she burned. But that seemed like too much trouble, and not very likely. "What kind of reparations?"

It clasped its hands, placed them on the tabletop. Its forehead furrowed. "Who are you now?" it asked.

"What business is it of yours?"

"I need to know how I hurt you so I can do whatever is possible to made amends."

I shook my head. "What you did to me didn't change me," I said. "I'm just who I am. A wife. A secretary. A daughter, a sister. A friend."

"Do you feel stupid?" it asked, and it was Carla's voice to the life, the undertone of sneer.

I looked at her. Her eyes were brown again. There was no sign of Radiant in her. My throat swelled and closed. I wondered what I had done to bring such torture down on me, to have her gone, and now to have her back. I felt the heat of tears in my eyes, the heat of flush on my face.

When she went away to college I began to have a life of my own, but every time she came back she sliced through any threads of progress or independence I had woven in her absence, and she came back just often enough for me to keep from building any strength. Most Christmases she returned, showing Dad her publications, her new scars from fieldwork; she was full of stories, shining with intellect, crushing in her accomplishments.

"Compared to you? Of course," I said.

Stupidity had shifted from being an embarrassment to being a defense. Eventually I had learned to like what it did for me. People didn't make demands, didn't expect much. Didn't know who I was. I was much safer that way.

I looked at my sister, my pink, dead sister. "So is everything the aliens told us a lie? Are you really alive in there?" I asked her, speaking to my nightmare. Though I had learned to like the damage she had done me, I still didn't want to thank her for it.

"No," she said, and her eyes lighted from within, violet banishing brown. "No," it said. "She is dead."

"How could you speak in her voice?"

"Her memories are still here," it said.

I covered my mouth with my hands. "What are you Radiants doing? Who are you being inside those bodies?" I whispered past my fingers.

"Whoever we find when we arrive. But away from their homes. We are here to study you, and this is the best way we know."

I lowered my hands slowly.

"You have all her memories and thoughts and feelings?" I asked after a long time while I tried to sort through my thoughts.

"All that were not overwritten by other thoughts and memories and feelings during her lifetime, or altered by chemistry, medication, or death."

"So you know how she treated me all my life. How could what you did to me possibly mean anything in that context?"

"I know I hurt you."

"It was nothing."

It reached across the picnic table and touched my hand. Its fingers were warm as a mother's touch.

"Don't!" I said, snatching my hand away.

"If it was nothing, why do you fear it still?"

"I don't want you to know me!"

"I know you," it said.

"No one knows me."

It clasped its hands in front of it and looked down at them. Its lowered eyelids hid its radiance; I could be sitting across the table from my sister. "I know you both," it whispered, and raised its lids to stare at me with purple eyes. "I know many of you."

"And we don't know you at all," I said. "How come your skin isn't gray?"

"Because we are shifting to another reality," it said.

"Is this the one where you take over all the bodies, living and dead? Are us Earth people totally screwed now?"

"No," it said. "There aren't very many of us, and that's not what we do." It smiled at me. "So many fears . . . We are here to preserve you."

"Preserve us?" I thought of butterflies on pins in boxes with glass tops, of museum displays, static and trapped. Of course, smart light had changed museums a lot. Technoids were still figuring out ways to display things with it.

"To study and remember you, and then to move on."

"You'll be leaving?" Radiants had been part of my life for almost as long as I could remember. What would life be like without them?

"Presently," it said.

"But first you walk around in corpses that look alive."

"A few of us, perhaps. Where we need to make amends."

"I still don't understand that part. You never told me what reparations might involve."

"I looked at you when you did not know how to say no. I offer you a look at me." It held out its hand.

*   *   *

Travel is so easy now because of smart light that I'm not surprised to see people from the other side of the world wandering the streets of Sparrow Creek, though I'm not sure what they find here that isn't easier to get to somewhere else.

The Radiants still relocate, though there are no visible signs that distinguish a Radiant from a living person any longer, except occasional flecks of light in the eyes.

Tony tells me that over time our xenophobia has lessened until it's safe for a Radiant to blend better, but I know this is not so. I listen to him because he likes to be listened to, and I think my own thoughts about Phases Three and Four, how the moment of arrival has the seed of leaving in it because of what you bring with you.

They give us smart light so that we will let them study us, and the smart light changes us until we begin to resemble every other people they have studied and we no longer interest them. Then they move on.

It is strange to know that I, who have lived inside the dim shell of stupidity, could drink smart light—I know now how to do it—and become a Radiant myself.

Here inside my head, I hold a million years of history, a thousand different life forms from as many planets, the memories of a hundred individuals of each life form. I could live forever and not have enough time to examine each one.

I don't know how it all fits inside my skull.

Well, maybe I do. When I look in the mirror now I see faint lavender rings around my irises. Coherent light lives inside me.

The memories I examine most often are Carla's. I never knew she thought I was pretty. I never knew she feared I was smart. I never knew she felt so hollow, small, and scared inside.

That's part of why she checked the alien donor box on her driver's license. She wanted to be useful. She longed to be brilliant.

Now she is part of a being of light.

I won't live long enough to be part of the spacefaring race we are destined to become if we follow the pattern of previous peoples the Radiants have contacted. That's all right with me. I've spent all my life within fifty miles of where I was born, and that's where I want to stay.

I can always travel in the comfort of my own head.

THE VENUS HUNTERS
BY J. G. BALLARD

When Dr. Andrew Ward joined the Hubble Memorial Institute at Mount Vernon Observatory he never imagined that the closest of his new acquaintances would be an amateur stargazer and spare-time prophet called Charles Kandinski, tolerantly regarded by the Observatory professionals as a madman. In fact, had either he or Professor Cameron, the Institute's Deputy Director, known just how far he was to be prepared to carry this friendship before his two-year tour at the Institute was over, Ward would certainly have left Mount Vernon the day he arrived and would never have become involved in the bizarre and curiously ironic tragedy which was to leave an ineradicable stigma upon his career.

*   *   *

Professor Cameron first introduced him to Kandinski. About a week after Ward came to the Hubble, he and Cameron were lunching together in the Institute cafeteria.

"We'll go down to Vernon Gardens for coffee," Cameron said when they finished dessert. "I want to get a shampoo for Edna's roses and then we'll sit in the sun for an hour and watch the girls go by." They strolled out through the terrace tables toward the parking lot. A mile away, beyond the conifers thinning out on the slopes above them, the three great Vernon domes gleamed like white marble against the sky. "Incidentally, you can meet the opposition."

"Is there another observatory at Vernon?" Ward asked as they set off along the drive in Cameron's Buick. "What is it—an Air Force weather station?"

"Have you ever heard of Charles Kandinski?" Cameron said. "He wrote a book called *The Landings from Outer Space*. It was published about three years ago."

Ward shook his head doubtfully. They slowed down past the check-point at the gates and Cameron waved to the guard. "Is that the man who claims to have seen extra-terrestrial beings? Martians or—"

"Venusians. That's Kandinski. Not only seen them," Professor Cameron added. "He's talked to them. Charles works at a cafe in Vernon Gardens. We know him fairly well."

"He runs the other observatory?"

"Well, an old 4-inch MacDonald Refractor mounted in a bucket of cement. You probably wouldn't think much of it, but I wish we could see with our two-fifty just a tenth of what he sees."

Ward nodded vaguely. The two observatories at which he had worked previously, Cape Town and the Milan Astrographic, had both attracted any number of cranks and charlatans eager to reveal their own final truths about the cosmos, and the prospect of meeting Kandinski interested him only slightly. "What is he?" he asked. "A practical joker, or just a lunatic?"

      *   *   *

Professor Cameron propped his glasses onto his forehead and negotiated a tight hairpin. "Neither," he said.

Ward smiled at Cameron, idly studying his plump cherubic face with its puckish mouth and keen eyes. He knew that Cameron enjoyed a modest reputation as a wit. "Has he ever claimed in front of you that he's seen a . . . Venusian?"

"Often," Professor Cameron said. "Charles lectures two or three times a week about the landings to the women's societies around here, and put himself completely at our disposal. I'm afraid we had to tell him he was a little too advanced for us. But wait until you meet him."

Ward shrugged and looked out at the long curving peach terraces lying below them, gold and heavy in the August heat. They dropped a thousand feet and the road widened and joined the highway which ran from Vernon Gardens across the desert to Santa Vera and the coast.

Vernon Gardens was the nearest town to the Observatory and most of it had been built within the last few years, evidently with an eye on the tourist trade. They passed a string of blue and pink-washed houses, a school constructed of glass bricks, and an abstract Baptist chapel. Along the main thoroughfare the shops and stores were painted in bright jazzy colors, the vivid awnings and neon signs like street scenery in an experimental musical.

Professor Cameron turned off into a wide tree-lined square and parked by a cluster of fountains in the center. He and Ward walked toward the cafes—Al's Fresco Diner, Ylla's, the Dome—which stretched down to the sidewalk. Around the square were a dozen gift-shops filled with cheap souvenirs: silverplate telescopes and models of the great Vernon dome masquerading as ink-stands and cigar-boxes, plus a juvenile omnium gatherum of miniature planetaria, space helmets and plastic 3-D star atlases.

The cafe to which they went was decorated in the same futuristic motifs. The chairs and tables were painted a drab aluminum grey, their limbs and panels cut in random geometric shapes. A silver rocket ship, ten feet long, its paint peeling off in rusty strips, reared up from a pedestal among the tables. Across it was painted the cafe's name.

'The Site Tycho.'

A large mobile had been planted in the ground by the sidewalk and dangled down over them, its vanes and struts flashing in the sun. Gingerly Professor Cameron pushed it away. "I'll swear that damn thing is growing," he confided to Ward. "I must tell Charles to prune it." He lowered himself into a chair by one of the open-air tables, put on a fresh pair of sunglasses and focused them at the long brown legs of a girl sauntering past.

*   *   *

Left alone for the moment, Ward looked around him and picked at a cellophane transfer of a ringed planet glued to the table-top. The Site Tycho was also used as a small science fiction exchange library. A couple of metal bookstands stood outside the cafe door, where a soberly dressed middle-aged man, obviously hiding behind his upturned collar, worked his way quickly through the rows of paperbacks. At another table a young man with an intent, serious face was reading a magazine. His high cerebrotonic forehead was marked across the temple by a ridge of pink tissue, which Ward wryly decided was a lobotomy scar.

"Perhaps we ought to show our landing permits," he said to Cameron when after three or four minutes no one had appeared to serve them. "Or at least get our pH's checked."

Professor Cameron grinned. "Don't worry, no customs, no surgery." He took his eyes off the sidewalk for a moment. "This looks like him now."

A tall, bearded man in a short-sleeved tartan shirt and pale green slacks came out of the cafe towards them with two cups of coffee on a tray.

"Hello, Charles," Cameron greeted him. "There you are. We were beginning to think we'd lost ourselves in a time-trap."

The tall man grunted something and put the cups down. Ward guessed that he was about fifty-five years old. He was well over six feet tall, with a massive sunburnt head and lean but powerfully muscled arms.

"Andrew, this is Charles Kandinski." Cameron introduced the two men. "Andrew's come to work for me, Charles. He photographed all those Cepheids for the Milan Conference last year."

Kandinski nodded. His eyes examined Ward critically but showed no signs of interest.

"I've been telling him all about you, Charles," Cameron went on, "and how we all follow your work. No further news yet, I trust?"

Kandinski's lips parted in a slight smile. He listened politely to Cameron's banter and looked out over the square, his great seamed head raised to the sky.

"Andrew's read your book, Charles," Cameron was saying. "Very interested. He'd like to see the originals of those photographs. Wouldn't you, Andrew?"

"Yes, I certainly would," Ward said.

*   *   *

Kandinski gazed down at him again. His expression was not so much penetrating as detached and impersonal, as if he were assessing Ward with an utter lack of bias, so complete, in fact, that it left no room for even the smallest illusion. Previously Ward had only seen this expression in the eyes of the very old. "Good," Kandinski said. "At present they are in a safe-deposit box at my bank, but if you are serious I will get them out."

Just then two young women wearing wide-brimmed Rapallo hats made their way through the tables. They sat down and smiled at Kandinski. He nodded to Ward and Cameron and went over to the young women, who began to chatter to him animatedly.

"Well, he seems popular with them," Ward commented. "He's certainly not what I anticipated. I hope I didn't offend him over the plates. He was taking you seriously."

"He's a little sensitive about them," Cameron explained. "The famous dustbin-lid flying saucers. You mustn't think I bait him, though. To tell the truth I hold Charles in great respect. When all's said and done, we're in the same racket."

"Are we?" Ward said doubtfully. "I haven't read his book. Does he say in so many words that he saw and spoke to a visitor from Venus?"

"Precisely. Don't you believe him?"

Ward laughed and looked through the coins in his pocket, leaving one on the table. "I haven't tried to yet. You say the whole thing isn't a hoax?"

"Of course not."

"How do you explain it then? Compensation-fantasy or—"

Professor Cameron smiled. "Wait until you know Charles a little better."

"I already know the man's messianic," Ward said dryly. "Let me guess the rest. He lives on yogurt, weaves his own clothes, and stands on his head all night, reciting the Bhagavadgita backwards."

"He doesn't," Cameron said, still smiling at Ward. "He happens to be a big man who suffers from barber's rash. I thought he'd have you puzzled."

*   *   *

Ward pulled the transfer off the table. Some science fantast had skillfully penciled in an imaginary topography on the planet's surface. There were canals, craters and lake systems named Verne, Wells, and Bradbury. "Where did he see this Venusian?" Ward asked, trying to keep the curiosity out of his voice.

"About twenty miles from here, out in the desert off the Santa Vera highway. He was picnicking with some friends, went off for a stroll in the sandhills and ran straight into the spaceship. His friends swear he was perfectly normal both immediately before and after the landing, and all of them saw the inscribed metallic tablet which the Venusian pilot left behind. Some sort of ultimatum, if I remember, warning mankind to abandon all its space programs. Apparently someone up there does not like us."

"Has he still got the tablet?" Ward asked.

"No. Unluckily it combusted spontaneously in the heat. But Charles managed to take a photograph of it."

Ward laughed. "I bet he did. It sounds like a beautifully organized hoax. I supposed he made a fortune out of his book?"

"About 150 dollars. He had to pay for the printing himself. Why do you think he works here? The reviews were too unfavorable. People who read science fiction apparently dislike flying saucers, and everyone else dismissed him as a lunatic." He stood up. "We might as well get back."

As they left the cafe Cameron waved to Kandinski, who was still talking to the young women. They were leaning forward and listening with rapt attention to whatever he was saying.

"What do the people in Vernon Gardens think of him?" Ward asked as they moved away under the trees.

"Well, it's a curious thing, almost without exception those who actually know Kandinski are convinced he's sincere and that he saw an alien spacecraft, while at the same time realizing the absolute impossibility of the whole story."

" 'I know God exists, but I cannot *believe* in him'?"

"Exactly. Naturally, most people in Vernon think he's crazy. About three months after he met the Venusian, Charles saw another UFO chasing its tail over the town. He got the Fire Police out, alerted the Radar Command chain and even had the National Guard driving around town ringing a bell. Sure enough, there were two white blobs diving about in the clouds. Unfortunately for Charles, they were caused by the headlights of one of the asparagus farmers in the valley doing some night spraying. Charles was the first to admit it, but at three o'clock in the morning no one was very pleased."

"Who is Kandinski, anyway?" Ward asked. "Where does he come from?"

"He doesn't make a profession of seeing Venusians, if that's what you mean. He was born in Alaska, for some years taught psychology at Mexico City University. He's been just about everywhere, had a thousand different jobs. A veteran of the private evacuations. Get his book."

*   *   *

Ward murmured noncommittally. They entered a small arcade and stood for a moment by the first shop, an aquarium called 'The Nouvelle Vague,' watching the Angel fish and Royal Brahmins swim dreamily up and down their tanks.

"It's worth reading," Professor Cameron went on. "Without exaggerating, it's really one of the most interesting documents I've ever come across."

"I'm afraid I have a closed mind when it comes to interplanetary bogeymen," Ward said.

"A pity," Cameron rejoined. "I find them fascinating. Straight out of the unconscious. The fish too," he added, pointing at the tanks. He grinned whimsically at Ward and ducked away into a horticulture store halfway down the arcade.

While Professor Cameron was looking through the sprays on the hormone counter, Ward went over to a newsstand and glanced at the magazines. The proximity of the observatory had prompted a large selection of popular astronomical guides and digests, most of them with illustrations of the Mount Vernon domes on their wrappers. Among them Ward noticed a dusty, dog-eared paperback, *The Landings from Outer Space*, by Charles Kandinski. On the front cover a gigantic space vehicle, at least the size of New York, tens of thousands of portholes ablaze with light, was soaring majestically across a brilliant backdrop of stars and spiral nebulae.

Ward picked up the book and turned to the end cover. Here there was a photograph of Kandinski, dressed in a dark lounge suit several sizes too small, peering stiffly into the eye-piece of his MacDonald.

Ward hesitated before finally taking out his wallet. He bought the book and slipped it into his pocket as Professor Cameron emerged from the horticulture store.

"Get your shampoo?" Ward asked.

Cameron brandished a brass insecticide gun, then slung it, buccaneer-like, under his belt. "My disintegrator," he said, patting the butt of the gun. "There's a positive plague of white ants in the garden, like something out of a science fiction nightmare. I've tried to convince Edna that their real source is psychological. Remember the story 'Leningen vs. the Ants'? A classic example of the forces of the Id rebelling against the Super Ego." He watched a girl in a black bikini and lemon-colored sunglasses move gracefully through the arcade and added meditatively: "You know, Andrew, like everyone else my real vocation was to be a psychiatrist. I spend so long analyzing my motives I've no time left to act."

"Kandinski's SuperEgo must be in difficulties," Ward remarked. "You haven't told me your explanation yet."

"What explanation?"

"Well, what's really at the bottom of this Venusian he claims to have seen?"

"Nothing is at the bottom of it. Why?"

Ward smiled helplessly. "You will tell me next that you really believe him."

Professor Cameron chuckled. They reached his car and climbed in. "Of course I do," he said.

＊　＊　＊

When, three days later, Ward borrowed Professor Cameron's car and drove down to the rail depot in Vernon Gardens to collect a case of slides which had followed him across the Atlantic, he had no intention of seeing Charles Kandinski again. He had read one or two chapters of Kandinski's book before going to sleep the previous night and dropped it in boredom. Kandinski's description of his encounter with the Venusian was not only puerile and crudely written but, most disappointing of all, completely devoid of imagination. Ward's work at the Institute was now taking up most of his time. The Annual Congress of the International Geophysical Association was being held at Mount Vernon in little under a month, and most of the burden of organizing the three-week program of lectures, semesters and dinners had fallen on Professor Cameron and himself.

But as he drove away from the depot past the cafes in the square he caught sight of Kandinski on the terrace of the Site Tycho. It was three o'clock, a time when most people in Vernon Gardens were lying asleep indoors, and Kandinski seemed to be the only person out in the sun. He was scrubbing away energetically at the abstract tables with his long hairy arms, head down so that his beard was almost touching the metal tops, like an aboriginal half-man prowling in dim bewilderment over the ruins of a futuristic city lost in an inversion of time.

On an impulse, Ward parked the car in the square and walked across to the Site Tycho, but as soon as Kandinski came over to his table he wished he had gone to another of the cafes. Kandinski had been reticent enough the previous day, but now that Cameron was absent he might well turn out to be a garrulous bore.

After serving him Kandinski sat down on a bench by the bookshelves and stared moodily at his feet. Ward watched him quietly for five minutes, as the mobiles revolved delicately in the warm air, deciding whether to approach Kandinski. Then he stood up and went over to the rows of magazines. He picked in a desultory way through half a dozen and turned to Kandinski. "Can you recommend any of these?"

Kandinski looked up. "Do you read science fiction?" he asked matter-of-factly.

"Not as a rule," Ward admitted. When Kandinski said nothing he went on: "Perhaps I'm too skeptical, but I can't take it too seriously."

Kandinski pulled at a blister on his palm. "No one suggests you should. What you mean is that you take it too seriously."

Accepting the rebuke with a smile at himself, Ward pulled out one of the magazines and sat down at a table next to Kandinski. On the cover was a placid suburban setting of snugly eaved houses, yew trees, and children's bicycles. Spreading slowly across the roof-tops was an enormous pulpy nightmare, blocking out the sun behind it and throwing a weird phosphorescent glow over the roofs and lawns. "You're probably right," Ward said, showing the cover to Kandinski. "I'd hate to want to take that seriously."

*   *   *

Kandinski waved it aside. "I have seen 11th-century illuminations of the pentateuch more sensational than any of these covers." He pointed to the cinema theater on the far side of the square, where the four-hour Biblical epic *Cain and Abel* was showing. Above the trees an elaborate technicolored hoarding showed Cain, wearing what appeared to be a suit of Roman armor, wrestling with an immense hydraheaded boa constrictor.

Kandinski shrugged tolerantly. "If Michelangelo were working for MGM today would he produce anything better?"

Ward laughed. "You may well be right. Perhaps the House of the Medicis should be re-christened '16th Century-Fox.' "

Kandinski stood up and straightened the shelves. "I saw you here with Godfrey Cameron," he said over his shoulder. "You're working at the Observatory?"

"At the Hubble."

Kandinski came and sat down beside Ward. "Cameron is a good man. A very pleasant fellow."

"He thinks a great deal of you," Ward volunteered, realizing that Kandinski was probably short of friends.

"You mustn't believe everything that Cameron says about me," Kandinski said suddenly. He hesitated, apparently uncertain whether to confide further in Ward, and then took the magazine from him. "There are better ones here. You have to exercise some discrimination."

"It's not so much the sensationalism that puts me off," Ward explained, "as the psychological implications. Most of the themes in these stories come straight out of the more unpleasant reaches of the unconscious."

Kandinski glanced sharply at Ward, a trace of amusement in his eyes. "That sounds rather dubious and, if I may say so, second-hand. Take the best of these stories for what they are: imaginative exercises on the theme of tomorrow."

"You read a good deal of science fiction?" Ward asked.

Kandinski shook his head. "Never. Not since I was a child."

"I'm surprised," Ward said. "Professor Cameron told me you had written a science fiction novel."

"Not a novel," Kandinski corrected.

"I'd like to read it," Ward went on. "From what Cameron said it sounded fascinating, almost Swiftian in concept. This spacecraft which arrives from Venus and the strange conversations the pilot holds with a philosopher he meets. A modern morality. Is that the subject?"

Kandinski watched Ward thoughtfully before replying. "Loosely, yes. But, as I said, the book is not a novel. It is a factual and literal report of a Venus landing which actually took place, a diary of the most significant encounter in history since Paul saw his vision of Christ on the road to Damascus." He lifted his huge bearded head and gazed at Ward without embarrassment. "As a matter of interest, as Professor Cameron probably explained to you, I was the man who witnessed the landing."

Still maintaining his pose, Ward frowned intently. "Well, in fact Cameron did say something of the sort, but . . ."

"But you found it difficult to believe?" Kandinski suggested ironically.

"Just a little," Ward admitted. "Are you seriously claiming that you did see a Venusian spacecraft?"

Kandinski nodded. "Exactly." Then, as if aware that their conversation had reached a familiar turning, he suddenly seemed to lose interest in Ward. "Excuse me." He nodded politely to Ward, picked up a length of hose-pipe connected to a faucet and began to spray one of the big mobiles.

* * *

Puzzled but still skeptical, Ward sat back and watched him critically, then fished in his pockets for some change. "I must say I admire you for taking it all so calmly," he told Kandinski as he paid him.

"What makes you think I do?"

"Well, if I'd seen, let alone spoken to a visitor from Venus I think I'd be running around in a flat spin, notifying every government and observatory in the world."

"I did," Kandinski said. "As far as I could. No one was very interested."

Ward shook his head and laughed. "It is incredible, to put it mildly."

"I agree with you."

"What I mean," Ward said, "is that it's straight out of one of these science fiction stories of yours."

Kandinski rubbed his lips with a scarred knuckle, obviously searching for some means of ending the conversation. "The resemblance is misleading. They are not my stories," he added parenthetically. "This cafe is the only one which would give me work, for a perhaps obvious reason. As for the incredibility, let me say that I was and still am completely amazed. You may think I take it all calmly, but ever since the landing I have lived in a state of acute anxiety and foreboding. But short of committing some spectacular crime to draw attention to myself I don't see now how I can convince anyone."

Ward gestured with his glasses. "Perhaps. But I'm surprised you don't realize the very simple reasons why people refuse to take you seriously. For example, why should you be the only person to witness an event of such staggering implications? Why have you alone seen a Venusian?"

"A sheer accident."

"But why should a spacecraft from Venus land here?"

"What better place than near Mount Vernon Observatory?"

"I can think of any number. The U.N. Assembly, for one."

Kandinski smiled lightly. "Columbus didn't make his first contacts with the North American Indians at the Iroquois-Sioux Tribal Conference."

"That may be," Ward admitted, beginning to feel impatient. "What did this Venusian look like?"

Kandinski smiled wearily at the empty tables and picked up his hose again. "I don't know whether you've read my book," he said, "but if you haven't you'll find it all there."

"Professor Cameron mentioned that you took some photographs of the Venusian spacecraft. Could I examine them?"

"Certainly," Kandinski replied promptly. "I'll bring them here tomorrow. You're welcome to test them in any way you wish."

That evening Ward had dinner with the Camerons. Professor Renthall, Director of the Hubble, and his wife completed the party. The table-talk consisted almost entirely of good-humored gossip about their colleagues retailed by Cameron and Renthall, and Ward was able to mention his conversation with Kandinski.

"At first I thought he was mad, but now I'm not so certain. There's something rather too subtle about him. The way he creates an impression of absolute integrity, but at the same time never gives you a chance to tackle him directly on any point of detail. And when you do manage to ask him outright about this Venusian his answers are far too pat. I'm convinced the whole thing is an elaborate hoax."

Professor Renthall shook his head. "No, it's no hoax. Don't you agree, Godfrey?"

Cameron nodded. "Not in Andrew's sense, anyway."

"But what other explanation is there?" Ward asked. "We know he hasn't seen a Venusian, so he must be a fraud. Unless you think he's a lunatic. And he certainly doesn't behave like one."

"What is a lunatic?" Professor Renthall asked rhetorically, peering into the facetted stem of his raised hock glass. "Merely a man with more understanding than he can contain. I think Charles belongs in that category."

"The definition doesn't explain him, sir," Ward insisted. "He's going to lend me his photographs and when I prove those are fakes I think I'll be able to get under his guard."

"Poor Charles," Edna Cameron said. "Why shouldn't he have seen a spaceship? I think I see them every day."

"That's just what I feel, dear," Cameron said, patting his wife's matronly, brocaded shoulder. "Let Charles have his Venusian if he wants to. Damn it, all it's trying to do is ban Project Apollo. An excellent idea, I have always maintained; only the professional astronomer has any business in space. After the Rainbow tests there isn't an astronomer anywhere in the world who wouldn't follow Charles Kandinski to the stake." He turned to Renthall. "By the way, I wonder what Charles is planning for the Congress? A Neptunian? Or perhaps a whole delegation from Proxima Centauri. We ought to fit him out with a space suit and a pavilion—'Charles Kandinski— New Worlds for Old'."

"Santa Claus in a space suit," Professor Renthall mused. "That's a new one. Send him a ticket."

* * *

The next weekend Ward returned the twelve plates to the Site Tycho.

"Well?" Kandinski asked.

"It's difficult to say," Ward answered. "They're all too heavily absorbed. They could be clever montages of light brackets and turbine blades. One of them looks like a close-up of a clutch plate. There's a significant lack of any really corroborative details, which you'd expect somewhere in so wide a selection." He paused. "On the other hand, they could be genuine."

Kandinski said nothing, took the paper package, and went off into the cafe.

The interior of the Site Tycho had been designed to represent the control room of a spaceship on the surface of the moon. Hidden fluorescent lighting glimmered through plastic wall fascia and filled the room with an eerie blue glow. Behind the bar a large mural threw the curving outline of the moon onto an illuminated starscape. The doors leading to the rest rooms were circular and bulged outwards like air locks, distinguished from each other by the symbols ♂ and ☿. The total effect was ingenious but somehow reminiscent to Ward of a twenty-fifth century cave.

He sat down at the bar and waited while Kandinski packed the plates away carefully in an old leather briefcase.

"I've read your book," Ward said. "I had looked at it the last time I saw you, but I read it again thoroughly." He waited for some comment upon this admission, but Kandinski went over to an old portable typewriter standing at the far end of the bar and began to type laboriously with one finger. "Have you seen any more Venusians since the book was published?" Ward asked.

"None," Kandinski said.

"Do you think you will?"

"Perhaps." Kandinski shrugged and went on with his typing.

"What are you working on now?" Ward asked.

"A lecture I am giving on Friday evening," Kandinski said. Two keys locked together and he flicked them back. "Would you care to come? Eight-thirty, at the high school near the Baptist chapel."

"If I can," Ward said. He saw that Kandinski wanted to get rid of him. "Thanks for letting me see the plates." He made his way out into the sun. People were walking about through the fresh morning air, and he caught the clean scent of peach blossom carried down the slopes into the town.

Suddenly Ward felt how enclosed and insane it had been inside the Tycho, and how apposite had been his description of it as a cave, with its residential magician incanting over his photographs like a down-at-heel Merlin manipulating his set of runes. He felt annoyed with himself for becoming involved with Kandinski and allowing the potent charisma of his personality to confuse him. Obviously Kandinski played upon the instinctive sympathy for the outcast, his whole pose of integrity and conviction a device for drawing the gullible toward him.

Letting the light spray from the fountains fall across his face, Ward crossed the square toward his car.

Away in the distance two thousand feet above, rising beyond a screen of fir trees, the three Mount Vernon domes shone together in the sun like a futuristic Taj Mahal.

＊　　　＊　　　＊

Fifteen miles from Vernon Gardens the Santa Vera highway circled down from the foot of Mount Vernon into the first low scrub-covered hills which marked the southern edge of the desert. Ward looked out at the long banks of coarse sand stretching away through the haze, their outlines blurring in the afternoon heat. He glanced at the book lying on the seat beside him, open at the map printed between its end covers, and carefully checked his position, involuntarily slowing the speed of the Chevrolet as he moved nearer to the site of the Venus landings.

In the fortnight since he had returned the photographs to the Site Tycho, he had seen Kandinski only once, at the lecture delivered the previous night. Ward had deliberately stayed away from the Site Tycho, but he had seen a poster advertising the lecture and driven down to the school despite himself.

The lecture was delivered in the gymnasium before an audience of forty or fifty people, most of them women, who formed one of the innumerable local astronomical societies. Listening to the talk around him, Ward gathered that their activities principally consisted of trying to identify more than half a dozen of the constellations. Kandinski had lectured to them on several occasions and the subject of this latest installment was his researches into the significance of the Venusian tablet he had been analyzing for the last three years.

When Kandinski stepped onto the dais there was a brief round of applause. He was wearing a lounge suit of a curiously archaic cut and had washed his beard, which bushed out above his string tie so that he resembled a Mormon patriarch or the homespun saint of some fervent evangelical community.

For the benefit of any new members, he prefaced his lecture with a brief account of his meeting with the Venusian, and then turned to his analysis of the tablet. This was the familiar ultimatum warning mankind to abandon its preparations for the exploration of space, for the ostensible reason that, just as the sea was a universal image of the unconscious, so space was nothing less than an image of psychosis and death, and that if he tried to penetrate the interplanetary voids man would only plunge to earth like a demented Icarus, unable to scale the vastness of the cosmic zero. Kandinski's real motives for introducing this were all too apparent—the expected success of Project Apollo and subsequent landings on Mars and Venus would, if nothing else, conclusively expose his fantasies.

However, by the end of the lecture Ward found that his opinion of Kandinski had experienced a complete about face.

As a lecturer Kandinski was poor, losing words, speaking in a slow ponderous style and trapping himself in long subordinate clauses, but his quiet, matter-of-fact tone and absolute conviction in the importance of what he was saying, coupled with the nature of his material, held the talk together. His analysis of the Venusian cryptograms, a succession of intricate philological theorems, was well above the heads of his audience, but what began to impress Ward, as much as the painstaking preparation which must have preceded the lecture, was Kandinski's acute nervousness in delivering it. Ward noticed that he suffered from an irritating speech impediment that made it difficult for him to pronounce 'Venusian,' and he saw that Kandinski, far from basking in the limelight, was delivering the lecture only out of a deep sense of obligation to his audience and was greatly relieved when the ordeal was over.

*   *   *

At the end Kandinski had invited questions. These, with the exception of the chairman's, all concerned the landing of the alien space vehicle and ignored the real subject of the lecture. Kandinski answered them all carefully, taking in good part the inevitable facetious questions. Ward noted with interest the audience's curious ambivalence, simultaneously fascinated by and resentful of Kandinski's exposure of their own private fantasies, an expression of the same ambivalence which had propelled so many of the mana-personalities of history toward their inevitable Calvarys.

Just as the chairman was about to close the meeting, Ward stood up.

"Mr. Kandinski. You say that this Venusian indicated that there was also life on one of the moons of Uranus. Can you tell us how he did this, if there was no verbal communication between you?"

Kandinski showed no surprise at seeing Ward. "Certainly; as I told you, he drew eight concentric circles in the sand, one for each of the planets. Around Uranus he drew five lesser orbits and marked one of these. Then he pointed to himself and to me and to a patch of lichen. From this I deduced, reasonably I maintain, that—"

"Excuse me, Mr. Kandinski," Ward interrupted. "You say he drew five orbits around Uranus? One for each of the moons?"

Kandinski nodded. "Yes. Five."

"That was in 1960," Ward went on. "Three weeks ago Professor Pineau at Brussels discovered a sixth moon of Uranus."

The audience looked around at Ward and began to murmur.

"Why should this Venusian have omitted one of the moons?" Ward asked, his voice ringing across the gymnasium.

Kandinski frowned and peered at Ward suspiciously. "I didn't know there was a sixth moon . . ." he began.

"Exactly!" someone called out. The audience began to titter.

"I can understand the Venusian not wishing to introduce any difficulties," Ward said, "but this seems a curious way of doing it."

Kandinski appeared at a loss. Then he introduced Ward to the audience. "Dr. Ward is a professional while I am only an amateur," he admitted. "I am afraid I cannot explain the anomaly. Perhaps my memory is at fault. But I am sure the Venusian drew only five orbits." He stepped down from the dais and strode out hurriedly, scowling into his beard, pursued by a few derisory hoots from the audience.

It took Ward fifteen minutes to free himself from the knot of admiring, white-gloved spinsters who cornered him between two vaulting horses. When he broke away he ran out to his car and drove into Vernon Gardens, hoping to see Kandinski and apologize to him.

*   *   *

Five miles into the desert Ward approached a nexus of rock cuttings and causeways which were part of an abandoned irrigation scheme. The colors of the hills were more vivid now, bright siliconic reds and yellows, crossed with sharp stabs of light from the exposed quartz veins. Following the map on the seat, he turned off the highway onto a rough track which ran along the bank of a dried-up canal. He passed a few rusting sections of picket fencing, a derelict grader half-submerged under the sand, and a collection of dilapidated metal shacks. The car bumped over the potholes at little more than ten miles an hour, throwing up clouds of hot ashy dust that swirled high into the air behind him.

Two miles along the canal the track came to an end. Ward stopped the car and waited for the dust to subside. Carrying Kandinski's book in front of him like a divining instrument, he set off on foot across the remaining three hundred yards. The contours around him were marked on the map, but the hills had shifted several hundred yards westward since the book's publication and he found himself wandering about from one crest to another, peering into shallow depressions only as old as the last sandstorm. The entire landscape seemed haunted by strange currents and moods; the sand-swirls surging down the aisles of dunes and the proximity of the horizon enclosed the whole place of stones with invisible walls.

Finally he found the ring of hills indicated and climbed a narrow saddle leading to its center. When he scaled the thirty-foot slope he stopped abruptly.

Down on his knees in the middle of the basin with his back to Ward, the studs of his boots flashing in the sunlight, was Kandinski. There was a clutter of tiny objects on the sand around him, and at first Ward thought he was at prayer, making his oblations to the tutelary deities of Venus. Then he saw that Kandinski was slowly scraping the surface of the ground with a small trowel. A circle about twenty yards in diameter had been marked off with pegs and string into a series of wedge-shaped allotments. Every few seconds Kandinski decanted a small heap of grit into one of the test tubes mounted in a wooden rack in front of him.

Ward put away the book and walked down the slope. Kandinski looked around and then climbed to his feet. The coating of red ash on his beard gave him a fiery, prophetic look. He recognized Ward and raised the trowel in greeting.

Ward stopped at the edge of the string perimeter. "What on earth are you doing?"

"I am collecting specimens." Kandinski bent down and corked one of the tubes. He looked tired but worked away steadily.

Ward watched him finish a row. "It's going to take you a long time to cover the whole area. I thought there weren't any gaps left in the Periodic Table."

"The spacecraft rotated at speed before it rose into the air. This surface is abrasive enough to have scratched off a few minute filings. With luck I may find one of them." Kandinski smiled thinly. "262. Venusiam, I hope."

Ward started to say: "But the transuranic elements decay spontaneously . . ." and then walked over to the center of the circle, where there was a round indentation, three feet deep and five across. The inner surface was glazed and smooth. It was shaped like an inverted cone and looked as if it had been caused by the boss of an enormous spinning top. "This is where the spacecraft landed?"

Kandinski nodded. He filled the last tube and then stowed the rack away in a canvas satchel. He came over to Ward and stared down at the hole. "What does it look like to you? A meteor impact? Or an oil drill, perhaps?" A smile showed behind his dusty beard. "The F-109's at the Air Force Weapons School begin their target runs across here. It might have been caused by a rogue cannon shell."

Ward stooped down and felt the surface of the pit, running his fingers thoughtfully over the warm fused silica. "More like a 500-pound bomb. But the cone is geometrically perfect. It's certainly unusual."

"Unusual?" Kandinski chuckled to himself and picked up the satchel.

"Has anyone else been out here?" Ward asked as they trudged up the slope?

"Two so-called experts." Kandinski slapped the sand off his knees. "A geologist from Gulf-Vacuum and an Air Force ballistics officer. You'll be glad to hear that they both thought I had dug the pit myself and then fused the surface with an acetylene torch." He peered critically at Ward. "Why did you come out here today?"

"Idle curiosity," Ward said. "I had an afternoon off and I felt like a drive."

*   *   *

They reached the crest of the hill and he stopped and looked down into the basin. The lines of string split the circle into a strange horological device, a huge zodiacal mandala, the dark patches in the arcs Kandinski had been working telling its stations.

"You were going to tell me why you came out here," Kandinski said as they walked back to the car.

Ward shrugged. "I suppose I wanted to prove something to myself. There's a problem of reconciliation." He hesitated, and then began: "You see, there are some things which are self-evidently false. The laws of common sense and everyday experience refute them. I know a lot of the evidence for many things we believe is pretty thin, but I don't have to embark on a theory of knowledge to decide that the moon isn't made of green cheese."

"Well?" Kandinski shifted the satchel to his other shoulder.

"This Venusian you've seen," Ward said. "The landing, the runic tablet. I can't believe them. Every piece of evidence I've seen, all the circumstantial details, the facts given in this book . . . they're all patently false." He turned to one of the middle chapters. "Take this at random—'A phosphorescent green fluid pulsed through the dorsal lung-chamber of the Prime's helmet, inflating two opaque fan-like gills . . . ' " Ward closed the book and shrugged helplessly. Kandinski stood a few feet away from him, the sunlight breaking across the deep lines of his face.

"Now I know what you say to my objections," Ward went on. "If you told a 19th-century chemist that lead could be transmuted into gold he would have dismissed you as a medievalist. But the point is that he'd have been right to do so—"

"I understand," Kandinski interrupted. "But you still haven't explained why you came out here today."

Ward stared out over the desert. High above, a stratojet was doing cuban eights into the sun, the spiral vapor trails drifting across the sky like gigantic fragments of an apocalyptic message. Looking around, he realized that Kandinski must have walked from the bus-stop on the highway. "I'll give you a lift back," he said.

        *   *   *

As they drove along the canal he turned to Kandinski. "I enjoyed your lecture last night. I apologize for trying to make you look a fool."

Kandinski was loosening his bootstraps. He laughed unreproachfully. "You put me in an awkward position. I could hardly have challenged you. I can't afford to subscribe to every astronomical journal. Though a sixth moon would have been big news." As they neared Vernon Gardens he asked: "Would you like to come in and look at the tablet analysis?"

Ward made no reply to the invitation. He drove around the square and parked under the trees, then looked up at the fountains, tapping his fingers on the windshield. Kandinski sat beside him, cogitating into his beard.

Ward watched him carefully. "Do you think this Venusian will return?"
Kandinski nodded. "Yes. I am sure he will."

* * *

Later they sat together at a broad rolltop desk in the room above the Tycho. Around the wall hung white cardboard screens packed with lines of cuneiform glyphics and Kandinski's progressive breakdown of their meaning.

Ward held an enlargement of the original photograph of the Venusian tablet and listened to Kandinski's explanation.

"As you see from this," Kandinski explained, "in all probability there are not millions of Venusians, as everyone would expect, but only three or four of them altogether. Two are circling Venus, a third Uranus and possibly a fourth is in orbit around Neptune. This solves the difficulty that puzzled you and antagonizes everyone else. Why should the Prime have approached only one person out of several hundred million and selected him on a completely random basis? Now obviously he had seen the Russian and American satellite capsules and assumed that our race, like his own, numbered no more than three or four, then concluded from the atmospheric H-bomb tests that we were in conflict and would soon destroy ourselves. This is one of the reasons why I think he will return shortly and why it is important to organize a worldwide reception for him on a governmental level."

"Wait a minute," Ward said. "He must have known that the population of this planet numbered more than three or four. Even the weakest telescope would demonstrate that."

"Of course, but he would naturally assume that the millions of inhabitants of the Earth belonged to an aboriginal subspecies, perhaps employed as work animals. After all, if he observed that despite this planet's immense resources the bulk of its population lived like animals, an alien visitor could only decide that they were considered as such."

"But space vehicles are supposed to have been observing us since the Babylonian era, long before the development of satellite rockets. There have been thousands of recorded sightings."

Kandinski shook his head. "None of them has been authenticated."

"What about the other landings that have been reported recently?"

Ward asked. "Any number of people have seen Venusians and Martians."

"Have they?" Kandinski asked skeptically. "I wish I could believe that. Some of the encounters reveal marvelous powers of invention, but no one can accept them as anything but fantasy."

"The same criticism has been leveled at your spacecraft," Ward reminded him.

Kandinski seemed to lose patience. "I *saw* it," he exclaimed, impotently tossing his notebook onto the desk. "I *spoke* to the Prime!"

Ward nodded noncommittally and picked up the photograph again. Kandinski stepped over to him and took it out of his hands. "Ward," he said carefully. "*Believe* me. You must. You know I am too big a man to waste myself on a senseless charade." His massive hands squeezed Ward's shoulders and almost lifted him off the seat. "*Believe* me. Together we can be ready for the next landings and alert the world. I am only Charles Kandinski, a waiter at a third-rate cafe, but you are Dr. Andrew Ward of Mount Vernon Observatory. They will listen to you. Try to realize what this may mean for mankind."

Ward pulled himself away from Kandinski and rubbed his shoulders.

"Ward, do you believe me? Ask yourself."

Ward looked up pensively at Kandinski towering over him, his red beard like the burning, unconsumed bush.

"I think so," he said quietly. "Yes, I do."

* * *

A week later the 23rd Congress of the International Geophysical Association opened at Mount Vernon Observatory. At 3:30 P.M., in the Hoyle Library amphitheater, Professor Renthall was to deliver the inaugural address welcoming the ninety-two delegates and twenty-five newspaper and agency reporters to the fortnight's program of lectures and discussions.

Shortly after eleven o'clock that morning Ward and Professor Cameron completed their final arrangements and escaped down to Vernon Gardens for an hour's relaxation.

"Well," Cameron said as they walked over to the Site Tycho, "I've got a pretty good idea of what it must be like to run the Waldorf-Astoria." They picked one of the sidewalk tables and sat down. "I haven't been here for weeks," Cameron said. "How are you getting on with the Man in the Moon?"

"Kandinski? I hardly ever see him," Ward said.

"I was talking to the *Time* magazine stringer about Charles," Cameron said, cleaning his sunglasses. "He thought he might do a piece about him."

"Hasn't Kandinski suffered enough of that sort of thing?" Ward asked moodily.

"Perhaps he has," Cameron agreed. "Is he still working on his crossword puzzle? The tablet thing, whatever he calls it."

Casually, Ward said: "He has a theory that it should be possible to see the lunar bases. Refueling points established there by the Venusians over the centuries."

"Interesting," Cameron commented.

"They're sited near Copernicus," Ward went on. "I know Vandone at Milan is mapping Archimedes and the Imbrium. I thought I might mention it to him at his semester tomorrow."

Professor Cameron took off his glasses and gazed quizzically at Ward. "My dear Andrew, what has been going on? Don't tell me you've become one of Charles' converts?"

Ward laughed and shook his head. "Of course not. Obviously there are no lunar bases or alien spacecraft. I don't for a moment believe a word Kandinski says." He gestured helplessly. "At the same time I admit I have become involved with him. There's something about Kandinski's personality. On the one hand I can't take him seriously—"

"Oh, I take him seriously," Cameron cut in smoothly. "Very seriously indeed, if not quite in the sense you mean." Cameron turned his back on the sidewalk crowds. "Jung's views on flying saucers are very illuminating, Andrew; they'd help you to understand Kandinski. Jung believes that civilization now stands at the conclusion of a Platonic Great Year, at the eclipse of the sign of Pisces which has dominated the Christian epoch, and that we are entering the sign of Aquarius, a period of confusion and psychic chaos.

He remarks that throughout history, at all times of uncertainty and discord, cosmic space vehicles have been seen approaching Earth, and that in a few extreme cases actual meetings with their occupants are supposed to have taken place."

*   *   *

As Cameron paused, Ward glanced across the tables for Kandinski, but a relief waiter served them and he assumed it was Kandinski's day off.

Cameron continued: "Most people regard Charles Kandinski as a lunatic, but as a matter of fact he is performing one of the most important roles in the world today, the role of a prophet alerting people to this coming crisis. The real significance of his fantasies, like that of the ban-the-bomb movements, is to be found elsewhere than on the conscious plane, as an expression of the immense psychic forces stirring below the surface of rational life, like the isotactic movements of the continental tables which heralded the major geological transformations."

Ward shook his head dubiously. "I can accept that a man such as Freud was a prophet, but Charles Kandinski—?"

"Certainly. Far more then Freud. It's unfortunate for Kandinski, and for the writers of science fiction for that matter, that they have to perform their task of describing the symbols of transformation in a so-called rationalist society, where a scientific, or at least a pseudo-scientific, explanation is required a priori. And because the true prophet never deals in what may be rationally deduced, people such as Charles are ignored or derided today."

"It's interesting that Kandinski compared his meeting with the Venusian with Paul's conversion on the road to Damascus," Ward said.

"He was quite right. In both encounters you see the same mechanism of blinding unconscious revelation. And you can see too that Charles feels the same overwhelming need to spread the Pauline revelation to the world. The anti-Apollo movement is only now getting underway, but within the next decade it will recruit millions, and men such as Charles Kandinski will be the fathers of its apocalypse."

"You make him sound like a titanic figure," Ward remarked quietly. "I think he's just a lonely, tired man obsessed by something he can't understand. Perhaps he simply needs a few friends to confide in."

Slowly shaking his head, Cameron tapped the table with his glasses. "Be warned, Andrew, you'll burn your fingers if you play with Charles' brand of fire. The mana-personalities of history have no time for personal loyalties—the founder of the Christian church made that pretty plain."

*   *   *

Shortly after seven o'clock that evening Charles Kandinski mounted his bicycle and set off out of Vernon Gardens. The small room in the seedy area where he lived always depressed him on his free days from the Tycho, and as he pedaled along he ignored the shouts from his neighbors sitting out on their balconies with their crates of beer. He knew that his beard and the high, ancient bicycle with its capacious wicker basket made him a grotesque, Quixotic figure, but he felt too preoccupied to care. That morning he had heard that the French translation of *The Landings from Outer Space*, printed at his own cost, had been completely ignored by the Paris press. In addition a jobbing printer in Santa Vera was pressing him for payment for 5,000 anti-Apollo leaflets that had been distributed the previous year.

Above all had come the news on the radio that the target date of the first manned moonflight had been advanced to 1965, and on the following day would take place the latest and most ambitious of the instrumented lunar flights. The anticipated budget for the Apollo program (in a moment of grim humor he had calculated that it would pay for the printing of some 1,000 billion leaflets) seemed to double each year, but so far he had found little success in his attempt to alert people to the folly of venturing into space. All that day he had felt sick with frustration and anger.

At the end of the avenue he turned onto the highway which served the asparagus farms lying in the twenty-mile strip between Vernon Gardens and the desert. It was a hot, empty evening and few cars or trucks passed him. On either side of the road the great lemon-green terraces of asparagus lay seeping in their moist paddy beds, and occasionally a marsh-hen clacked overhead and dived out of sight.

Five miles along the road he reached the last farmhouse above the edge of the desert. He cycled on to where the road ended two hundred yards ahead, dismounted and left the bicycle in a culvert. Slinging his camera over one shoulder, he walked off across the hard ground into the mouth of a small valley.

The boundary between the desert and the farm-strip was irregular. On his left, beyond the rocky slopes, he could hear a motor-reaper purring down one of the mile-long spits of fertile land running into the desert, but the barren terrain and the sense of isolation began to relax him and he forgot the irritations that had plagued him all day.

A keen naturalist, he saw a long-necked sand crane perched on a spur of shale fifty feet from him and stopped and raised his camera. Peering through the finder he noticed that the light had faded too deeply for a photograph. Curiously, the sand crane was clearly silhouetted against a circular glow of light which emanated from beyond a low ridge at the end of the valley. This apparently sourceless corona fitfully illuminated the darkening air, as if coming from a lighted mineshaft.

Putting away his camera, Kandinski walked forward, within a few minutes reached the ridge, and began to climb it. The face sloped steeply, and he pulled himself up by the hefts of brush and scrub, kicking away footholds in the rocky surface.

*   *   *

Just before he reached the crest he felt his heart surge painfully with the exertion, and he lay still for a moment, a sudden feeling of dizziness spinning in his head. He waited until the spasm subsided, shivering faintly in the cool air, an unfamiliar undertone of uneasiness in his mind. The air seemed to vibrate strangely with an intense inaudible music that pressed upon his temples. Rubbing his forehead, he lifted himself over the crest.

The ridge he had climbed was U-shaped and about two hundred feet across, its open end away from him. Resting on the sandy floor in its center was an enormous metal disc, over one hundred feet in diameter and thirty feet high. It seemed to be balanced on a huge conical boss, half of which had already sunk into the sand. A fluted rim ran around the edge of the disc and separated the upper and lower curvatures, which were revolving rapidly in opposite directions, throwing off magnificent flashes of silver light.

Kandinski lay still, as his first feelings of fear retreated and his courage and presence of mind returned. The inaudible piercing music had faded, and his mind felt brilliantly clear. His eyes ran rapidly over the space-ship, and he estimated that it was over twice the size of the craft he had seen three years earlier. There were no markings or ports on the carapace, but he was certain it had not come from Venus.

Kandinski lay watching the spacecraft for ten minutes, trying to decide upon his best course of action. Unfortunately he had smashed the lens of his camera. Finally, pushing himself backward, he slid slowly down the slope. When he reached the floor he could still hear the whine of the rotors. Hiding in the pools of shadow, he made his way up the valley, and two hundred yards from the ridge he broke into a run.

He returned the way he had come, his great legs carrying him across the ruts and boulders, seized his bicycle from the culvert and ped-aled rapidly toward the farmhouse.

A single light shone in an upstairs room and he pressed one hand to the bell and pounded on the screen door with the other, nearly tearing it from its hinges. Eventually a young woman appeared. She came down the stairs reluctantly, uncertain what to make of Kandinski's beard and ragged, dusty clothes.

"Telephone!" Kandinski bellowed at her, gasping wildly as he caught back his breath.

The girl at last unlatched the door and backed away from him nerv-ously. Kandinski lurched past her and staggered blindly around the dark-ened hall. "Where is it?" he roared.

The girl switched on the lights and pointed into the sitting room. Kandinski pushed past her and rushed over to it.

*   *   *

Ward played with his brandy glass and discreetly loosened the collar of his dress shirt, listening to Dr. MacIntyre of Greenwich Observatory, four seats away on his right, make the third of the after-dinner speeches. Ward was to speak next, and he ran through the opening phrases of his speech, glancing down occasionally to con his notes. At thirty-four he was the youngest member to address the Congress banquet, and by no means unimpressed by the honor. He looked at the venerable figures to his left and right at the top table, their black jackets and white shirt fronts reflected in the table silver, and saw Professor Cameron wink at him reassuringly.

He was going through his notes for the last time when a steward bent over his shoulder. "Telephone for you, Dr. Ward."

"I can't take it now," Ward whispered. "Tell them to call later."

"The caller said it was extremely urgent, Doctor. Something about some people from the Neptune arriving."

"The Neptune?"

"I think that's a hotel in Santa Vera. Maybe the Russian delegates have turned up after all."

Ward pushed his chair back, made his apologies and slipped away.

Professor Cameron was waiting in the alcove outside the banquetting hall when Ward stepped out of the booth. "Anything the trouble, Andrew? It's not your father, I hope——"

"It's Kandinski," Ward said hurriedly. "He's out in the desert, near the farm-strip. He says he's seen another space vehicle."

"Oh, is that all." Cameron shook his head. "Come on, we'd better get back. The poor fool!"

"Hold on," Ward said. "He's got it under observation now. It's on the ground. He told me to call General Wayne at the air base and alert the Strategic Air Command." Ward chewed his lip. "I don't know what to do."

Cameron took him by the arm. "Andrew, come on. MacIntyre's winding up."

"What can we do, though?" Ward asked. "He seemed all right, but then he said that he thought they were hostile. That sounds a little sinister."

"Andrew!" Cameron snapped. "What's the matter with you? Leave Kandinski to himself. You can't go now. It would be unpardonable rudeness."

"I've got to help Kandinski," Ward insisted. "I'm sure he needs it this time." He wrenched himself away from Cameron.

"Ward!" Professor Cameron called. "For God's sake, come back!" He followed Ward out onto the balcony and watched him run down the steps and disappear across the lawn into the darkness.

*   *   *

As the wheels of the car thudded over the deep ruts, Ward cut the headlights and searched the dark hills which marked the desert's edge. The warm glitter of Vernon Gardens lay behind him and only a few isolated lights shone in the darkness on either side of the road. He passed the farmhouse from which he assumed Kandinski had telephoned, then drove on slowly until he saw the bicycle Kandinski had left for him.

It took him several minutes to mount the huge machine, his feet well clear of the pedals for most of their stroke. Laboriously he covered a hundred yards, and after careening helplessly into a clump of scrub was forced to dismount and continue on foot.

Kandinski had told him that the ridge was about a mile up the valley. It was almost night and the starlight reflected off the hills lit the valley with fleeting, vivid colors. He ran on heavily, the only sounds he could hear those of a thresher rattling like a giant metal insect half a mile behind him. Filling his lungs, he pushed on across the last hundred yards.

*   *   *

Kandinski was still lying on the edge of the ridge, watching the spaceship and waiting impatiently for Ward. Below him in the hollow the upper and lower rotor sections swung around more slowly, at about one revolution per second. The spaceship had sunk a further ten feet into the desert floor and he was now on the same level as the observation dome. A single finger of light poked out into the darkness, circling the ridge walls in jerky sweeps.

Then out of the valley behind him he saw someone stumbling along toward the ridge at a broken run. Suddenly a feeling of triumph and exhilaration came over him, and he knew that at last he had his witness.

*   *   *

Ward climbed up the slope to where he could see Kandinski. Twice he lost his grip and slithered downward helplessly, tearing his hands on the gritty surface. Kandinski was lying flat on his chest, his head just above the ridge. Covered by dust, he was barely distinguishable from the slope itself.

"Are you all right?" Ward whispered. He pulled off his bow tie and ripped open his collar. When he had controlled his breathing he crawled up besides Kandinski.

"Where?" he asked.

Kandinski pointed down into the hollow.

Ward raised his head, levering himself up on his elbows. For a few seconds he peered out into the darkness, and then drew his head back.

"You see it?" Kandinski whispered. His voice was short and labored. When Ward hesitated before replying he suddenly seized Ward's wrist in a vice-like grip. In the faint light reflected by the white dust on the ridge Ward could see plainly his bright inflamed eyes.

"Ward! Can you see it?"

Ward nodded. "Yes," he said. "Yes, I see it."

The powerful fingers remained clamped to his wrist as he lay beside Kandinski and gazed down into the darkness.

* * *

Below the compartment window one of Ward's fellow passengers was being seen off by a group of friends, and the young women in bright hats and bandanas and the men in slacks and beach sandals made him feel that he was leaving a seaside resort at the end of a holiday. From the window he could see the observatory domes of Mount Vernon rising out of the trees, and he identified the white brickwork of the Hoyle Library a thousand feet below the summit. Edna Cameron had brought him to the station, but he had asked her not to come onto the platform, and she had said goodbye and driven off. Cameron himself he had seen only once, when he had collected his books from the Institute.

Trying to forget it all, Ward noted thankfully that the train would leave within five minutes. He took his bankbook out of his wallet and counted the last week's withdrawals. He winced at the largest item, 600 dollars which he had transferred to Kandinski's account to pay for the cablegrams.

Deciding to buy something to read, he left the car and walked back to the newsstand. Several of the magazines contained what could only be described as discouraging articles about himself, and he chose two or three newspapers.

Just then someone put a hand on his shoulder. He turned and saw Kandinski.

"Are you leaving?" Kandinski asked quietly. He had trimmed his beard so that only a pale vestige of the original bloom remained, revealing his high bony cheekbones. His face seemed almost fifteen years younger, thinner and more drawn, but at the same time composed, like that of a man recovering slowly from the attack of some intermittent fever.

"I'm sorry, Charles," Ward said as they walked back to the car. "I should have said goodbye to you but I thought I'd better not."

Kandinski's expression was subdued but puzzled. "Why?" he asked. "I don't understand."

Ward shrugged. "I'm afraid everything here has more or less come to an end for me, Charles. I'm going back to Princeton until the spring. Freshman physics." He smiled ruefully at himself. "Boyle's Law, Young's Modulus, getting right back to fundamentals. Not a bad idea, perhaps."

"But why are you leaving?" Kandinski pressed.

"Well, Cameron thought it might be tactful of me to leave. After our statement to the Secretary-General was published in the *New York Times* I became very much *persona non grata* at the Hubble. The trustees were on Professor Renthall again this morning."

Kandinski smiled and seemed relieved. "What does the Hubble matter?" he scoffed. "We have more important work to do. You know, Ward, when Mrs. Cameron told me just now that you were leaving I couldn't believe it."

"I'm sorry, Charles, but it's true."

"Ward," Kandinski insisted. "You can't leave. The Primes will be returning soon. We must prepare for them."

"I know, Charles, and I wish I could stay." They reached the car and Ward put his hand out. "Thanks for coming to see me off."

Kandinski held his hand tightly. "Andrew, tell me the truth. Are you afraid of what people will think of you? Is that why you want to leave? Haven't you enough courage and faith in yourself?"

"Perhaps that's it," Ward conceded, wishing the train would start. He reached for the rail and began to climb into the car but Kandinski held him.

"Ward, you can't drop your responsibilities like this!"

"Please, Charles," Ward said, feeling his temper rising. He pulled his hand away but Kandinski seized him by the shoulder and almost dragged him off the car.

Ward wrenched himself away. "Leave me alone!" he snapped fiercely. "I saw your spaceship, didn't I?"

Kandinski watched him go, a hand picking at his vanished beard, completely perplexed.

Whistles sounded, and the train began to edge forward.

"Goodbye, Charles," Ward called down. "Let me know if you see anything else."

He went into the car and took his seat. Only when the train was twenty miles from Mount Vernon did he look out of the window.

THE ONE THAT GOT AWAY
BY KRISTINE KATHRYN RUSCH

It happened at the Thursday night blackjack tournament, and we were miffed. Not because it happened, but because of *when* it happened. And to get to that will take a bit of explaining, both about the tournament and about us.

There are about ten of us, and we call ourselves the Tuesday/Thursday regulars because we never miss a tournament. The local Native American casino—the Spirit Winds—held an open tournament every Tuesday and Thursday. Anyone could play if he put up twenty bucks, and if he won, he got a share of the pot. The pot consisted of the buy-in fees, and the buy-back fees plus another hundred added by the casino. The casino made no money on the tournament. The game was a freebie designed to get people into the casino—and it got me there twice a week.

Me, and nine others. There were more regulars than us, of course, but we were the ones who never skipped a week. I was a pretty good player—I'd made a living counting cards in the mid-seventies—and I'd swear that Tigo Jones had professional card-playing experience as well. Five more of the regulars played basic strategy, and the rest, well, they relied upon luck or God or their moods to supply their strategy. It worked for them every once in a while.

In blackjack, you learn to honor luck.

The good players just try to minimize it. They try to rely on skill. But luck can win out, in the end, if you're not careful.

On most nights, pot's only worth about two hundred to the winner, a hundred to second place, and fifty to third, with four dinner comps to sop the folks who made it to the final round. What that means is that there's good money in this for me and Tigo because we place every four tournaments we play. A few regulars are losing money each time they play, and about five—those basic strategy guys—are giving their gambling fund an occasional shot in the arm.

It's all in good fun, and we've become a family of sorts—the kind of family that barflies make or old ladies make when they work on church social after church social. We look after each other, and we gossip about each other, and we tolerate each other, whether we like each other or not.

We also know who's crazy and who isn't, and, except for Joey, the kid who is pissing his inheritance away twenty dollars at a time, no one who shows up for the blackjack tournaments at Spirit Winds is crazy.

Or, at least, that's what we hope.

* * *

That night, I noticed a few strange things before I even made it to Spirit Winds. For one thing, the ocean was so black it was impossible to see. Now, the ocean is never black. It reflects light—and even if the sky is completely dark, the ocean isn't because it's reflecting the light of nearby homes. In fact, I like the ocean on cloudy nights because it has a luminescence all its own, a glow that makes it look alive from within.

The second strange thing was that there was no wind. None. Zero, zip, zilch. We usually have a breeze in Seavy Village and often have more than that. The ocean again. It is a major part of our lives.

And the final strange thing was the power outage that swept through the neighborhoods like anxious fingers pinching out candles. I didn't know about that until later—the casino has backup generators—and if I had known, well, it would have made no difference.

I would have been at the tournament anyway.

I have nothing better to do.

You see, I call myself retired, but really what I am is hiding out. I'm good enough to play in big tournaments, but when Spirit Winds holds its semi-annual $10,000 tournament, I'm conveniently out of town. That way, I don't have to fill out a 1099, and I don't have to show three pieces of ID, and all the correct tax information. Because I don't have three valid pieces of ID, and I haven't filed taxes since 1978, the year I fled Nevada with the wrong kind of folks at my heels. I moved too fast to get any fake ID, and so I lived off cash for far too long. By the time I had settled down, I didn't know anybody in that business anymore. The government had closed the loopholes making fake IDs simple for anyone with half a brain, and I really didn't want to put fingers out to the criminal element, since it was the criminal element I'd been running from.

I confessed to a local banker with hippie sympathies, let him think I had been underground since my college activist days, and had him set me up a checking account. It's amazing what a man can do with a checking account—the lies he can tell to get him a real life in a small town.

But it couldn't get me a driver's license, nor could it get me a credit card. I still use cash much of the time, and a lot of that cash comes from my safety deposit box in the aforementioned bank. The gambling at the small casino is just incidental. I figure I'm old enough now that no one would recognize me and my problem is so out of date that the folks who were looking for me are either dead or in prison. But I have learned to be cautious by nature. I don't rub anyone the wrong way.

And I never, ever call attention to myself.

*　　*　　*

The tournament was big that night, bigger than it had ever been. Later I learned the reason: the power outage. The casino was packed on a Thursday because much of Seavy Village had lost their lights, their heat, and their cable. I had been in the casino since mid-afternoon. I'd been on a roll at one of the regular tables, parlaying my lucky hundred dollar chip into six thousand. Normally that puts you in tax declaration territory, but I would get five hundred on one table, then pocket it, and move to the next. I was hot that afternoon, and it felt good.

Lucky streaks are important. Knowing how to maximize them is even more important, and that's what I was doing. Perfecting the old skills.

When I reached six grand, my brain shut off, and I decided to replenish it with food. I had a solitary dinner at the buffet, and then wandered to the tournament tables.

There were a lot of unfamiliar faces around the table, and I was burdened with a small fortune in chips, stuck in my pockets and my fanny pack. I couldn't take anything to the car because I didn't have one, and I also didn't have time to walk home. I'd been in that situation before, and I'd learned not to be too friendly. The last time I'd told one of the regulars about my run and a pit boss overheard. I had to spend a good fifteen minutes making a show of losing the money at various tables.

Normally the pit bosses don't tell on me. They tolerate me and Tigo and the other local professionals. It's the out-of-towners they kick out of the casino. Oregonians and their dislike of "foreigners." Gotta love 'em.

That night, though, I wasn't taking any chances. I leaned against one of the slot machines and smoked a cigarette, adding to the thick, slightly bluish air already growing around the tables. The casino is new and modern—no tokens for slots, only cash and cards—high ceilings, good traffic flow. The place feels more like a spa than a casino, especially the casinos of my heyday. I still miss the chink-chink of tokens as they clink out of the machines. I'm not sure I'll ever get used to those electronic beeps. But not even the modern recycling system was taking care of the cigarette smoke. In a blue-collar town like Seavy Village, card players get nervous when more than $50 is on the line.

That night, forty players had signed up for the tournament, and the pot tipped a grand for the first time since the casino opened.

*   *   *

I'll leave out the detailed descriptions of the rounds, although I can recite all of it, every card, every bet, from the first round, the semi-final round, and the buy-back round. I know by what percentage Tigo beat the odds when he doubled down on eighteen and got a three. I know the exact moment luck abandoned Cherise and it wasn't when she drew a twenty to the dealer's twenty-one. I even know that I made a small mistake on the twenty-ninth hand, and if the cards hadn't gone my way, I would have been out—deservedly so—and it would have peeved me to no end.

I rarely make mistakes.

I can't afford it.

No. I won't say much about the game except that tempers flared early, even among the regulars, because of the amount of money on the table. And people left angry when they were eliminated because everyone could taste their share of the pot.

When it came to the final hand, only the players and the regulars were left.

Tigo and I were on the table, of course, along with the idiot Joey whose luck was running better than usual, and Smoky Butler who was a dealer at another casino on the other side of the coast range. The rest of the players weren't regulars. Two were bad betters and even worse strategists who managed to get the right cards at the right time, and the other one was a black-haired woman who'd caught all of our attention.

She looked like she should be in Monte Carlo, not Seavy Village, Oregon. She wore a black cocktail dress cut in a modified V that revealed more cleavage than I had seen in years. Her hair was pulled into a chignon and over it she wore a cloe hat complete with small veil. Her lips were dark red, and she smoked a cigarette through a cigarette holder.

And she wasn't lucky.

She was good.

Almost as good as me.

The cards were running hot and cold that night, and our pal Joey's luck ran out first. He was off the table in five hands. Then we lost the first of the two bad betters. The second was holding in, but not worth our time. He was out by the eleventh hand.

The rest of us, though. The rest of us had a game.

For our buy-in, the casino gives us $500 in tournament chips (which you can't carry to the real tables) per game. The winner, of course, is the person with the most chips after fifteen hands.

By end of the eleventh hand, I had fifteen hundred eighty-five dollars in phony chips.

Tigo had fifteen hundred seventy-five.

Smoky Butler had fifteen hundred fifty.

And the woman, well, she had two thousand even.

For the first time since I'd left Nevada, I was in a blackjack game where everyone knew how to play. That meant they knew how to draw cards, they knew how to bet, and they knew strategy.

I damned near licked my lips and rubbed my hands together in glee. Instead, I crouched over my chips as if I were protecting them from prying eyes.

We all put out our bets.

The lady put out a hundred.

Smoky put out a hundred fifty.

Tigo a hundred twenty-five.

And me, a hundred fifteen.

Then Rosco, the dealer, began the hand. I was first base (a revolving position), and he gave me an ace of clubs.

Followed by an ace of diamonds for Tigo, an ace of spades for Smoky, and an ace of hearts for the lady.

"They should be playing poker," someone said from behind me.

Rosco gave himself a three of hearts. Then he reached toward the shue for my next card.

At that moment, the lights went out. The place was pitch black except for several small red dots made by the tips of a hundred cigarettes. I fell across my cards and chips, and Rosco yelled, "Freeze!" to the tournament players. The pit bosses were yelling and the dealers were shouting orders, and some old lady near the slots was wailing at the top of her lungs.

All the time, I kept thinking that this shouldn't be happening. It couldn't be happening. The casino had generators. They should have kicked in. (At the time, I didn't know they'd already kicked in, which meant that they shouldn't have gone off—at least, not all at once.)

Then the lights came back up, or I thought they did, until I realized that the overhead lights in the casino were white, not green. Everyone looked as if they were peering at each other through a fish tank. Even the mystery lady looked green. She was holding her cigarette holder over her chips, and glaring at us all angrily, as if we had caused the problem.

The pit bosses were looking mighty scared. I don't know how much money they had to protect, in chips mostly because the cash disappeared into slots beneath the tables, but I knew it was a lot. And there were more civilians in the casino than pit bosses. Security guards had stationed themselves near the casino banks, and other employees had fanned themselves around the room.

I had never seen anything like it, but it made sense. The casino had to have a drill policy for all types of emergencies.

The place was hot and smoky and everything was green. I kept my hands over my chips and scanned for the source of the light.

As I did, a wind came up. First it licked my hair—or what's left of it—and then it cleared the smoke. At first, I thought the air recycling system had turned back on. Then I realized something greater was happening here.

The source of the green lights were small dervishes the size of my coffee saucers at home. They looked like the alien spaceship out of E.T., only shrunk down into toy specials for MacDonalds' Happy Meals. Except they worked. Their top was a dark cone, and their base was a rotating series of lights, all various shades of green.

And there must have been thousands of them in that small space. Maybe even millions of them.

They hovered over various tables, avoided the slot machines, and disappeared into the back. The poker room was filled with them. I could see them from my vantage point, lined up like tiny aircraft carriers facing a city, the poker players backing against the wall, hands up.

Five crafts found their places over our table, and a sixth placed itself above the dealer. The woman pulled a small pistol from her handbag, and a pit boss immediately grabbed it from her—firearms are illegal on Indian land. He pointed it, wobbling for a moment, at one of the little crafts, then Rosco said, "If you shoot one and it explodes and we get that green goo all over us and we die, you're going to regret that."

"He'll regret it more if the bullet hits one of us," Smoky said.

"It could ricochet," Tigo added.

The pit boss let the weapon fall to his side. The woman glared at him.

"I wouldn't have missed," she said, as if she blamed him for taking away her opportunity.

The little crafts were above us, whirling and creating the breeze. Rosco had his hand on the money slot. So, it seemed, did every other dealer in the place. We all stared at the things.

"What are they?" Tigo whispered.

I took the question as rhetorical, and apparently everyone else did too because no one answered him.

One of the pit bosses was on the phone, talking with the 911 dispatch. He was whispering loudly, so loudly he may as well have been shouting: "No, really, I'm not kidding. Please . . ."

Aside from the whirs, the soft mumbles of scared patrons, and the wailing woman, the casino was eerily quiet. No electronic beeps and buzzes, no blaring music, no tinkling chords of winning slots. The silence unnerved me more than anything.

"What do they want?" Tigo whispered.

"Ask them," Smoky snapped.

"I feel like I'm in a James Bond movie," the woman said, and that started a ripple of panic through the pit bosses. They apparently hadn't thought of the things as high-tech theft devices.

"If you were in a James Bond movie, my dear," I said, "you'd have better lighting." No one looked good in that ugly green. Not even the most beautiful woman in the place.

Then, as if on cue, green lights flared out of the bottom of the tiny crafts. I backed away from the table, chips forgotten. So did everyone else. Rosco let go of his hold on the money slot, and one of the pit bosses screamed at him but—I noted—did not make a move toward the money, the table or any of the lights.

The lights hit the table and I expected to see big burning holes appear. I was ready to run for cover—all of this going through my mind in the half second it took, mind you—when I realized what was going on.

The cards rose off the surface, whirling and twirling as if they were in a tornado. For a moment, the entire casino was filled with swirling cards. It looked like an elaborate fan dance, or as if green sea gulls were swarming the beach or like an electronic kaleidoscope performance designed especially for us.

Then one by one the cards slid into the crafts through a slot in the sides. They made a slight ca-thunk! as they entered. Then the green tractor lights—what else could they be called?—went out, and the little green ships whirled away.

The doormen and the folks in the parking lot at the time all say the little ships sped out the doors and into a larger ship that had been hovering over the ocean. A number of green slots opened on it, letting the little ships through, and then they disappeared into the night.

The ocean, which had been dark, regained its luminesence, and slowly the lights flickered on all over town.

At least, that's what the outdoor folks said.

Inside, it was chaos. People started shouting and screaming, and that wailing woman continued. A few people stampeded toward the door, and one relatively fit young man got trampled just enough to later attempt a suit against the casino.

Then the lights came back on. The slot machines groaned as they started up, then beeped through their start-up protocol. The slot players, the video poker players, and the keno players all continued with their games except for a few sensible folks who decided to call it a night and left.

I have no idea what happened inside the poker room, but at the tournament table, we counted our chips. The pit bosses put the game on hold as they made sure the money was fine.

It soon became clear the only thing missing from the casino were the cards.

All of them.

Including the decks stored in the back rooms, and the discards waiting to be trucked off the place, and even the little souvenir cards in the gift shop.

Gone.

All gone.

The pit boss who had called 911 was off the phone, saying the police were going to arrive soon, but I suspected it would take them some time. If, as people were saying, things were a mess all over town, it would take the police a while to get anywhere.

"We still have money on the table," Smoky said.

"And a game to finish," Tigo said.

"How do you propose we do that with no cards?" Rosco asked.

"We know what was dealt," the woman said

"But we don't know the order in the rest of the shue," I said.

"We're going to shuffle a new shue and start over," Rosco said, "just as soon as we get cards."

"We need the other three players," Tigo said. I glanced around me. Joe was standing behind me as he usually did after he got knocked out of a tournament, but the others were nowhere to be seen.

"We're going to have to put this game on hold until the cops arrive anyway," the pit boss said.

"Until we get cards," Rosco added.

"Besides, everyone'll have to report what they saw," Smoky said.

At that point, the woman and I both stood up. "I think my luck has just run out," the woman said.

"Mine, too," I said.

We left the table and headed toward the door.

"Hey!" Tigo said behind us. "We can't replay the game without you guys!"

"I think the game is forfeit," the woman said.

"Yeah, have the casino put the pot in for next week," I said, knowing they never would.

Then she and I walked through the casino, side by side. The conversations were strangely muted, only a few people discussing what they saw. As we stepped outside, we ran into chaos, cars cramming the parking lot, attendants staring at the sky, a warm bath of light all over the town.

A familiar bath of light.

I had missed it more than I realized.

I turned to her. "There's a nice coffee place about a block from here. Care for a walk?"

"I'd love it," she said.

And we had a nice cup of coffee, and a nice evening, and a nice night, and an even better morning. I never learned her name and she never learned mine, but we both knew that we had left the casino for the exact same reason.

We didn't need to see the police.

Or the media.

Or anyone else, for that matter.

"What do you think they wanted with the cards?" she asked long around midnight.

"I don't know," I said. "Maybe they use bigger shues than we do."

And a little later, I said, "That, by far, has to be the strangest thing I ever saw in a casino."

"Really?" she responded. "I've seen stranger."

But she never elaborated and I didn't ask her to.

Some stories are better kept close to the vest.

You see, that isn't the strangest thing I'd ever seen in a casino either.

But it's the only one I'll admit to.

And I only do that because I'm a regular and it's a shared group experience. A bit of local legend—the one game that never finished, the pot that got away.

Well away. The casino had to shut down both the poker and black-jack tables for two days while it ordered cards from all over the country. During that time, regulars gave interviews on every show from CNN to *Hard Copy*. Except for me.

I laid low for a while even after my lady left. Laid low and watched the skies.

And wondered—

What would have happened on the thirteenth hand if we had all blackjacked on the twelfth?

What would have happened then?

PART

II

ALIEN

INVASIONS

TO SERVE MAN
BY DAMON KNIGHT

The Kanamit were not very pretty, it's true. They looked something like pigs and something like people, and that is not an attractive combination. Seeing them for the first time shocked you; that was their handicap. When a thing with the countenance of a fiend comes from the stars and offers a gift, you are disinclined to accept.

I don't know what we expected interstellar visitors to look like—those who thought about it at all, that is. Angels, perhaps, or something too alien to be really awful. Maybe that's why we were all so horrified and repelled when they landed in their great ships and we saw what they really were like.

The Kanamit were short and very hairy—thick, bristly brown-gray hair all over their abominably plump bodies. Their noses were snoutlike and their eyes small, and they had thick hands of three fingers each. They wore green leather harness and green shorts, but I think the shorts were a concession to our notions of public decency. The garments were quite modishly cut, with slash pockets and half-belts in the back. The Kanamit had a sense of humor, anyhow.

There were three of them at this session of the U.N., and, lord, I can't tell you how queer it looked to see them there in the middle of a solemn plenary session—three fat piglike creatures in green harness and shorts, sitting at the long table below the podium, surrounded by the packed arcs of delegates from every nation. They sat correctly upright, politely watching each speaker. Their flat ears drooped over the earphones. Later on, I believe, they learned every human language, but at this time they knew only French and English.

They seemed perfectly at ease—and that, along with their humor, was a thing that tended to make me like them. I was in the minority; I didn't think they were trying to put anything over.

The delegate from Argentina got up and said that his government was interested in the demonstration of a new cheap power source, which the Kanamit had made at the previous session, but that the Argentine government could not commit itself as to its future policy without a much more thorough examination.

It was what all the delegates were saying, but I had to pay particular attention to Señor Valdes, because he tended to sputter and his diction was bad. I got through the translation all right, with only one or two momentary hesitations, and then switched to the Polish-English line to hear how Grigori was doing with Janciewicz. Janciewicz was the cross Grigori had to bear, just as Valdes was mine.

Janciewicz repeated the previous remarks with a few ideological variations, and then the Secretary-General recognized the delegate from France, who introduced Dr. Denis Lévêque, the criminologist, and a great deal of complicated equipment was wheeled in.

Dr. Lévêque remarked that the question in many people's minds had been aptly expressed by the delegate from the U.S.S.R. at the preceding session, when he demanded, "What is the motive of the Kanamit? What is their purpose in offering us these unprecedented gifts, while asking nothing in return?"

The doctor then said, "At the request of several delegates and with the full consent of our guests, the Kanamit, my associates and I have made a series of tests upon the Kanamit with the equipment which you see before you. These tests will now be repeated."

A murmur ran through the chamber. There was a fusillade of flash-bulbs, and one of the TV cameras moved up to focus on the instrument board of the doctor's equipment. At the same time, the huge television screen behind the podium lighted up, and we saw the blank faces of two dials, each with its pointer resting at zero, and a strip of paper tape with a stylus point resting against it.

The doctor's assistants were fastening wires to the temples of one of the Kanamit, wrapping a canvas-covered rubber tube around his fore-arm, and taping something to the palm of his right hand.

In the screen, we saw the paper tape begin to move while the stylus traced a slow zigzag pattern along it. One of the needles began to jump rhythmically; the other flipped halfway over and stayed there, wavering slightly.

"These are the standard instruments for testing the truth of a state-ment," said Dr. Lévêque. "Our first object, since the physiology of the Kanamit is unknown to us, was to determine whether or not they react to these tests as human beings do. We will now repeat one of the many exper-iments which were made in the endeavor to discover this."

He pointed to the first dial. "This instrument registers the subject's heartbeat. This shows the electrical conductivity of the skin in the palm of his hand, a measure of perspiration, which increases under stress. And this—" pointing to the tape-and-stylus device—"shows the pattern and intensity of the electrical waves emanating from his brain. It has been shown, with human subjects, that all these readings vary markedly depending upon whether the subject is speaking the truth."

He picked up two large pieces of cardboard, one red and one black. The red one was a square about three feet on a side; the black was a rectangle three and a half feet long. He addressed himself to the Kanama.

"Which of these is longer than the other?"

"The red," said the Kanama.

Both needles leaped wildly, and so did the line on the unrolling tape.

"I shall repeat the question," said the doctor. "Which of these is longer than the other?"

"The black," said the creature.

This time the instruments continued in their normal rhythm.

"How did you come to this planet?" asked the doctor.

"Walked," replied the Kanama.

Again the instruments responded, and there was a subdued ripple of laughter in the chamber.

"Once more," said the doctor. "How did you come to this planet?"

"In a spaceship," said the Kanama, and the instruments did not jump.

The doctor again faced the delegates. "Many such experiments were made," he said, "and my colleagues and myself are satisfied that the mechanisms are effective. Now—" he turned to the Kanama—"I shall ask our distinguished guest to reply to the question put at the last session by the delegate of the U.S.S.R.—namely, what is the motive of the Kanamit people in offering these great gifts to the people of Earth?"

The Kanama rose. Speaking this time in English, he said, "On my planet there is a saying, 'There are more riddles in a stone than in a philosopher's head.' The motives of intelligent beings, though they may at times appear obscure, are simple things compared to the complex workings of the natural universe. Therefore I hope that the people of Earth will understand, and believe, when I tell you that our mission upon your planet is simply this—to bring to you the peace and plenty which we ourselves enjoy, and which we have in the past brought to other races throughout the galaxy. When your world has no more hunger, no more war, no more needless suffering, that will be our reward."

And the needles had not jumped once.

The delegate from the Ukraine jumped to his feet, asking to be recognized, but the time was up and the Secretary-General closed the session.

I met Grigori as we were leaving the chamber. His face was red with excitement. "Who promoted that circus?" he demanded.

"The tests looked genuine to me," I told him.

"A circus!" he said vehemently. "A second-rate farce! If they were genuine, Peter, why was debate stifled?"

"There'll be time for debate tomorrow, surely."

"Tomorrow the doctor and his instruments will be back in Paris. Plenty of things can happen before tomorrow. In the name of sanity, man, how can anybody trust a thing that looks as if it ate the baby?"

I was a little annoyed. I said, "Are you sure you're not more worried about their politics than their appearance?"

He said, "Bah," and went away.

The next day reports began to come in from government laboratories all over the world where the Kanamit's power source was being tested. They were wildly enthusiastic. I don't understand such things myself, but it seemed that those little metal boxes would give more electrical power than an atomic pile, for next to nothing and nearly forever. And it was said that they were so cheap to manufacture that everybody in the world could have one of his own. In the early afternoon there were reports that seventeen countries had already begun to set up factories to turn them out.

The next day the Kanamit turned up with plans and specimens of a gadget that would increase the fertility of any arable land by 60 to 100 percent. It speeded the formation of nitrates in the soil, or something. There was nothing in the newscasts anymore about stories about the Kanamit. The day after that, they dropped their bombshell.

"You now have potentially unlimited power and increased food supply," said one of them. He pointed with his three-fingered hand to an instrument that stood on the table before him. It was a box on a tripod, with a parabolic reflector on the front of it. "We offer you today a third gift which is at least as important as the first two."

He beckoned to the TV men to roll their cameras into close-up position. Then he picked up a large sheet of cardboard covered with drawings and English lettering. We saw it on the large screen above the podium; it was all clearly legible.

"We are informed that this broadcast is being relayed throughout your world," said the Kanama. "I wish that everyone who has equipment for taking photographs from television screens would use it now."

The Secretary-General leaned forward and asked a question sharply, but the Kanama ignored him.

"This device," he said, "generates a field in which no explosive, of whatever nature, can detonate."

There was an uncomprehending silence.

The Kanama said, "It cannot now be suppressed. If one nation has it, all must have it." When nobody seemed to understand, he explained bluntly, "There will be no more war."

That was the biggest news of the millennium, and it was perfectly true. It turned out that the explosions the Kanama was talking about included gasoline and diesel explosions. They had simply made it impossible for anybody to mount or equip a modern army.

We could have gone back to bows and arrows, of course, but that wouldn't have satisfied the military. Besides, there wouldn't be any reason to make war. Every nation would soon have everything.

Nobody ever gave another thought to those lie-detector experiments, or asked the Kanamit what their politics were. Grigori was put out; he had nothing to prove his suspicions.

I quit my job with the U.N. a few months later, because I foresaw that it was going to die under me anyhow. U.N. business was booming at the time, but after a year or so there was going to be nothing for it to do. Every nation on Earth was well on the way to being completely self-supporting; they weren't going to need such arbitration.

I accepted a position as translator with the Kanamit Embassy, and it was there that I ran into Grigori again. I was glad to see him, but I couldn't imagine what he was doing there.

"I thought you were on the opposition," I said. "Don't tell me you're convinced the Kanamit are all right."

He looked rather shamefaced. "They're not what they look, anyhow," he said.

It was as much of a concession as he could decently make, and I invited him down to the embassy lounge for a drink. It was an intimate kind of place, and he grew confidential over the second daiquiri.

"They fascinate me," he said. "I hate them instinctively still—that hasn't changed—but I can evaluate it. You were right, obviously; they mean us nothing but good. But do you know—" he leaned across the table—"the question of the Soviet delegate was never answered."

I am afraid I snorted.

"No, really," he said. "They told us what they wanted to do—'to bring to you the peace and plenty which we ourselves enjoy.' But they didn't say *why*."

"Why do missionaries—"

"Missionaries be damned!" he said angrily. "Missionaries have a religious motive. If these creatures have a religion, they haven't once mentioned it. What's more, they didn't send a missionary group; they sent a diplomatic delegation—a group representing the will and policy of their whole people. Now just what have the Kanamit, as a people or a nation, got to gain from our welfare?"

I said, "Cultural—"

"Cultural cabbage soup! No, it's something less obvious than that, something obscure that belongs to their psychology and not to ours. But trust me, Peter, there is no such thing as a completely disinterested altruism. In one way or another, they have something to gain."

"And that's why you're here," I said. "To try to find out what it is."

"Correct. I wanted to get on one of the ten-year exchange groups to their home planet, but I couldn't; the quota was filled a week after they made the announcement. This is the next best thing. I'm studying their language, and you know that language reflects the basic assumptions of the people who use it. I've got a fair command of the spoken lingo already. It's not hard, really, and there are hints in it. Some of the idioms are quite similar to English. I'm sure I'll get the answer eventually."

"More power," I said, and we went back to work.

I saw Grigori frequently from then on, and he kept me posted about his progress. He was highly excited about a month after that first meeting; said he'd got hold of a book of the Kanamit's and was trying to puzzle it out. They wrote in ideographs, worse than Chinese, but he was determined to fathom it if it took him years. He wanted my help.

Well, I was interested in spite of myself, for I knew it would be a long job. We spent some evenings together, working with material from Kanamit bulletin boards and so forth, and with the extremely limited English-Kanamit dictionary they issued to the staff. My conscience bothered me about the stolen book, but gradually I became absorbed by the problem. Languages are my field, after all. I couldn't help being fascinated.

We got the title worked out in a few weeks. It was *How to Serve Man*, evidently a handbook they were giving out to new Kanamit members of the embassy staff. They had new ones in, all the time now, a shipload about once a month; they were opening all kinds of research laboratories, clinics and so on. If there was anybody on Earth besides Grigori who still distrusted those people, he must have been somewhere in the middle of Tibet.

It was astonishing to see the changes that had been wrought in less than a year. There were no more standing armies, no more shortages, no unemployment. When you picked up a newspaper you didn't see H-bomb or Satellite leaping out at you; the news was always good. It was a hard thing to get used to. The Kanamit were working on human biochemistry, and it was known around the embassy that they were nearly ready to announce methods of making our race taller and stronger and healthier — practically a race of supermen — and they had a potential cure for heart disease and cancer.

I didn't see Grigori for a fortnight after we finished working out the title of the book; I was on a long-overdue vacation in Canada. When I got back, I was shocked by the change in his appearance.

"What on earth is wrong, Grigori?" I asked. "You look like the very devil."

"Come down to the lounge."

I went with him, and he gulped a stiff Scotch as if he needed it.

"Come on, man, what's the matter?" I urged.

"The Kanamit have put me on the passenger list for the next exchange ship," he said. "You, too, otherwise I wouldn't be talking to you."

"Well," I said, "but—"

"They're not altruists."

I tried to reason with him. I pointed out they'd made Earth a paradise compared to what it was before. He only shook his head.

Then I said, "Well, what about those lie-detector tests?"

"A farce," he replied, without heat. "I said so at the time, you fool. They told the truth, though, as far as it went."

"And the book?" I demanded, annoyed. "What about that—How to Serve Man? That wasn't put there for you to read. They mean it. How do you explain that?"

"I've read the first paragraph of that book," he said. "Why do you suppose I haven't slept for a week?"

I said, "Well?" and he smiled a curious, twisted smile.

"It's a cookbook," he said.

PICTURES DON'T LIE
BY KATHERINE MACLEAN

The man from the *News* asked, "What do you think of the aliens, Mister Nathen? Are they friendly? Do they look human?"

"Very human," said the thin young man.

Outside, rain sleeted across the big windows, blurring and dimming the view of the airfield where *they* would arrive. On the concrete runways, the puddles were pockmarked with rain, and the grass growing untouched between the runways of the unused airfield glistened wetly, bending before gusts of wind.

Back at a respectful distance from where the huge spaceship would land were the gray shapes of trucks, where TV camera crews huddled inside their mobile units, waiting. Farther back in the deserted sandy landscape, behind distant sand hills, artillery was ranged in a great circle, and in the distance across the horizon, bombers stood ready at airfields, guarding the world against possible treachery from the first alien ship ever to land from space.

"Do you know anything about their home planet?" asked the man from the *Herald*.

The *Times* man stood with the others, listening absently; thinking of questions but reserving them. Joseph R. Nathen, the thin young man with the straight black hair and the tired lines on his face, was being treated with respect by his interviewers. He was obviously on edge, and they did not want to harry him with too many questions. They wanted to keep his goodwill. Tomorrow he would be one of the biggest celebrities ever to appear in headlines.

"No, nothing directly."

"Any ideas or deductions?" *Herald* persisted.

"Their world must be Earth-like to them," the weary-looking young man answered uncertainly. "The environment evolves the animal. But only in relative terms, of course." He looked at them with a quick glance and then looked away evasively, his lank black hair beginning to cling to his forehead with sweat. "That doesn't necessarily mean anything."

"Earth-like," muttered a reporter, writing it down as if he had noticed nothing more in the reply.

The *Times* man glanced at the *Herald*, wondering if he had noticed, and received a quick glance in exchange.

The *Herald* asked Nathen, "You think they are dangerous, then?"

It was the kind of question assuming much, which usually broke reticence and brought forth quick facts—when it hit the mark. They all knew of the military precautions, although they were not supposed to know.

The question missed. Nathen glanced out the window vaguely. "No, I wouldn't say so."

"You think they are friendly, then?" said the *Herald*, equally positive on the opposite tack.

A fleeting smile touched Nathen's lips. "Those I know are."

There was no lead in this direction, and they had to get the basic facts of the story before the ship came. The *Times* asked, "What led up to your contacting them?"

Nathen answered after a hesitation. "Static. Radio static. The Army told you my job, didn't they?"

The Army had told them nothing at all. The officer who had conducted them in for the interview stood glowering watchfully, as if he objected by instinct to telling the public anything.

Nathen glanced at him doubtfully. "My job is radio decoding for the Department of Military Intelligence. I use a directional pickup, tune in on foreign bands, record any scrambled or coded messages I hear, and build automatic decoders and descramblers for all the basic scramble patterns."

The officer cleared his throat but said nothing.

The reporters smiled, noting that down.

Security regulations had changed since arms inspection had been legalized by the U.S. Complete information being the only public security against secret rearmament, spying and prying had come to seem a public service. Its aura had changed. It was good public relations to admit to it.

Nathen continued, "I started directing the pickup at stars in my spare time. There's radio noise from stars, you know. Just stuff that sounds like spatter static, and an occasional squawk. People have been listening to it for a long time and researching, trying to work out why stellar radiation on those bands comes in such jagged bursts. It didn't seem natural."

He paused and smiled uncertainly, aware that the next thing he would say was the thing that would make him famous—an idea that had come to him while he listened—an idea as simple and as perfect as the one that came to Newton when he saw the apple fall.

"I decided it wasn't natural. I tried decoding it."

Hurriedly he tried to explain it away and make it seem obvious. "You see, there's an old intelligence trick: speeding up a message on a record until it sounds just like that, a short squawk of static, and then broadcasting it. Undergrounds use it. I'd heard that kind of screech before."

"You mean they broadcast at us in code?" asked the *News*.

"It's not exactly code. All you need to do is record it and slow it down. They're not broadcasting at us. If a star has planets, inhabited planets, and there is broadcasting between them, they would send it on a tight beam to save power." He looked for comprehension. "You know, like a spotlight. Theoretically, a tight beam can go on forever without losing power. But aiming would be difficult from planet to planet. You can't expect a beam to stay on target over such distances more than a few seconds at a time. So they'd naturally compress each message into a short half-second- or one-second-long package and send it a few hundred times in one long blast to make sure it is picked up during the instant the beam swings across the target."

He was talking slowly and carefully, remembering that this explanation was for the newspapers. "When a stray beam swings through our section of space, there's a sharp peak in noise level from that direction. The beams are swinging to follow their own planets at home, and the distance between there and here exaggerates the speed of swing tremendously, so we wouldn't pick up more than a bip as it passes."

"How do you account for the number of squawks coming in?" the Times asked. "Do stellar systems rotate on the plane of the galaxy?" It was a private question; he spoke impulsively from excitement.

The radio decoder grinned, the lines of strain vanishing from his face for a moment. "Maybe we're intercepting everybody's telephone calls, and the whole galaxy is swarming with races that spend all day yakking at each other over the radio. Maybe the human type is a standard model."

"It would take something like that," the Times agreed. They smiled at each other.

The News asked "How did you happen to pick up television instead of voices?"

"Not by accident," Nathen explained patiently. "I'd recognized a scanning pattern, and I wanted pictures. Pictures are understandable in any language."

*   *   *

Near the interviewers, a Senator paced back and forth, muttering his memorized speech of welcome and nervously glancing out the wide streaming windows into the gray sleeting rain.

Opposite the windows of the long room was a small raised platform flanked by the tall shapes of TV cameras and sound pickups on booms, and darkened floodlights, arranged and ready for the Senator to make his speech of welcome to the aliens and the world. A shabby radio sending set stood beside it without a case to conceal its parts, two cathode television tubes flickering naked on one side and the speaker humming on the other. A vertical panel of dials and knobs jutted up before them, and a small hand-mike sat ready on the table before the panel. It was connected to a boxlike, expensively cased piece of equipment with "Radio Lab, U.S. Property" stenciled on it.

"I recorded a couple of package screeches from Sagittarius and began working on them," Nathen added. "It took a couple of months to find the synchronizing signals and set the scanners close enough to the right time to even get a pattern. When I showed the pattern to the department, they gave me full time to work on it and an assistant to help. It took eight months to pick out the color bands and assign them the right colors, to get anything intelligible on the screen."

The shabby-looking mess of exposed parts was the original receiver that they had labored over for ten months, adjusting and readjusting to reduce the maddening rippling plaids of unsynchronized color scanners to some kind of sane picture.

"Trial and error," said Nathen, "but it came out all right. The wide band-spread of the squawks had suggested color TV from the beginning."

He walked over and touched the set. The speaker bipped slightly, and the gray screen flickered with a flash of color at the touch. The set was awake and sensitive, tuned to receive from the great interstellar spaceship which now circled the atmosphere.

Between the pauses in Nathen's voice, the Times found himself unconsciously listening for the sound of roaring, swiftly approaching rocket jets.

The Post asked, "How did you contact the spaceship?"

"I scanned and recorded a film copy of *Rite of Spring*, the Disney-Stravinsky combination, and sent it back along the same line we were receiving from. Just testing. It wouldn't get there for a good number of years, if it got there at all, but I thought it would please the library to get a new record in.

"Two weeks later, when we caught and slowed a new batch of recordings, we found an answer. It was obviously meant for us. It was a flash of the Disney being played to a large audience, and then the audience sitting and waiting before a blank screen. The signal was very clear and loud. We'd intercepted a spaceship. They were asking for an encore, you see. They liked the film and wanted more. . . ."

He smiled at them in sudden thought. "You can see them for yourself. It's all right down the hall where the linguists are working on the automatic translator."

The listening officer frowned and cleared his throat, and the thin young man turned to him quickly. "No security reason why they should not see the broadcast, is there? Perhaps you should show them." He said to the reporters reassuringly, "It's right down the hall. You will be informed the moment the spaceship approaches."

The interview was very definitely over. The lank-haired, nervous young man turned away and seated himself at the radio set while the officer swallowed his objections and showed them dourly down the hall to a closed door.

They opened it and fumbled into a darkened room crowded with empty folding chairs and dominated by a glowing bright screen. The door closed behind them, bringing total darkness.

There was the sound of reporters fumbling their way into seats around him, but the *Times* man remained standing, aware of an enormous surprise, as if he had been asleep and wakened to find himself in the wrong country.

The bright colors of the double image seemed the only real thing in the darkened room. Even blurred as they were, he could see that the action was subtly different, the shapes subtly not right.

He was looking at aliens.

The impression was of two humans in disguise; humans moving oddly, half-dancing, half-crippled. Carefully, afraid the images would go away, he reached up to his breast pocket, took out his polarized glasses, rotated one lens at right angles to the other, and put them on.

Immediately, the two beings came into sharp focus, real and solid, and the screen became a wide, illusively near window through which he watched them.

They were conversing with each other in a gray-walled room, discussing something with restrained excitement. The large man in the green tunic closed his purple eyes for an instant at something the other said and grimaced, making a motion with his fingers as if shoving something away from him.

Mellerdrammer.

The second, smaller, with yellowish-green eyes, stepped closer, talking more rapidly in a lower voice. The first stood very still, not trying to interrupt.

Obviously, the proposal was some advantageous treachery, and he wanted to be persuaded. The *Times* groped for a chair and sat down.

Perhaps gesture is universal: desire, a leaning forward; aversion, a leaning back; tension, relaxation. Perhaps these actors were masters. The scenes changed, a corridor, a parklike place in what he began to realize was a spaceship, a lecture room. There were others talking and working, speaking to the man in the green tunic, and never was it unclear what was happening or how they felt.

They talked a flowing language with many short vowels and shifts of pitch, and they gestured in the heat of talk, their hands moving with an odd lagging difference of motion, not slow but somehow drifting.

He ignored the language, but after a time the difference in motion began to arouse his interest. Something in the way they walked. . . .

With an effort he pulled his mind from the plot and forced his attention to the physical difference. Brown hair in short silky crew cuts, varied eye colors, the colors showing clearly because their irises were very large, their round eyes set very widely apart in tapering light brown faces. Their necks and shoulders were thick in a way that would indicate unusual strength for a human, but their wrists were narrow and their fingers long and thin and delicate.

There seemed to be more than the usual number of fingers.

Since he came in, a machine had been whirring and a voice muttering beside him. He called his attention from counting fingers and looked around. Beside him sat an alert-looking man wearing earphones, watching and listening with hawklike concentration. Beside him was a tall streamlined box. From the screen came the sound of the alien language. The man abruptly flipped a switch on the box, muttered a word into a small handmicrophone, and flipped the switch back with nervous rapidity.

He reminded the Times man of the earphoned interpreters at the U.N. The machine was probably a vocal translator, and the mutterer a linguist adding to its vocabulary. Near the screen were two other linguists taking notes.

*   *   *

The Times remembered the Senator pacing in the observatory room, rehearsing his speech of welcome. The speech would not be just an empty pompous gesture. It would be translated mechanically and understood by the aliens.

On the other side of the glowing window that was the stereo screen, the large protagonist in the green tunic was speaking to a pilot in a gray uniform. They stood in a brightly lit canary-yellow control room in a spaceship.

The Times tried to pick up the thread of the plot. Already he was interested in the fate of the hero, and liked him. That was the effect of good acting probably, for part of the art of acting is to win affection from the audience, and this actor might be the matinee idol of whole solar systems.

Controlled tension, betraying itself by a jerk of the hands, a too-quick answer to a question. The uniformed one, not suspicious, turned his back and busied himself at some task involving a map lit with glowing red points, his motions sharing the same fluid dragging grace of the others, as if they were underwater or on a slow-motion film. The other was watching a switch, a switch set into a panel, moving closer to it, talking casually— background music coming and rising in thin chords of tension.

There was a close-up of the alien's face watching the switch, and the Times noted that his ears were symmetrical half circles, almost perfect, with no earholes visible. The voice of the uniformed one answered, a brief word in a preoccupied deep voice. His back was still turned. The other glanced at the switch, moving closer to it, talking casually, the switch coming closer and closer stereoscopically. It was in reach, filling the screen. His hand came into view, darting out, closed over the switch—

There was a sharp clap of sound, and his hand opened in a frozen shape of pain. Beyond him, as his gaze swung up, stood the figure of the uniformed officer, unmoving, a weapon rigid in his hand, in the startled position in which he had turned and fired, watching with widening eyes as the man in the green tunic swayed and fell.

The tableau held, the uniformed one drooping, looking down at his hand holding the weapon which had killed, and music began to build in from the background. Just for an instant, the room and the things within it flashed into one of those bewildering color changes which were the bane of color television, and switched to a color negative of itself, a green man standing in a violet control room, looking down at the body of a green man in a red tunic. It held for less than a second; then the color-band alternator fell back into phase, and the colors reversed to normal.

Another uniformed man came and took the weapon from the limp hand of the other, who began to explain dejectedly in a low voice while the music mounted and covered his words and the screen slowly went blank, like a window that slowly filmed over with gray fog.

The music faded.

In the dark, someone clapped appreciatively.

The earphoned man beside the Times shifted his earphones back from his ears and spoke briskly. "I can't get any more. Either of you want a replay?"

There was a short silence until the linguist nearest the set said, "I guess we've squeezed that one dry. Let's run the tape where Nathen and that ship's radio boy are diddling around, CQing and tuning their beams. I have a hunch the boy is talking routine ham talk and giving the old radio count, one-two-three-testing. If he is, we have number words."

There was some fumbling in the semidark, and then the screen came to life again.

*   *   *

It showed a flash of an audience sitting before a screen and gave a clipped chord of some familiar symphony. "Crazy about Stravinsky and Mozart," remarked the earphoned linguist to the Times, resettling his earphones. "Can't stand Gershwin. Can you beat that?" He turned his attention back to the screen as the right sequence came on.

The Post, who was sitting just in front of him, turned to the Times and said, "Funny how much they look like people." He was writing, making notes to telephone his report. "What color hair did that character have?"

"I didn't notice." He wondered if he should remind the reporter that Nathen had said he assigned the color bands on guess, choosing the colors that gave the most plausible images. The guests, when they arrived, could turn out to be bright green with blue hair. Only the gradations of color in the picture were sure, only the similarities and contrasts, the relationship of one color to another.

From the screen came the sound of the alien language again. This race averaged deeper voices than human. He liked deep voices. Could he write that?

No, there was something wrong with that, too. How had Nathen established the right sound-track pitch? Was it a matter of taking the modulation as it came in, or some sort of heterodyning up and down by trial and error? Probably.

It might be safer to assume that Nathen had simply preferred deep voices.

As he sat there, doubting, an uneasiness he had seen in Nathen came back to memory. The tightness and uncertainty of Nathen's gestures. . . . He was afraid of something.

"What I still don't get, is why he went to all the trouble of building a special TV set to pick up their TV shows, instead of just talking to them on the radio," the News complained aloud. "They're good shows, but what's the point?"

Nobody bothered to answer. Pictures can be understood. Pictures need no translation. Pictures don't lie. Nathen's reasoning was obvious to the others.

On the screen now was the obviously unstaged and genuine scene of a young alien working over a bank of apparatus. He turned and waved, and opened his mouth in the comical O shape which the Times was beginning to recognize as their equivalent of a grin, then went back to trying to explain something about the equipment, in elaborate awkward gestures and carefully mouthed words.

The Times got up quietly, went out into the bright, white stone corridor, and walked back the way he had come, thoughtfully folding his stereo glasses and putting them away.

No one stopped him. Secrecy restrictions were ambiguous here. The reticence of the Army seemed a matter of habit, a reflex response of the Intelligence Department, in which all this had originated, rather than any reasoned policy of keeping the landing a secret.

The main room was more crowded than when he had left it. The TV camera and sound crew stood near their apparatus, the Senator had found a chair and was reading, and at the far end of the room eight men were grouped in a circle of chairs, arguing something with impassioned concentration. The Times recognized a few he knew personally, eminent names in science, workers in field theory.

A stray phrase reached him: "—reference to the universal constants as ratio—" It was probably a discussion of ways of converting formulas from one mathematics to another for a rapid exchange of information.

They had reason to be intent, aware of the flood of insights that novel viewpoints could bring if they could grasp them. He would have liked to go over and listen, but there was too little time left before the spaceship was due, and he had a question to ask.

The land-rigged transceiver was still humming, tuned to the sending band of the circling ship, and the young man who had started it all was sitting on the edge of the TV platform, with his chin resting in one hand. He did not look up as the *Times* approached, but it was the indifference of preoccupation, not discourtesy.

The *Times* sat down on the edge of the platform beside him and took out a pack of cigarettes, then remembered the coming TV broadcast and the ban on smoking. He put them away, thoughtfully watching the diminishing rain spray against the streaming windows.

"What's wrong?" he asked.

Nathen showed that he was aware and friendly by a slight motion of his head.

"You tell me."

"Hunch," said the *Times* man. "Sheer hunch. Everything sailing along too smoothly, everyone taking too much for granted."

Nathen relaxed slightly. "I'm still listening."

"Something about the way they move. . . ."

Nathen shifted to glance at him.

"That's bothered me, too."

"Are you sure they're adjusted to the right speed?"

Nathen clenched his hands out in front of him and looked at them consideringly. "I don't know. When I turn the tape faster, they're all rushing, and you begin to wonder why their clothes don't stream behind them, why the doors close so quickly and yet you can't hear them slam, why things fall so fast. If I turn it slower, they all seem to be swimming." He gave the *Times* a considering sidewise glance. "Didn't catch the name."

Country-bred guy, thought the *Times*. "Jacob Luke, *Times*," he said, extending his hand.

Nathen gave the hand a quick, hard grip, identifying the name. "Sunday Science Section editor. I read it. Surprised to meet you here."

"Likewise." The Times smiled. "Look, have you gone into this rationally, with formulas?" He found a pencil in his pocket. "Obviously there's something wrong with our judgment of their weight–to-speed–to-momentum ratio. Maybe it's something simple like low gravity aboard ship, with magnetic shoes. Maybe they are floating slightly."

"Why worry?" Nathen cut in. "I don't see any reason to try to figure it out now." He laughed and shoved back his black hair nervously. "We'll see them in twenty minutes."

"Will we?" asked the Times slowly.

There was a silence while the Senator turned a page of his magazine with a slight crackling of paper, and the scientists argued at the other end of the room. Nathen pushed at his lank black hair again, as if it were trying to fall forward in front of his eyes and keep him from seeing.

"Sure." The young man laughed suddenly, talked rapidly. "Sure we'll see them. Why shouldn't we, with all the Government ready with welcome speeches, the whole Army turned out and hiding over the hill, reporters all around, newsreel cameras—everything set up to broadcast the landing to the world. The President himself shaking hands with me and waiting in Washington—"

He came to the truth without pausing for breath.

He said, "Hell, no, they won't get here. There's some mistake somewhere. Something's wrong. I should have told the brass hats yesterday when I started adding it up. Don't know why I didn't say anything. Scared, I guess. Too much top rank around here. Lost my nerve."

He clutched the Times man's sleeve. "Look, I don't know what—"

A green light flashed on the sending-receiving set. Nathen didn't look at it, but he stopped talking.

∗ ∗ ∗

The loudspeaker on the set broke in a voice speaking in the alien's language. The Senator started and looked nervously at it, straightening his tie. The voice stopped.

Nathan turned and looked at the loudspeaker. His worry seemed to be gone.

"What is it?" the *Times* asked anxiously.

"He says they've slowed enough to enter the atmosphere now. They'll be here in five to ten minutes, I guess. That's Bud. He's all excited. He says holy smoke, what a murky-looking planet we live on." Nathen smiled. "Kidding."

The *Times* was puzzled. "What does he mean, murky? It can't be raining over much territory on Earth." Outside, the rain was slowing, and bright blue patches of sky were shining through breaks in the cloud blanket, glittering blue light from the drops that ran down the windows. Murky? He tried to think of an explanation. "Maybe they're trying to land on Venus." The thought was ridiculous, he knew. The spaceship was following Nathen's sending beam. It couldn't miss Earth. "Bud" had to be kidding.

The green light on the set glowed again, and they stopped speaking, waiting for the message to be recorded, slowed, and replayed. The cathode screen came to life suddenly with a picture of the young man sitting at his sending-set, his back turned, watching a screen at one side which showed a glimpse of a huge dark plain approaching. As the ship plunged down toward it, the illusion of solidity melted into a boiling turbulence of black clouds. They expanded in an ink swirl, looked huge for an instant, and then blackness swallowed the screen. The young alien swung around to face the camera, speaking a few words as he moved, made the O of a smile again, then flipped the switch and the screen went gray.

Nathen's voice was suddenly toneless and strained. "He said something like break out the drinks, here they come."

"The atmosphere doesn't look like that," the *Times* said at random, knowing he was saying something too obvious even to think about. "Not Earth's atmosphere."

Some people drifted up. "What did they say?"

"Entering the atmosphere, ought to be landing in five or ten minutes," Nathen told them.

A ripple of heightened excitement ran through the room.

Cameramen began adjusting the lens angles again, turning on mikes and checking them, turning on the floodlights. The scientists rose and stood near the window, still talking. The reporters trooped in from the hall and went to the windows to watch for the great event. The three linguists came in, trundling a large wheeled box that was the mechanical translator, supervising while it was hitched into the sound broadcasting system.

"Landing where?" the *Times* asked Nathen brutally. "Why don't you do something?"

"Tell me what to do and I'll do it," Nathen said quietly, not moving.

It was not sarcasm. Jacob Luke of the *Times* looked sidewise at the strained whiteness of his face and moderated his tone. "Can't you contact them?"

"Not while they're landing."

"What now?" The *Times* took out a pack of cigarettes, remembered the rule against smoking, and put it back.

"We just wait." Nathen leaned his elbow on one knee and his chin in his hand.

They waited.

*   *   *

All the people in the room were waiting. There was no more conversation. A bald man in the scientist group was automatically buffing his fingernails over and over and inspecting them without seeing them, another absently polished his glasses, held them up to the light, put them on, and then a moment later took them off and began polishing again. The television crew concentrated on their jobs, moving quietly and efficiently, with perfectionist care, minutely arranging things which did not need to be arranged, checking things that had already been checked.

This was to be one of the great moments of human history, and they were all trying to forget that fact and remain impassive and wrapped up in the problems of their jobs, as good specialists should.

After an interminable age the *Times* consulted his watch. Three minutes had passed. He tried holding his breath a moment, listening for a distant approaching thunder of jets. There was no sound.

The sun came out from behind the clouds and lit up the field like a great spotlight on an empty stage.

Abruptly the green light shone on the set again, indicating that a squawk message had been received. The recorder recorded it, slowed it, and fed it back to the speaker. The speaker clicked, and the sound was very loud in the still, tense room.

The screen remained gray, but Bud's voice spoke a few words in the alien language. He stopped, the speaker clicked, and the light went out. When it was plain that nothing more would occur and no announcement was to be made of what was said, the people in the room turned back to the windows. Talk picked up again.

Somebody told a joke and laughed alone.

One of the linguists remained turned toward the loudspeaker, then looked at the widening patches of blue sky showing out the window, his expression puzzled. He had understood.

"'It's dark,'" the thin Intelligence Department decoder translated, low-voiced, to the man from the *Times*. "'Your atmosphere is *thick*.' That's precisely what Bud said."

Another three minutes. The *Times* caught himself about to light a cigarette and swore silently, blowing the match out and putting the cigarette back into its package. He listened for the sound of the rocket jets. It was time for the landing, yet he heard no blasts.

The green light came on in the transceiver.

Message in.

Instinctively he came to his feet. Nathen abruptly was standing beside him. Then the message came in the voice he was coming to think of as Bud. It spoke and paused. Suddenly the *Times* knew.

"We've landed." Nathen whispered the words.

The wind blew across the open spaces of white concrete and damp soil that was the empty airfield, swaying the wet, shiny grass. The people in the room looked out, listening for the roar of jets, looking for the silver bulk of a spaceship in the sky.

Nathen moved, seating himself at the transmitter, switching it on to warm up, checking and balancing dials. Jacob Luke of the *Times* moved softly to stand behind his right shoulder, hoping he could be useful. Nathen made a half motion of his head, as if to glance back at him, unhooked two of the earphone sets hanging on the side of the tall streamlined box that was the automatic translator, plugged them in, and handed one back over his shoulder to the *Times* man.

The voice began to come from the speaker again.

Hastily, Jacob Luke fitted the earphones over his ears. He fancied he could hear Bud's voice tremble. For a moment it was just Bud's voice speaking the alien language, and then, very distant and clear in his earphones, he heard the recorded voice of the linguist say an English word, then a mechanical click and another clear word in the voice of one of the other translators, then another as the alien's voice flowed from the loudspeaker, the cool single words barely audible, overlapping and blending with it like translating thought, skipping unfamiliar words, yet quite astonishingly clear.

"Radar shows no buildings or civilization near. The atmosphere around us registers as thick as glue. Tremendous gas pressure, low gravity, no light at all. You didn't describe it like this. Where are you, Joe? This isn't some kind of trick, is it?" Bud hesitated, was prompted by a deeper official voice, and jerked out the words:

"If it is a trick, we are ready to repel attack."

           *   *   *

The linguist stood listening. He whitened slowly and beckoned the other linguists over to him and whispered to them.

Joseph Nathen looked at them with unwarranted bitter hostility while he picked up the hand-mike, plugging it into the translator. "Joe calling," he said quietly into it in clear, slow English. "No trick. We don't know where you are. I am trying to get a direction fix from your signal. Describe your surroundings to us if at all possible."

Nearby, the floodlights blazed steadily on the television platform, ready for the official welcome of the aliens to Earth. The television channels of the world had been alerted to set aside their scheduled programs for an unscheduled great event. In the long room the people waited, listening for the swelling sound of rocket jets.

This time, after the light came on, there was along delay. The speaker sputtered, and sputtered again, building to a steady scratching behind which they could barely sense a dim voice. It came through in a few tinny words and then wavered back to inaudibility. The machine translated in their earphones.

"Tried . . . seemed . . . repair. . . ." Suddenly it came in clearly. "Can't tell if the auxiliary blew, too. Will try it. We might pick you up clearly on the next try. I have the volume down. Where is the landing port? Where are you?"

Nathen put down the hand-mike and carefully set a dial on the recording box and flipped a switch, speaking over his shoulder. "This sets it to repeat what I said the last time. It keeps repeating." Then he sat with unnatural stillness, his head still half turned, as if he had suddenly caught a glimpse of answer and was trying to understand it.

The green warning light cut in, the recording clicked, and the play-back of Bud's face and voice appeared on the screen.

"We heard a few words, Joe, and then the receiver blew again. We're adjusting a viewing screen to pick up the long waves that go through the murk and convert them to visible light. We'll be able to see out soon. The engineer says that something is wrong with the stern jets, and the Captain has had me broadcast to help call to our nearest space base." He made the mouth O of a grin. "The message won't reach it for some years. I trust you, Joe, but get us out of here, will you? They're buzzing that the screen is finally ready. Hold everything."

*   *   *

The screen went gray, and the green light went off.

The *Times* considered the lag required for the help call, the speaking and recording of the message just received, the time needed to reconvert a viewing screen.

"They work fast." He shifted uneasily and added at random, "Something wrong with the time factor. All wrong. They work *too* fast."

The green light came on again immediately. Nathen half turned to him, sliding his words hastily into the gap of time as the message was recorded and slowed. "They're close enough for our transmission power to blow their receiver."

If it was on Earth, why the darkness around the ship?

"Maybe they see in the high ultraviolet—the atmosphere is opaque to that band," the Times suggested hastily as the speaker began to talk in the young extraterrestrial's voice.

His voice *was* really shaking now. "Stand by for the description." They tensed, waiting. The Times brought a map of the state before his mind's eye.

"A half circle of cliffs around the horizon. A wide, muddy lake, swarming with swimming things. Huge, strange white foliage all around the ship, and incredibly huge pulpy monsters attacking and eating each other on all sides. We almost landed in the lake, right on the soft edge. The mud can't hold the ship's weight, and we're sinking. The engineer says we might be able to blast free, but the tubes are mud-clogged and might blow up the ship. When can you reach us?"

The description fitted nowhere on the map of the state. It fitted nowhere on a map of Earth. Pulpy monsters. . . . Times thought of the Carboniferous era. Dinosaurs? Cliffs . . . a muddy lake . . . monsters. . . . Where?

"Right away," Nathen said. "We can reach them right away." Nathen obviously had seen something.

"Where are they?" the Times asked him quietly.

Nathen pointed to the antenna position indicators. The Times let his eyes follow the converging imaginary lines of focus out the window to the sunlit airfield, the empty airfield, the white drying concrete runways and green waving grass where the lines met.

Where the lines met. The spaceship was there!

The fear of something unknown gripped him suddenly.

The spaceship was broadcasting again. *"Where are you? Answer if possible! We are sinking! Where are you?"*

He saw that Nathen knew. "What is it?" the Times asked hoarsely. "How will we get them out of there? Are they in another dimension, or the past, or in another world, or what?"

*   *   *

Nathen was smiling bitterly, and Times remembered that he had a good friend in the spaceship.

"My guess is that they evolved on a high-gravity planet with a thin atmosphere near a blue-white sun. Sure they see in the ultraviolet. Blue-white stars are normal. Our sun is small and dim and yellow, not normal. Our atmosphere is so thick, like under water. . . ." He brought his gaze back to Jacob Luke of the Times without seeing him, seeing only some picture in his own mind. "We are giants, do you understand? Big, slow, stupid. . . ."

"Where is the spaceship?"

"Slow. . . ." Nathen laughed harshly. "A good joke on us, the weird place we live in, the thing it did to us."

The receiver squawked. The decoder machine caught the squawk, slowed it, and replayed it immediately, spacing the tumbled frightened voice with cool English words.

"Where are you?" called the young voice from the alien spaceship. "Hurry, please, we're sinking."

The Times man took off the earphones and came to his feet. "We've got to hurry." He gripped Nathen's shoulder to get his attention. "Just tell me. Where are they?"

Nathen looked up into Times' face. "I want you to understand. We'll rescue them," he said quietly. "You were right about their way of moving, right about them moving at different speeds. This business I told you about them squawk-coding, speeding up their messages for better transmission. I was wrong."

"What do you mean?"

"They don't speed up their broadcasts."

"They don't—?"

Suddenly, in his mind's eye, the Times man began to see again the play he had just seen—but the actors were moving at blurring speed, the words jerking out in fluting, dizzying streams, thoughts and decisions passing with unnoticeable rapidity, rippling faces in a twisting blue of expressions, doors slamming wildly, shatteringly, as the actors leaped in and out of rooms.

No—faster, faster—he wasn't visualizing it as rapidly as it was, an hour of talk and action in one second of "squawk," a narrow peak of "noise" interfering with one single word of an Earth broadcast! Faster . . . faster. . . . It was impossible. Matter could not stand such stress. Inertia— momentum—abrupt weight. . . .

It was insane. "Why?" he asked. "How?"

Nathen laughed again, harshly. "Get them out? There isn't a lake or a big river within a hundred miles of here! Where did you think they were?"

A shiver of unreality went down the Times man's spine. Automatically and inanely, he found himself delving in his pocket for a cigarette while he tried to understand what had happened. "Where are they, then? Why can't we see their spaceship?"

Nathen picked up the microphone in a gesture that showed the bitterness of his disappointment.

"We'll need a magnifying glass for that."

BETELGEUSE BRIDGE
BY WILLIAM TENN

You tell them, Alvarez, old boy; you know how to talk to them. This isn't my kind of public relations. All I care about is that they get the pitch exactly right, with all the implications and complications and everything just the way they really were.

If it hurts, well, let them yell. Just use your words and get it right. Get it all.

You can start with the day the alien spaceship landed outside Baltimore. Makes you sick to think how we never tumbled, doesn't it, Alvarez? No more than a hop, skip, and a jet from the Capitol dome, and we thought it was just a lucky accident.

Explain why we thought it was so lucky. Explain about the secrecy it made possible, the farmer who telephoned the news was placed in special and luxurious custody, how a hand-picked cordon of M.P.s paced five square miles off into an emergency military reservation a few hours later, how Congress was called into secret session and the way it was all kept out of the newspapers.

How and why Trowson, my old sociology prof, was consulted once the problem became clear. How he blinked at the brass hats and striped pants and came up with the answer.

Me. I was the answer.

How my entire staff and I were plucked out of our New York offices, where we were quietly earning a million bucks, by a flying squad of the F.B.I. and air-mailed to Baltimore. Honestly, Alvarez, even after Trowson explained the situation to me, I was still irritated. Government hush-hush always makes me uncomfortable. Though I don't have to tell you how grateful I was for it later.

The spaceship itself was such a big surprise that I didn't even wet my lips when the first of the aliens *slooshed* out. After all those years of stream-lined cigar shapes the Sunday supplement artists had dreamed up, that colorful and rococo spheroid rearing out of a barley field in Maryland looked less like an interplanetary vessel than an oversized ornament for a what-not table. Nothing that seemed like a rocket jet anywhere.

"And there's your job." The prof pointed. "Those two visitors."

They were standing on a flat metal plate surrounded by the highest the republic had elected or appointed. Nine feet of slimy green trunk tapering up from a rather wide base to a pointed top, and dressed in a tiny pink-and-white shell. Two stalks with eyes on them that swung this way and that, and seemed muscular enough to throttle a man. And a huge wet slash of a mouth that showed whenever an edge of the squirming base lifted from the metal plate.

"Snails," I said. "*Snails!*"

"Or slugs," Trowson amended. "Gastropodal mollusks in any case." He gestured at the roiling white bush of hair that sprouted from his head. "But, Dick, that vestigial bit of coiled shell is even less an evolutionary memento than this. They're an older—and smarter—race."

"Smarter?"

He nodded. "When our engineers got curious, they were very courteously invited inside to inspect the ship. They came out with their mouths hanging."

I began to get uncomfortable. I ripped a small piece off my manicure. "Well, naturally, prof, if they're so alien, so different—"

"Not only that. Superior. Get that, Dick, because it'll be very important in what you have to do. The best engineering minds that this country can assemble in a hurry are like a crowd of South Sea Islanders trying to analyze the rifle and compass from what they know of spears and wind storms. These creatures belong to a galaxy-wide civilization composed of races *at least* as advanced as they; we're a bunch of backward hicks in an unfrequented hinterland of space that's about to be opened to exploration. Exploitation, perhaps, if we can't measure up. We have to give a very good impression and we have to learn fast."

A dignified official with a briefcase detached himself from the nodding, smiling group around the aliens and started for us.

"*Whew!*" I commented brilliantly. "Fourteen ninety-two, repeat performance." I thought for a moment, not too clearly. "But why send the Army and Navy after *me*? I'm not going to be able to read blueprints from—from—"

"Betelgeuse. Ninth planet of the star Betelgeuse. No, Dick, we've already had Dr. Warbury out here. They learned English from him in two hours, although he hasn't identified a word of theirs in three days! And people like Lopez, like Mainzer, are going quietly psychotic trying to locate their power source. We have the best minds we can get to do the learning. Your job is different. We want you as a top-notch advertising man, a public-relations executive. You're the good impression part of the program."

The official plucked at my sleeve and I shrugged him away. "Isn't that the function of government glad-handers?" I asked Trowson.

"No. Don't you remember what you said when you first saw them? *Snails!* How do you think this country is going to take to the idea of snails— giant snails—who sneer condescendingly at our skyscraper cities, our atomic bombs, and our most advanced mathematics? We're a conceited kind of monkey. Also, we're afraid of the dark."

There was a gentle official tap on my shoulder. I said "*Please!*" impatiently. I watched the warm little breeze ruffle Professor Trowson's slept-in clothes and noticed the tiny red streaks in his weary eyes.

" 'Mighty Monsters from Outer Space.' Headlines like that, Prof?"

"Slugs with superiority complexes. Dirty slugs, more likely. We're lucky they landed in this country, and so close to the Capitol too. In a few days we'll have to call in the heads of other nations. Then, sometime soon after, the news will be out. We don't want our visitors attacked by mobs drunk on superstition, planetary isolation, or any other form of tabloid hysteria. We don't want them carrying stories back to their civilization of being shot at by a suspendered fanatic who screamed, 'Go back where you come from, you furrin seafood!' We want to give them the impression that we are a fairly amiable, fairly intelligent race, that we can be dealt with reasonably well."

I nodded. "Yeah. So they'll set up trading posts on this planet instead of garrisons. But what do I do in all this?"

He punched my chest gently. "You, Dick—you do a job of public relations. You sell these aliens to the American people!"

*   *   *

The official had maneuvered around in front of me. I recognized him. He was the Undersecretary of State.

"Would you step this way, please?" he said. "I'd like to introduce you to our distinguished guests."

So he stepped, and I stepped, and we scrunched across the field and clanked across the steel plate and stood next to our gastropodic guests.

"Ahem," said the Undersecretary politely.

The nearer snail bent an eye toward us. The other eye drew a bead on the companion snail, and then the great slimy head arched and came down to our level. The creature raised, as it were, one cheek of its foot and said, with all the mellowness of air being pumped through a torn inner tube, "Can it be that you wish to communicate with my unworthy self, respected sir?"

I was introduced. The thing brought two eyes to bear on me. The place where its chin should have been dropped to my feet and snaked around there for a second. Then it said, "You, honored sir, are our touch-stone, the link with all that is great in your noble race. Your condescension is truly a tribute."

All this tumbled out while I was muttering "How," and extending a diffident hand. The snail put one eyeball in my palm and the other on the back of my wrist. It didn't shake; it just put the things there and took them away again. I had the wit not to wipe my hands on my pants, which was my immediate impulse. The eyeball wasn't exactly dry, either.

I said, "I'll do my best. Tell me, are you—uh—ambassadors, sort of? Or maybe just explorers?"

"Our small worth justifies no titles," said the creature, "yet we are both; for all communication is ambassadorship of a kind, and any seeker after knowledge is an explorer."

I was suddenly reminded of an old story with the punchline, "Ask a foolish question and you get a foolish answer." I also wondered suddenly what snails eat.

The second alien glided over and eyed me. "You may depend upon our utmost obedience," it said humbly. "We understand your awesome function and we wish to be liked to whatever extent it is possible for your admirable race to like such miserable creatures as ourselves."

"Stick to that attitude and we'll get along," I said.

*   *   *

By and large, they were a pleasure to work with. I mean there was no temperament, no upstaging, no insistence on this camera angle or that mention of a previously published book or the other wishful biographical apocrypha about being raised in a convent, like with most of my other clients.

On the other hand, they weren't easy to talk to. They'd take orders, sure. But ask them a question. Any question:

"How long did the trip take you?"

"'How long' in your eloquent tongue indicates a frame of reference dealing with duration. I hesitate to discuss so complex a problem with one as learned as yourself. The velocities involved make it necessary to answer in relative terms. Our lowly and undesirable planet recedes from this beauteous system during part of its orbital period, advances toward it during part. Also, we must take into consideration the direction and velocity of our star in reference to the cosmic expansion of this portion of the continuum. Had we come from Cygnus, say, or Bootes, the question could be answered somewhat more directly; for those bodies travel in a contiguous arc skewed from the ecliptic plane in such a way that—"

Or a question like, "Is your government a democracy?"

"A democracy is a rule of the people, according to your rich etymology. We could not, in our lowly tongue, have expressed it so succinctly and movingly. One must govern oneself, of course. The degree of governmental control on the individual must vary from individual to individual and in the individual from time to time. This is so evident to as comprehensive a mind as yours that I trust you forgive me my inanities. The same control applies, naturally, to individuals considered in the mass. When faced with a universal necessity, the tendency exists among civilized species to unite to fill the need. Therefore, when no such necessity exists, there is less reason for concerted effort. Since this applies to all species, it applies even to such as us. On the other hand—"

See what I mean? A little of that got old quickly with me. I was happy to keep my nose to my own grindstone.

*　　*　　*

The Government gave me a month for the preparatory propaganda. Originally, the story was to break in two weeks, but I got down on my hands and knees and bawled that a publicity deadline required at least five times that. So they gave me a month.

Explain that carefully, Alvarez. I want them to understand exactly what a job I faced. All those years of lurid magazine covers showing extremely nubile females being menaced in three distinct colors by assorted monstrosities; those horror movies, those invasion-from-outer-space novels, those Sunday supplement fright splashes—all those sturdy psychological ruts I had to retrack. Not to mention the shudders elicited by mention of "worms," the regulation distrust of even human "furriners," the superstitious dread of creatures who had no visible place to park a soul.

Trowson helped me round up the men to write the scientific articles, and I dug up the boys who could pseudo them satisfactorily. Magazine mats were ripped apart to make way for yarns speculating gently on how far extraterrestrial races might have evolved beyond us, how much more ethical they might have become, how imaginary seven-headed creatures could still apply the Sermon on the Mount. Syndicated features popped up describing "Humble Creatures Who Create Our Gardens," "Snail Racing, the Spectacular New Spectator Sport," and so much stuff on "The Basic Unity of All Living Things" that I began to get uncomfortable at even a vegetarian dinner. I remember hearing there was a perceptible boom in mineral waters and vitamin pills. . . .

And all this, mind you, without a word of the real story breaking. A columnist did run a cute and cryptic item about someone having finally found meat on the flying saucers, but half an hour of earnest discussion in an abandoned fingerprint file room prejudiced him against further comment along this line.

The video show was the biggest problem. I don't think I could have done it on time with anything less than the resources and influence of the United States Government behind me. But a week before the official announcement, I had both the video show and the comic strip in production.

I think fourteen—though maybe it was more—of the country's best comedy writers collaborated on the project, not to mention the horde of illustrators and university psychologists who combined to sweat out the delightful little drawings. We used the drawings as the basis for the puppets on the TV show, and I don't think anything was ever so gimmicked up with Popular Appeal—and I do mean Popular—as "Andy and Dandy."

Those two fictional snails crept into the heart of America like a virus infection: overnight, everybody was talking about their anthropomorphic antics, repeating their quotable running gags and adjuring each other not to miss the next show. ("You can't miss it, Steve; it's on every channel anyway. Right after supper.") I had the tie-ins, too: Andy and Dandy dolls for the girls, snail scooters for the boys, everything from pictures on cocktail glasses to kitchen decalcomanias. Of course, a lot of the tie-ins didn't come off the production line till after the Big Announcement.

When we gave the handouts to the newspapers, we "suggested" what headlines to use. They had a choice of ten. Even the *New York Times* was forced to shriek "REAL ANDY AND DANDY BLOW IN FROM BETELGEUSE," and under that a four-column cut of blond Baby Ann Joyce with the snails.

Baby Ann had been flown out from Hollywood for the photograph. The cut showed her standing between the two aliens and clutching an eye stalk of each in her trusting, chubby hands.

The nicknames stuck. Those two slimy intellectuals from another star became even more important than the youthful evangelist who was currently being sued for bigamy.

Andy and Dandy had a ticker-tape reception in New York. They obligingly laid a cornerstone for the University of Chicago's new library. They posed for the newsreels everywhere, surrounded by Florida oranges, Idaho potatoes, Milwaukee beer. They were magnificently cooperative.

From time to time I wondered what they thought of us. They had no facial expressions, which was scarcely odd, since they had no faces. Their long eye stalks swung this way and that as they rode down shrieking Broadway in the back seat of the mayor's car; their gelatinous body-foot would heave periodically and the mouth under it make a smacking noise, but when the photographers suggested that they curl around the barely clad beauties, the time video rigged up a Malibu Beach show, Andy and Dandy wriggled over and complied without a word. Which is more than I can say for the barely clad beauties.

And when the winning pitcher presented them with an autographed baseball at that year's World Series, they bowed gravely, their pink shell tops glistening in the sunlight, and said throatily into the battery of microphones: "We're the happiest fans in the universe!"

The country went wild over them.

"But we can't keep them here," Trowson predicted. "Did you read about the debate in the U.N. General Assembly yesterday? We are accused of making secret alliances with non-human aggressors against the best interests of our own species."

I shrugged. "Well, let them go overseas. I don't think anyone else will be more successful extracting information from them than we were."

Professor Trowson wriggled his short body up on a corner of his desk. He lifted a folderful of typewritten notes and grimaced as if his tongue were wrapped in wool.

"Four months of careful questioning," he grumbled. "Four months of painstaking interrogation by trained sociologists using every free moment the aliens had, which admittedly wasn't much. Four months of organized investigation, of careful data sifting." He dropped the folder disgustedly to the desk and some of the pages splashed out. "And we know more about the social structure of Atlantis than Betelgeuse IX."

We were in the wing of the Pentagon assigned to what the brass hats, in their own cute way, had christened Project Encyclopedia. I strolled across the large, sunny office and glanced at the very latest organizational wall chart. I pointed to a small rectangle labeled "Power Source Sub-Section" depending via a straight line from a larger rectangle marked "Alien Physical Science Inquiry Section." In the small rectangle, very finely printed, were the names of an army major, a WAC corporal, and Drs. Lopez, Vinthe, and Mainzer.

"How're they doing?" I asked.

"Not much better, I'm afraid." Trowson turned away with a sigh from peering over my shoulder. "At least I deduce that from the unhappy way Mainzer bubbles into his soup spoon at lunch. Conversation between sub-sections originating in different offices on the departmental level is officially discouraged, you know. But I remember Mainzer from the university cafeteria. He bubbled into his soup the very same way when he was stuck on his solar refraction engine."

"Think Andy and Dandy are afraid we're too young to play with matches? Or maybe apelike creatures are too unpleasant-looking to be allowed to circulate in their refined and esthetic civilization?"

"I don't know, Dick." The prof ambled back to his desk and leafed irritably through his sociological notes. "If anything like that is true, why would they give us free run of their ship? Why would they reply so gravely and courteously to every question? If only their answers weren't so vague in our terms! But they are such complex and artistically minded creatures, so chockful of poetic sentiment and good manners that it's impossible to make mathematical or even verbal sense out of their vast and circumlocutory explanations. Sometimes, when I think of their highly polished manners and their seeming lack of interest in the structure of their society, when I put that together with their spaceship, which looks like one of those tiny jade carvings that took a lifetime to accomplish—"

He trailed off and began riffling the pages like a Mississippi steamboat gambler going over somebody else's deck of cards.

"Isn't it possible we just don't have enough stuff as yet to understand them?"

"Yes. In fact, that's what we always come back to. Warbury points to the tremendous development in our language since the advent of technical vocabularies. He says that this process, just beginning with us, already affects out conceptual approach as well as our words. And, naturally, in a race so much further along— But if we could only find a science of theirs which bears a faint resemblance to one of ours!"

I felt sorry for him, standing there blinking futilely out of gentle, academic eyes.

"Cheer up, Prof. Maybe by the time old Suckfoot and his pal come back from the Grand Tour, you'll have unsnarled a sophistry and we'll be off this 'Me, friend; you come from across sea in great bird with many wings' basis that we seem to have wandered into."

And there you are, Alvarez: a cheap advertising small-brain like me, and I was that close. I should have said something then. Bet you wouldn't have nodded at me heavily and said, "I hope so, Dick. I desperately hope so." But, come to think of it, not only Trowson was trotting up that path. So was Warbury. So were Lopez, Vinthe, and Mainzer. So was I, among others.

*   *   *

I had a chance to relax when Andy and Dandy went abroad. My job wasn't exactly over, but the public relations end was meshing right along, with me needed only once in a while to give a supervisory spin. Chiefly, I maintained close contact with my opposite number in various other sovereign states, giving out experienced advice on how to sell the Boys from Betelgeuse. They had to adjust it to their own mass phobias and popular myths; but they were a little happier about it than I had been without any clear idea of what public behavior to expect of our visitors.

Remember, when I'd started, I hadn't even been sure those snails were housebroken.

I followed them in the newspapers. I pasted the pictures of the Mikado receiving them next to their nice comments on the Taj Mahal. They weren't nearly so nice to the Akhund of Swat, but then when you think of what the Akhund said about them . . .

They tended to do that everywhere, giving just a little better than they got. For example, when they were presented with those newly created decorations in Red Square (Dandy got the Order of Extraterrestrial Friends of Soviet Labor, while, for some abstruse reason, the Order of Heroic Interstellar Champion of the Soviet People was conferred upon Andy), they came out with a long, ringing speech about the scientific validity of communist government. It made for cheering, flower-tossing crowds in the Ukraine and Poland but a certain amount of restiveness in these United States.

But before I had to run my staff into overtime hours, whipping up press releases which recapitulated the aliens' statement before the joint houses of Congress and their lovely, sentimental comments at Valley Forge, the aliens were in Berne, telling the Swiss that only free enterprise could have produced the yodel, the Incabloc escapement in watches, and such a superb example of liberty; hadn't they had democracy long enough to have had it first, and wasn't it wonderful?

By the time they reached Paris I had the national affection pretty much under control again, although here and there a tabloid still muttered peevishly in its late city final. But, as always, Andy and Dandy put the clincher on. Even then I wondered whether they really liked DeRoges's latest abstraction for itself alone.

But they bought the twisted sculpture, paying for it, since they had no cash of their own, with a thumb-sized gadget which actually melted marble to any degree of pattern delicacy the artist desired, merely by being touched to the appropriate surface. DeRoges threw away his chisels blissfully, but six of the finest minds in France retired to intensive nervous break-downs after a week of trying to solve the tool's working principles.

It went over big here:

ANDY AND DANDY
PASS AS THEY GO

Betelgeuse Businessmen
Show Appreciation
for Value Received.

This newspaper notes with pleasure the sound shopper's ethics behind the latest transaction of our distin-guished guests from the elemental void. Understanding the inexorable law of supply and demand, these represen-tatives of an advanced economic system refuse to succumb to the "gimmies." If certain other members of the human race were to examine carefully the true implications of . . .

* * *

So when they returned to the United States after being presented at the British court, they got juicy spreads in all the newspapers, a tug-whistle reception in New York harbor and the mayor's very chiefest deputy there on City Hall steps to receive them.

And even though people were more or less accustomed to them now, they were somehow never shoved off page one. There was the time a certain furniture polish got a testimonial out of them in which the aliens announced that they'd had particularly happy and glossy results on their tiny shell toppers with the goo; and they used the large financial rewards of the testimonial to buy ten extremely rare orchids and have them sunk in plastic. And there was the time . . .

I missed the television show on which it broke. I had gone to a side-street movie theater that night to see a revival of one of my favorite Chaplin pictures; and I'd never enjoyed the ostentatious greet-the-great hysterics of *Celebrity Salon* anyway. I hadn't any idea of how long the M.C., Bill Bancroft, had waited to get Andy and Dandy on his program, and how much he was determined to make it count when the big night arrived.

Reconstructed and stripped of meaningless effusion, it went something like this:

Bancroft asked them if they weren't anxious to get home to the wife and kiddies. Andy explained patiently, for perhaps the thirty-fourth time, that, since they were hermaphrodites, they had no family in any humanly acceptable sense. Bancroft cut into the explanation to ask them what ties they *did* have. Chiefly the revitalizer, says Andy politely.

Revitalizer? What's a revitalizer? Oh, a machine they have to expose themselves to every decade or so, says Dandy. There's at least one revitalizer in every large city on their home planet.

Bancroft makes a bad pun, waits for the uproarious audience to regain control, then asks: And this revitalizer—just what does it do? Andy goes into a long-winded explanation, the gist of which is that the revitalizers stir up cytoplasm in animal cells and refresh them.

I see, cracks Bancroft; the pause every decade that refreshes. And then, after being refreshed, you have what as a result? "Oh," muses Dandy, "you might say we have no fear of cancer or any degenerative disease. Besides that, by exposing ourselves to revitalizers at regular intervals throughout our lifetime and refreshing our body cells, we quintuple our life expectancy. We live five times longer than we should. That's about what the revitalizer does, you might say," says Dandy. Andy, after thinking a bit, agrees. "That's about it."

Pandemonium, and not mild. Newspaper extras in all languages, including the Scandinavian. Lights burning late at night in the U.N. Headquarters with guards twenty deep around the site.

When President of the Assembly Sadhu asked them why they'd never mentioned revitalizers before, they did the snail equivalent of shrugging and said the Betelgeuse IX equivalent of nobody ever asked them.

President Sadhu cleared his throat, waved all complications aside with his long brown fingers, and announced, "That is not important. Not now. We must have revitalizers."

It seemed to take the aliens awhile to understand that. When they finally became convinced that we, as a species, were utterly entranced with the prospect of two to four centuries of life instead of fifty or sixty years, they went into a huddle.

But their race didn't make these machines for export, they explained regretfully. Just enough to service their population. And while they could see as how we might like and must obviously deserve to have these gadgets, there was none to ferry back from Betelgeuse.

Sadhu didn't even look around for advice. "What would your people want?" he asked. "What would they like in exchange for manufacturing these machines for us? We will pay almost any price within the power of this entire planet." A rumbling, eager "yes" in several languages rolled across the floor of the Assembly.

Andy and Dandy couldn't think of a thing. Sadhu begged them to try. He personally escorted them to their spaceship, which was now parked in a restricted area in Central Park. "Good night, gentlemen," said President of the Assembly Sadhu. "Try—please try hard to think of an exchange."

They stayed inside their ship for almost six days while the world almost went insane with impatience. When I think of all the fingernails bitten that week by two billion people . . .

"Imagine!" Trowson whispered to me. He was pacing the floor as if he fully intended to walk all the way to Betelgeuse. "We'd just be children on a quintupled life scale, Dick. All my achievement and education, all yours, would be just the beginning! A man could learn five professions in such a life—and think what he could accomplish in one!"

I nodded, a little numb. I was thinking of the books I could read, the books I might write, if the bulk of my life stretched ahead of me and the advertising profession was just a passing phase at the beginning of it. Then again, somehow I'd never married, never had a family. Not enough free time, I had felt. And now, at forty, I was too set in my ways. But a man can unset a lot in a century . . .

In six days the aliens came out. With a statement of price.

They believed they could persuade their people to manufacture a supply of revitalizers for use if— An IF writ very large indeed.

Their planet was woefully short of radioactive minerals, they explained apologetically. Barren worlds containing radium, uranium, and thorium had been discovered and claimed by other races, but the folk of Betelgeuse IX were forbidden by their ethics to wage aggressive war for territorial purposes. We had plenty of radioactive ore, which we used chiefly for war and biological research. The former was patently undesirable and the latter would be rendered largely unnecessary by the revitalizers.

So, in exchange, they wanted our radioactive elements. All of them, they stated humbly.

＊　　＊　　＊

All right, we were a little surprised, even stunned. But the protests never *started* to materialize. There was an overwhelming chorus of "sold!" from every quadrant of the globe. A couple of generals here, a few militaristic statesmen there managed to raise direly pointing forefingers before they were whisked out of position. A nuclear physicist or two howled about the future of subatomic research, but the peoples of the Earth howled louder.

"Research? How much research can you do in a lifetime of three hundred years?"

Overnight, the United Nations became the central office of a planet-wide mining concession. National boundaries were superseded by pitchblende deposits and swords were beaten into pickaxes. Practically anyone with a good, unable arm enlisted in the shovel brigades for two or more months out of the year. Camaraderie flew on the winds of the world.

Andy and Dandy politely offered to help. They marked out on detail contour maps the spots to be mined, and that included areas never suspected of radioactivity. They supplied us with fantastic but clear line drawings of devices for extracting the stuff from the ores in which it assayed poorly, and taught us the exact use of these devices, if not their basic principle.

They hadn't been joking. They wanted it all.

Then, when everything was running smoothly, they buzzed off for Betelgeuse to handle their part of the bargain.

* * *

Those two years were the most exhilarating of my life. And I'd say everyone feels the same, don't they, Alvarez? The knowledge that the world was working together, cheerfully, happily, for life itself. I put my year in at the Great Slave Lake, and I don't think anyone of my age and weight lifted more pitchblende.

Andy and Dandy came back in two huge ships, manned by weird snail-like robots. The robots did everything, while Andy and Dandy went on being lionized. From the two ships, almost covering the sky, the robots ferried back and forth in strange, spiral aircraft, bringing revitalizers down, carrying refined radioactive elements aloft. No one paid the slightest attention to their methods of instantaneous extraction from large quantities of ore: we were interested in just one throbbing thought—the revitalizers.

They worked. And that, so far as most of us were concerned, was that.

The revitalizers *worked*. Cancer disappeared; heart disease and kidney disease became immediately arrested. Insects which were introduced into the square one-story lab structures lived for a year instead of a few months. And humans—doctors shook their heads in wonder over people who had gone through.

All over the planet, near every major city, the long, patient, slowly moving lines stood outside the revitalizers, which were rapidly becoming something else.

"Temples!" shouted Mainzer. "They look on them as temples. A scientist investigating their operation is treated by the attendants like a dangerous lunatic in a nursery. Not that a man can find a clue in those ridiculously small motors. I no longer ask what their power source can be. Instead, I ask if they have a power source at all!"

"The revitalizers are very precious now, in the beginning," Trowson soothed him. "After a while the novelty will wear off and you'll be able to investigate at your leisure. Could it be solar power?"

"No!" Mainzer shook his huge head positively. "Not solar power. Solar power I am sure I could recognize. As I am sure that the power supply of their ships and whatever runs these—these revitalizers are two entirely separate things. On the ships I have given up. But the revitalizers I believe I could solve. If only they would let me examine them. Fools! So terribly afraid I might damage one, and they would have to travel to another city for their elixir!"

We patted his shoulder, but we weren't really interested. Andy and Dandy left that week, after wishing us well in their own courteous and complex fashion. Whole population groups blew kisses at their mineral-laden ships.

Six months after they left, the revitalizers stopped.

*   *   *

"Am I certain?" Trowson snorted at my dismayed face. "One set of statistics proves it: look at your death rate. It's back to pre-Betelgeuse normal. Or ask any doctor. Any doctor who can forget his U.N. security oath, that is. There'll be really wild riots when the news breaks, Dick."

"But why?" I asked him. "Did we do something wrong?"

He started a laugh that ended with his teeth clicking frightenedly together. He rose and walked to the window, staring out into the star-diseased sky. "We did something wrong, all right. We trusted. We made the same mistake all natives have made when they met a superior civilization. Mainzer and Lopez have taken one of the revitalizer engine units apart. There was just a trace of it left, but this time they found the power source. Dick, my boy, the revitalizers were run on the fuel of completely pure radioactive elements!"

I needed a few moments to file that properly. Then I sat down in the easy chair very, very carefully. I made some hoarse, improbable sounds before croaking: "Prof, do you mean they wanted that stuff for themselves, for their own revitalizers? That everything they did on this planet was carefully planned so that they could con us with a maximum of friendliness all around? It doesn't seem—it just can't—Why, with their superior science, they could have conquered us if they'd cared to. They could have—"

"No, they couldn't have," Trowson whipped out. He turned to face me and flung his arms across each other. "They're a decadent, dying race; they wouldn't have attempted to conquer us. Not because of their ethics—this huge, horrible swindle serves to illustrate that aspect of them—but because they haven't the energy, the concentration, the interest. Andy and Dandy are probably representative of the few remaining who have barely enough git-up-and-go to trick backward peoples out of the all-important, life-sustaining revitalizer fuel."

The implications were just beginning to soak into my cortex. Me, the guy who did the most complete and colossal public-relations job of all time—I could just see what my relations with the public would be like if I was ever connected with this shambles.

"And without atomic power, Prof, we won't have space travel!"

He gestured bitterly. "Oh, we've been taken, Dick; the whole human race has been had. I know what you're going through, but think of me! I'm the failure, the man responsible. I'm supposed to be a sociologist! How could I have missed? How? It was all there: the lack of interest in their own culture, the overintellectualization of esthetics, the involved methods of thought and expression, the exaggerated etiquette, even the very first thing of theirs we saw—their ship—was too heavily stylized and intricately designed for a young, trusting civilization.

"They *had* to be decadent; every sign pointed to that conclusion. And of course the fact that they resort to the methods of fueling their revitalizers that we've experienced—when if we had their science, what might we not do, what substitutes might we not develop! No wonder they couldn't explain their science to us; I doubt if they understand it fully themselves. They are the profligate, inadequate and sneak-thief heirs of what was once a soaring race!"

I was following my own unhappy images. "And we're still hicks. Hicks who've been sold the equivalent of the Brooklyn Bridge by some dressed-up sharpies from Betelgeuse."

Trowson nodded. "Or a bunch of poor natives who have sold their island home to a group of European explorers for a handful of brightly colored glass beads."

But of course we were both wrong, Alvarez. Neither Trowson nor I had figured on Mainzer or Lopez or the others. Like Mainzer said, a few years earlier and we would have been licked. But man had entered the atomic age some time before 1945, and people like Mainzer and Vinthe had done nuclear research back in the days when radioactive elements abounded on Earth. We had that and we had such tools as the cyclotron, the betatron. And, if our present company will pardon the expression, Alvarez, we are a young and vigorous race.

All we had to do was the necessary research.

The research was done. With a truly effective world government, with a population not only interested in the problem but recently experienced in working together—and with the grim incentive we had, Alvarez, the problem, as you know, was solved.

We developed artificial radioactives and refueled the revitalizers. We developed atomic fuels out of the artificial radioactives and we got space travel. We did it comparatively fast, and we weren't interested in a ship that just went to the moon or Mars. We wanted a starship. And we wanted it so bad, so fast, that we have it now too.

Here we are. Explain the situation to them, Alvarez, just the way I told it to you, but with all the knee-bending and gobbledegook that a transplanted Brazilian with twelve years oriental trading experience can put into it. You're the man to do it—I can't talk like that. It's the only language those decadent slugs understand, so it's the only way we can talk to them. So talk to them, these slimy snails, these oysters on the quarter shell, those smart-alecky slugs. Don't forget to mention to them that the supply of radioactives they got from us won't last forever. Get that down in fine detail.

Then stress the fact that we've got artificial radioactives, and that they've got some things we know we want and lots of other things we mean to find out about.

Tell them, Alvarez, that we've come to collect tolls on that Brooklyn Bridge they sold us.

EIGHT O'CLOCK IN THE MORNING
BY RAY NELSON

At the end of the show the hypnotist told his subjects, "Awake."

Something unusual happened.

One of the subjects awoke all the way. This had never happened before. His name was George Nada and he blinked out at the sea of faces in the theatre, at first unaware of anything out of the ordinary. Then he noticed, spotted here and there in the crowd, the nonhuman faces, the faces of the Fascinators. They had been there all along, of course, but only George was really awake, so only George recognized them for what they were. He understood everything in a flash, including the fact that if he were to give any outward sign, the Fascinators would instantly command him to return to his former state, and he would obey.

He left the theatre, pushing out into the neon night, carefully avoiding giving any indication that he saw the green, reptilian flesh or the multiple yellow eyes of the rulers of Earth. One of them asked him, "Got a light, buddy?" George gave him a light, then moved on.

At intervals along the street George saw the posters hanging with photographs of the Fascinators' multiple eyes and various commands printed under them, such as, "Work eight hours, play eight hours, sleep eight hours," and "Marry and Reproduce." A TV set in the window of a store caught George's eye, but he looked away in the nick of time. When he didn't look at the Fascinator in the screen, he could resist the command, "Stay tuned to this station."

George lived alone in a little sleeping room, and as soon as he got home, the first thing he did was to disconnect the TV set. In other rooms he could hear the TV sets of his neighbours, though. Most of the time the voices were human, but now and then he heard the arrogant, strangely bird-like croaks of the aliens. "Obey the government," said one croak. "We are the government," said another. "We are your friends, you'd do anything for a friend, wouldn't you?"

"Obey!"

"Work!"

Suddenly the phone rang.

George picked it up. It was one of the Fascinators.

"Hello," it squawked. "This is your control, Chief of Police Robinson. You are an old man, George Nada. Tomorrow morning at eight o'clock, your heart will stop. Please repeat."

"I am an old man," said George. "Tomorrow morning at eight o'clock, my heart will stop."

The control hung up.

"No it won't," whispered George. He wondered why they wanted him dead. Did they suspect that he was awake? Probably. Someone might have spotted him, noticed that he didn't respond the way the others did. If George were alive at one minute after eight tomorrow morning, then they would be sure.

No use waiting here for the end, he thought.

He went out again. The posters, the TV, the occasional commands from passing aliens did not seem to have absolute power over him, though he still felt strongly tempted to obey, to see these things the way his master wanted him to see them. He passed an alley and stopped. One of the aliens was alone there, leaning against the wall. George walked up to him.

"Move on," grunted the thing, focusing his deadly eyes on George.

George felt his grasp on awareness waver. For a moment the reptilian head dissolved into the face of a lovable old drunk. Of course the drunk would be lovable. George picked up a brick and smashed it down on the old drunk's head with all his strength. For a moment the image blurred, then the blue-green blood oozed out of the face and the lizard fell, twitching and writhing. After a moment it was dead.

George dragged the body into the shadows and searched it. There was a tiny radio in its pocket and a curiously shaped knife and fork in another. The tiny radio said something in an incomprehensible language. George put it down beside the body, but kept the eating utensils.

I can't possibly escape, thought George. Why fight them?

But maybe he could.

What if he could awaken others? That might be worth a try.

He walked twelve blocks to the apartment of his girlfriend, Lil, and knocked on her door. She came to the door in her bathrobe.

"I want you to wake up," he said.

"I'm awake," she said. "Come on in."

He went in. The TV was playing. He turned it off.

"No," he said. "I mean really wake up." She looked at him without comprehension, so he snapped his fingers and shouted, "*Wake up!* The masters command that you wake up!"

"Are you off your rocker, George?" she asked suspiciously. "You sure are acting funny." He slapped her face. "Cut that out!" she cried. "What the hell are you up to anyway?"

"Nothing," said George, defeated. "I was just kidding around."

"Slapping my face wasn't just kidding around!" she cried.

There was a knock at the door.

George opened it

It was one of the aliens.

"Can't you keep the noise down to a dull roar?" it said.

The eyes and reptilian flesh faded a little and George saw the flickering image of a fat middle-aged man in shirt-sleeves. It was still a man when George slashed its throat with the eating knife, but it was an alien before it hit the floor. He dragged it into the apartment and kicked the door shut.

"What do you see there?" he asked Lil, pointing to the many-eyed snake thing on the floor.

"Mister . . . Mister Coney," she whispered, her eyes wide with horror. "You . . . just killed him, like it was nothing at all."

"Don't scream," warned George, advancing on her.

"I won't, George. I swear I won't, only please, for the love of God, put down that knife." She backed away until she had her shoulder blades pressed to the wall.

George saw that it was no use.

"I'm going to tie you up," said George. "First tell me which room Mister Coney lived in."

"The first door on your left as you go toward the stairs," she said. "George . . . Georgie. Don't torture me. If you're going to kill me, do it clean. Please, George, please."

He tied her up with bedsheets and gagged her, then searched the body of the Fascinator. There was another one of the little radios that talked a foreign language, another set of eating utensils, and nothing else.

George went next door.

When he knocked, one of the snake things answered, "Who is it?"

"Friend of Mister Coney. I wanna see him," said George.

"He went out for a second, but he'll be right back." The door opened a crack, and four yellow eyes peeped out. "You wanna come in and wait?"

"OK," said George, not looking at the eyes.

"You alone here?" he asked, as it closed the door, its back to George. "Yeah, why?"

He slit its throat from behind, then searched the apartment.

He found human bones and skulls, a half-eaten hand.

He found tanks with huge fat slugs floating in them.

The children, he thought, and killed them all.

There were guns too, of a sort he had never seen before. He discharged one by accident, but fortunately it was noiseless. It seemed to fire little poisoned darts.

He pocketed the gun and as many boxes of darts as he could and went back to Lil's place. When she saw him she writhed in helpless terror.

"Relax, honey," he said, opening her purse. "I just want to borrow your car keys."

He took the keys and went downstairs to the street.

Her car was still parked in the same general area in which she always parked it. He recognized it by the dent in the right fender. He got in, started it, and began driving aimlessly. He drove for hours, thinking—desperately searching for some way out. He turned on the car radio to see if he could get some music, but there was nothing but news and it was all about him, George Nada, the homicidal maniac. The announcer was one of the masters, but he sounded a little scared. Why should he be? What could one man do?

George wasn't surprised when he saw the roadblock, and he turned off on a side street before he reached it. No little trip to the country for you, Georgie boy, he thought to himself.

They had just discovered what he had done back at Lil's place, so they would probably be looking for Lil's car. He parked it in an alley and took the subway. There were no aliens on the subway, for some reason. Maybe they were too good for such things, or maybe it was just because it was so late at night.

When one finally did get on, George got off.

He went up to the street and went into a bar. One of the Fascinators was on the TV, saying over and over again, "We are your friends. We are your friends. We are your friends." The stupid lizard sounded scared. Why? What could one man do against all of them?

George ordered a beer, then it suddenly struck him that the

Fascinator on the TV no longer seemed to have any power over him. He looked at it again and thought, It has to believe it can master me to do it. The slightest hint of fear on its part and the power to hypnotize is lost. They flashed George's picture on the TV screen and George retreated to the phone booth. He called his control, the Chief of Police.

"Hello, Robinson?" he asked.

"Speaking."

"This is George Nada. I've figured out how to wake people up."

"What? George, hang on. Where are you?" Robinson sounded almost hysterical.

He hung up and paid and left the bar. They would probably trace his call.

He caught another subway and went downtown.

It was dawn when he entered the building housing the biggest of the city's TV studios. He consulted the building directory and then went up in the elevator. The cop in front of the studio entrance recognized him. "Why, you're Nada!" he gasped.

George didn't like to shoot him with the poison dart gun, but he had to.

He had to kill several more before he got into the studio itself, including all the engineers on duty. There were a lot of police sirens outside, excited shouts, and running footsteps on the stairs. The alien was sitting before the TV camera saying, "We are your friends. We are your friends," and didn't see George come in. When George shot him with the needle gun he simply stopped in mid-sentence and sat there dead. George stood near him and said, imitating the alien croak, "Wake up. Wake up. See us as we are and kill us!"

It was George's voice the city heard that morning, but it was the Fascinator's image, and the city did awake for the very first time and the war began.

George did not live to see the victory that finally came. He died of a heart attack at exactly eight o'clock.

NIGHT OF THE COOTERS
BY HOWARD WALDROP

This story is in memory of Slim Pickens (1919–1983)

Sheriff Lindley was asleep on the toilet in the Pachuco County courthouse when someone started pounding on the door.

"Bert! Bert!" the voice yelled as the sheriff jerked awake.

"Gol Dang!" said the lawman. The Waco newspaper slid off his lap onto the floor.

He pulled his pants up with one hand and the toilet chain on the waterbox overhead with the other. He opened the door. Chief Deputy Sweets stood before him, a complaint slip in his hand.

"Dang it, Sweets!" said the sheriff. "I told you never to bother me in there. It's the hottest Thursday in the history of Texas! You woke me up out of a hell of a dream!"

The deputy waited, wiping sweat from his forehead. There were two big circles, like half-moons, under the arms of his blue chambray shirt.

"I was fourteen, maybe fifteen years old, and I was a Aztec or a Mixtec or somethin'," said the sheriff. "Anyways, I was buck-naked, and I was standin' on one of them ball courts with the little-bitty stone rings twenty foot up one wall, and they was presentin' me to Moctezuma. I was real proud, and the sun was shinin', but it was real still and cool down there in the Valley of the Mexico. I looks up at the grandstand, and there's Moctezuma and all his high muckety-mucks with feathers and stuff hangin' off 'em, and more gold than a circus wagon. And there was these other guys, conquistadors and stuff, with beards and rusty helmets, and I-talian priests with crosses you coulda barred a livery-stable door with. One of Moctezuma's men was explainin' how we was fixin' to play ball for the gods and things.

"I knew in my dream I was captain of my team. I had a name that sounded like a bird fart in Aztec talk, and they mentioned it and the name of the captain of the other team, too. Well, everything was goin' all right, and I was prouder and prouder, until the guy doing the talkin' let slip that whichever team won was gonna be paraded around Tenochtitlán and given women and food and stuff like that, and then tomorrow A.M. they was gonna be cut up and simmered real slow and served up with chilis and onions and tomatoes.

"Well, you never seed such a fight as broke out then! They was a-yellin', and a priest was swingin' a cross, and spears and axes were flyin' around like it was an Irish funeral.

"Next thing I know, you're a-bangin' on the door and wakin' me up and bringin' me back to Pachuco County! What the hell do you want?"

"Mr. De Spain wants you to come over to his place right away."

"He does, huh?"

"That's right, Sheriff. He says he's got some miscreants he wants you to arrest."

"Everybody else around here has desperadoes. De Spain has miscreants. I'll be so danged glad when the town council gets around to movin' the city limits fifty foot the other side of his place, I won't know what to do! Every time anybody farts too loud, he calls me."

Lindley and Sweets walked back to the office at the other end of the courthouse. Four deputies sat around with their feet propped up on desks. They rocked forward respectfully and watched as the sheriff went to the hat pegs.

On one of the dowels was a sweat-stained hat with turned-down points at front and back. The sidebrims were twisted in curves. The hat angled up to end in a crown that looked like the business end of a Phillips screwdriver. Under the hat was a holster with a Navy Colt .41 that looked like someone had used it to drive railroad spikes all the way to the Continental Divide. Leaning under them was a 10-gauge pump shotgun with the barrel sawed off just in front of the foregrip.

On the other peg was an immaculate new round-top Stetson of brown felt with a snakeskin band half as wide as a fingernail running around it.

The deputies stared.

Lindley picked up the Stetson.

The deputies rocked back in their chairs and resumed yakking.

"Hey, Sweets!" said the sheriff at the door. "Change that damn calendar on your desk. It ain't Wednesday, August seventeenth; it's Thursday, August eighteenth."

"Sure thing, Sheriff."

"And you boys try not to play checkers so loud you wake the judge up, okay?"

"Sure thing, Sheriff."

Lindley went down the courthouse steps onto the rock walk. He passed the two courthouse cannons he and the deputies fired off three times a year—March second, July Fourth and Robert E. Lee's birthday. Each cannon had a pyramid of ornamental cannonballs in front of it.

Waves of heat came off the cannons, the ammunition, the telegraph wires overhead, and, in the distance, the rails of the twice-a-day spur line from Waxahachie.

The town was still as a rusty shovel. The 45-star United States flag hung like an old, dried dishrag from its stanchion. From looking at the town you couldn't tell the nation was about to go to war with Spain over Cuba, that China was full of unrest, and that five thousand miles away a crazy German count was making airships.

Lindley had seen enough changes in his sixty-eight years. He had been born in the bottom of an Ohio keelboat in 1830; was in Bloody Kansas when John Brown came through; fought for the Confederacy, first as a corporal, then a sergeant major, from Chickamauga to the Wilderness; and had seen more skirmishes with hostile tribes than most people would ever read about in a dozen Wide-Awake Library novels.

It was as hot as under an upside-down washpot on a tin shed roof. The sheriff's wagon horse seemed asleep as it trotted, head down, puffs hanging in the still air like brown shrubs made of dust around its hooves.

There were ten, maybe a dozen people in sight in the whole town. Those few on the street moved like molasses, only as far as they had to, from shade to shade. Anybody with sense was asleep at home with wet towels hung over the windows, or sitting as still as possible with a funeral-parlor fan in their hands.

The sheriff licked his big droopy mustache and hoped nobody nodded to him. He was already too hot and tired to tip his hat. He leaned back in the wagon seat and straightened his bad leg (a Yankee souvenir) against the boot board. His grey suit was like a boiling shroud. He was too hot to reach up and flick the dust off his new hat.

He had become sheriff in the special election three years ago, to fill out Sanderson's term when the governor had appointed the former sheriff attorney general. Nothing much had happened in the county since then.

"Gee-hup," he said.

The horse trotted three steps before going back into its walking trance.

Sheriff Lindley didn't bother her again until he pulled up at De Spain's big place and said, "Whoa, there."

The black man who did everything for De Spain opened the gate.

"Sheriff," he said.

"Luther," said Lindley, nodding his head.

"Around back, Mr. Lindley."

There were two boys—raggedly town kids, the Strother boy and one of the poor Chisums—sitting on the edge of the well. The Chisum kid had been crying.

De Spain was hot and bothered. He was only half dressed, with suit pants, white shirt, vest and stockings on but no shoes or coat. He hadn't macassared his hair yet. He was pointing a rifle with a barrel big as a drainpipe at the two boys.

"Here they are, Sheriff. Luther saw them down in the orchard. I'm sure he saw them stealing my peaches, but he wouldn't tell me. I knew something was up when he didn't put my clothes in the usual place next to the window where I like to dress. So I looked out and saw them. They had half a potato sack full by the time I crept around the house and caught them. I want to charge them with trespass and thievery."

"Well, well," said the sheriff, looking down at the sackful of evidence. He turned and pointed toward the black man.

"You want me to charge Luther here with collusion and abetting a crime?" Neither Lindley's nor Luther's faces betrayed any emotion.

"Of course not," said De Spain. "I've told him time and time again he's too soft on filchers. If this keeps happening, Ill hire another boy who'll enforce my orchard with buckshot, if need be."

De Spain was a young man with eyes like a Weimaraner's. As Deputy Sweets said, he had the kind of face you couldn't hit just once. He owned half the town of Pachuco City. The other half paid him rent.

"Get in the wagon, boys," said the sheriff.

"Aren't you going to cover them with your weapon?" asked De Spain.

"You should know by now, Mr. De Spain, that when I wear this suit I ain't got nothin' but a three-shot pocket pistol on me. Besides"—he looked at the two boys in the wagon bed—"they know if they give me any guff, I'll jerk a bowknot in one of 'em and bite the other'n's ass off."

"I don't think there's a need for profanity," said De Spain.

"It's too damn hot for anything else," said Lindley. "I'll clamp 'em in the *juzgado* and have Sweets run the papers over to your office tomorrow mornin'."

"I wish you'd take them out one of the rural roads somewhere and flail the tar out of them to teach them about property rights," said De Spain.

The sheriff tipped his hat back and looked up at De Spain's three-story house with the parlor so big you could hold a rodeo in it. Then he looked back at the businessman, who'd finally lowered the rifle.

"Well, I know you'd like that," said Lindley. "I seem to remember that most of the fellers who wrote the Constitution were pretty well off, but some of the other rich people thought they had funny ideas. But they were really pretty smart. One of the things they were smart about was the Bill of Rights. You know, Mr. De Spain, the reason they put in the Bill of Rights wasn't to give all the little people without jobs or money a lot of breaks with the law. Why they put that in there was for if the people without jobs or money ever got upset and turned on *them*, they could ask for the same justice everybody else got."

De Spain looked at him with disgust. "I've never liked your home-spun parables, and I don't like the way you sheriff this county."

"I don't doubt that," said Lindley. "You've got sixteen months, three weeks and two days to find somebody to run against me. Good evening, Mr. De Spain."

He climbed onto the wagon seat.

"Luther."

"Sheriff."

He turned the horse around as De Spain and the black man took the sack of peaches through the kitchen door into the house.

*   *   *

The sheriff stopped the wagon near the railroad tracks where the houses began to deviate from the vertical.

"Jody. Billy Roy." He looked at them with eyes like chips of flint. "You're the dumbest pair of squirts that *ever* lived in Pachuco City! First off, half those peaches were still green. You'd have got belly-aches, and your mothers would have beaten you within an inch of your lives and given you so many doses of Black Draught you'd shit over ten-rail fences all week.

"Now listen to what I'm sayin', 'cause I'm only gonna say it once. If I ever hear of *either* of you stealing anything, anywhere in this county, I'm going to put you *both* in school."

"No, sheriff, please, no!" Their eyes were wide as horses'.

"I'll put you in there every morning and come and get you out seven long hours later, and I'll have the judge issue a writ keeping you there till you're *twelve years old*. And if you try to run away, I'll follow you to the ends of the earth with Joe Sweeper's bloodhounds, and I'll bring you back."

They were crying now.

"You git home."

They were running before they left the wagon.

*   *   *

Somewhere between the second piece of cornbread and the third helping of snap beans, a loud rumble shook the ground.

"Goodness' Sakes!" said Elsie, his wife of twenty-three years. "What can that be?"

"I expect that's Elmer, out by the creek. He came in last week and asked if he could blast on the place. I told him it didn't matter to me as long as he did it between sunup and sundown and didn't blow his whole family of rug-rats and yard-apes up.

"Jake, down at the mercantile, said Elmer bought enough dynamite to blow up Fort Worth if he'd a mind to—all but the last three sticks in the store. Jake had to reorder for stump-blowin' time."

"Whatever could he want with all that much?"

"Oh, that damn fool has the idea the vein in that old mine what played out in '83 might start up again on his property. He got to talking with the Smith boy, oh, hell, what's his name—?"

"Leo?"

"Yeah, Leo, the one that studies down in Austin, learns abut stars and rocks and all that shit ..."

"Watch your language, Bertram!"

"Oh, hell! Anyway, that boy must have put a bug up Elmer's butt about that—"

"Bertram!" said Elsie, putting down her knife and fork.

"Oh, hell, anyway. I guess Elmer'll blow the side off his hill and bury his house before he's through."

*　　*　　*

The sheriff was reading a week-old copy of the *Waco Herald* while Elsie washed up the dishes. He sure missed *Brann's Iconoclast*, the paper he used to read, which had ceased publication when the editor was gunned down on a Waco street by an irate Baptist four months before.

The Waco paper had a little squib from London, England, about there having been explosions on Mars ten nights in a row last month, and whether it was a sign of life on that planet or some unusual volcanic activity.

Sheriff Lindley had never given volcanoes (except those in the Valley of the Mexico) or the planet Mars much thought.

Hooves came pounding down the road. He put down his paper. "*Sheriff, sheriff!*" he said in a high, mocking voice.

"What?" asked Elsie. Then she heard the hooves and began to dry her hands on the towel on the nail above the sink.

The horse stopped out front; bare feet slapped up to the porch; small fists pounded on the door.

"Sheriff! Sheriff!" yelled a voice Lindley recognized as belonging to either Tommy or Jimmy Atkinson.

He strode to the door and opened it.

"Tommy, what's all the hooraw?"

"Jimmy. Sheriff, something fell on our pasture, tore it all to hell, knocked down the tree, killed some of our cattle, Tommy can't find his dog, Mother sent—"

"Hold on! Something fell on your place? Like what?"

"I don't know! Like a big rock, only sparks was flyin' off it, and it roared and blew up! It's at the north end of the place, and—"

"Elsie, run over and get Sweets and the boys. Have them go get Leo Smith if he ain't gone back to college yet. Sounds to me like Pachuco County's got its first shootin' star. Hold on, Jimmy, I'm comin' right along.

We'll take my wagon; you can leave your pony here."

"Oh, hurry, Sheriff! It's big! It killed our cattle and tore up the fences—"

"Well, I can't arrest it for that," said Lindley. He put on his Stetson. "And I thought Elmer'd blowed hisself up. My, my, ain't never seen a shooting star before ..."

*   *   *

"Damn if it don't look like somebody threw a locomotive through here," said the sheriff.

The Atkinson place used to have a sizable hill and the tallest tree in the county on it. Now it had half a hill and a big stump and beyond, a huge crater. Dirt had been thrown up in a ten-foot-high pile around it.

There was a huge, rounded, grey object buried in the dirt and torn caliche at the bottom. Waves of heat rose from it, and grey ash, like old charcoal, fell off it into the shimmering pit.

Half the town was riding out in wagons and on horseback as the news spread. The closest neighbors were walking over in the twilight, wearing their go-visiting clothes.

"Well, well," said the sheriff, looking down. "So that's what a meteor looks like."

Leo Smith was already in the pit, walking around.

"I figured you'd be here sooner or later," said Lindley.

"Hello, Sheriff," said Leo. "It's still too hot to touch. Part of a cow's buried under the back end."

The sheriff looked over at the Atkinson family. "You folks is danged lucky. That thing coulda come down smack on your house or, what's worse, your barn. What time it fall?"

"Straight up and down six o'clock," said Mrs. Atkinson. "We was setting' down to supper. I saw it out of the corner of my eye; then all tarnation came down. Rocks must have been falling for ten minutes!"

"It's pretty spectacular, Sheriff," said Leo. "I'm going into town to telegraph off to the professors at the University. They'll sure want to look at this."

"Any reason other than general curiosity?" asked Lindley.

"I've only seen pictures and handled little bitty parts of one," said Leo, "but it doesn't look usual. They're generally like big rocks, all stone or iron. The outside of this one's soft and crumbly. Ashy, too."

There was a slight pop and a stove-cooling noise from the thing.

"Well, you can come back into town with me if you want to. Hey, Sweets!"

The chief deputy came over.

"A couple of the boys better stay here tonight, keep people from falling in the hole. I guess if Leo's gonna wire the University, you better keep anybody from knockin' chunks off it. It'll probably get pretty crowded. If I was the Atkinsons, I'd start chargin' a nickel a look."

"Sure thing, Sheriff."

Kerosene lanterns and carriage lights were moving toward the Atkinsons' in the coming darkness.

"I'll be out here early tomorrow mornin' to take another gander. I gotta serve a process paper on old Theobald before he lights out for his chores. If I sent one o' you boys, he'd as soon shoot you as say howdy."

"Sure thing, Sheriff."

He and Leo and Jimmy Atkinson got in the wagon and rode off toward the quiet lights of town far away.

*   *   *

There was a new smell in the air.

The sheriff noticed it as he rode toward the Atkinson ranch by the south road early the next morning. There was an odor like when something goes wrong at the telegraph office.

Smoke was curling up from the pasture. Maybe there was a scrub fire started from the heat of the falling star.

He topped the last rise. Before him lay devastation the likes of which he hadn't seen since the retreat from Atlanta.

"Great Gawd Ahmighty!" he said.

There were dead horses and charred wagons all around. The ranch house was untouched, but the barn was burned to the ground. There were crisscrossed lines of burnt grass that looked like they'd been painted with a tarbrush.

He saw no bodies anywhere. Where was Sweets? Where was Luke, the other deputy? Where had the people from the wagons gone? What had happened?

Lindley looked at the crater. There was a shiny rod sticking out of it, with something round on the end. From here it looked like one of those carnival acts where a guy spins a plate on the end of a dowel rod, only this glinted like metal in the early sun. As he watched, a small cloud of green steam rose above it from the pit.

He saw a motion behind an old tree uprooted by a storm twelve years ago. It was Sweets. He was yelling and waving the sheriff back.

Lindley rode his horse into a small draw, then came up into the open.

There was movement over at the crater. He thought he saw something. Reflected sunlight flashed by his eyes, and he thought he saw a rounded silhouette. He heard a noise like sometimes gets in bobwire on a windy day.

He heard a humming sound then, smelled the electric smell real strong. Fire started a few feet from him, out of nowhere, and moved toward him.

Then his horse exploded.

The air was an inferno, he was thrown spinning—

He must have blacked out. He had no memory of what went next. When he came to, he was running as fast as he ever had toward the uprooted tree.

Fire jumped all around. Luke was shooting over the tree roots with his pistol. He ducked. A long section of the trunk was washed over with flames and sparks.

Lindley dove behind the root tangle.

"What the ding-dong is goin' on?" he asked as he tried to catch his breath. He still had his new hat on, but his britches and coat were singed and smoking.

"God damn, Bert! I don't know," said Sweets, leaning around Luke. "We was out here all night; it was a regular party; most of the time we was up on the lip up there. Maybe thirty or forty people comin' and goin' all the time. We was all talking and hoorawing, and then we heard something about an hour ago. We looked down, and I'll be damned if the whole top of that thing didn't come off like a Mason jar!

"We was watching, and these damn things started coming out— they looked like big old leather balls, big as horses, with snakes all out the front—"

"What?"

"Snakes. Yeah, tentacles Leo called them, like an octy-puss. Leo'd come back from town and was here when them boogers came out. Martians he said they was, things from Mars. They had big old eyes, big as your head! Everybody was pushing and shoving; then one of them pulled out one of them gun things, real slow like, and he just started burning up everything in sight.

"We all ran back for whatever cover we could find—it took 'em a while to get up the dirt pile. They killed horses, dogs, anything they could see. Fire was everywhere. They use that thing just like the volunteer firemen use them water hoses in Waco!"

"Where's Leo?"

Sweets pointed to the draw that ran diagonally to the west. "We watched awhile, finally figured they couldn't line up on the ditch all the way to the rise. Leo and the others got away up the draw—he was gonna telegraph the University about it. The bunch that got away was supposed to send people out to the town road to warn people. You probably would have run into them if you hadn't been coming from Theobald's place.

"Anyway, soon as them things saw people were gettin' away, they got mad as hornets. That's when they lit up the Atkinsons' barn."

A flash of fire leapt in the roots of the tree, jumped back thirty feet into the burnt grass behind them, then moved back and forth in a curtain of sparks.

"Man, that's what I call a real smoke pole," said Luke.

"Well," Lindley said. "This just won't do. These things done attacked citizens in my jurisdiction, and they killed my horse."

He turned to Luke.

"Be real careful, and get back to town, get the posse up. Telegraph the Rangers and tell 'em to burn leather gettin' here. Then get ahold of Skip Whitworth and have him bring out The Gun."

* * *

Skip Whitworth sat behind the tree trunk and pulled the cover from the six-foot rifle at his side. Skip was in his late fifties. He had been a sniper in the War for Southern Independence when he had been in his twenties. He had once shot at a Yankee general just as the officer was bringing a forkful of beans up to his mouth. When the fork got there, there was only some shoulders and a gullet for the beans to drop into.

That had been from a mile and a half away, from sixty feet up a pine tree.

The rifle was an .80-caliber octagonal-barrel breechloader that used two and a half ounces of powder and a percussion cap the size of a jawbreaker for each shot. It had a telescopic sight running the entire length of the barrel.

"They're using that thing on the end of that stick to watch us," said Lindley. "I had Sweets jump around, and every time he did, one of those cooters would come up with that fire gun and give us what-for."

Skip said nothing. He loaded his rifle, which had a breechblock lever the size of a crowbar on it, then placed another round—cap, paper cartridge, ball—next to him.

He drew a bead and pulled the trigger. It sounded like dynamite had gone off in their ears.

The wobbling pole snapped in two halfway up. The top end flopped around back into the pit.

There was a scrabbling noise above the whirring from the earthen lip. Something round came up.

Skip had smoothly opened the breech, put in the ball, torn the cartridge with his teeth, put in the cap, closed the action, pulled back the hammer, and sighted before the shape reached the top of the dirt.

Metal glinted in the middle of the dark thing.

Skip fired.

There was a *squeech*; the whole top of the round thing opened up; it spun around and backward, things in its front working like a daddy longlegs thrown on a roaring stove.

Skip loaded again. There were flashes of light from the crater. Something came up shooting, fire leaping like hot sparks from a blacksmith's anvil, the air full of flames and smoke.

Skip fired again.

The fire gun flew up in the air. Snakes twisted, writhed, disappeared.

It was very quiet for a few seconds.

Then there was the renewed whining of machinery and noises like a pile driver, the sounds of filing and banging. Steam came up over the crater lip.

"Sounds like a steel foundry in there," said Sweets.

"I don't like it one bit," said Bert. "Be danged if I'm gonna let 'em get the drop on us. Can you keep them down?"

"How many are there?" asked Skip.

"Luke and Sweets saw four or five before all hell broke loose this morning. Probably more of 'em than that was inside."

"I've got three more shots. If they poke up, I'll get 'em."

"I'm going to town, then out to Elmer's. Sweets'll stay with you awhile.

"If you run outta bullets, light up out the draw. I don't want nobody killed. Sweets, keep an eye out for the posse. I'm telegraphin' the Rangers again, then goin' to get Elmer and his dynamite. We're gonna fix their little red wagon for certain."

"Sure thing, Sheriff."

The sun had just passed noon.

＊　　＊　　＊

Leo looked haggard. He had been up all night, then at the telegraph office sending off messages to the University. Inquiries had begun to come in from as far east as Baton Rouge. Leo had another, from Percival Lowell out in Flagstaff, Arizona Territory.

"Everybody at the University thinks it's wonderful," said Leo.

"People in Austin would," said the sheriff.

"They're sure these things are connected with Mars and those bright flashes of gas last month. Seems something's happened in England, starting about a week ago. No one's been able to get through to London for two or three days."

"You telling me Mars is attacking London, England, and Pachuco City, Texas?" asked the sheriff.

"It seems so," said Leo. He took off his glasses and rubbed his eyes.

"'Scuse me, Leo," said Lindley. "I got to get another telegram off to the Texas Rangers."

"That's funny," said Argyle, the telegraph operator. "The line was working just a second ago." He kept tapping his key and fiddling with his coil box.

Leo peered out the window. "Hey!" he said. "Where's the 3:14?" He looked at the railroad clock. It was 3:25.

In sixteen years of rail service, the train had been four minutes late, and that was after a mud slide in the storm twelve years ago.

"Uh-oh," said the sheriff.

*　　*　　*

They were turning out Elmer's yard with a wagon load of dynamite. The wife and eleven of the kids were watching.

"Easy, Sheriff," said Elmer, who, with two of his boys and most of their guns, was riding in back with the explosives. "Jake sold me everything he had. I just didn't notice till we got back here with that stuff that some of it was already sweating."

"Holy shit!" said Lindley. "You mean we gotta go a mile an hour out there? Let's get out and throw the bad stuff off."

"Well, it's all mixed in," said Elmer. "I was sorta gonna set it all up on the hill and put one blasting cap in the whole load."

"Jesus. You woulda blowed up your house and Pachuco City, too."

"I was in a hurry," said Elmer, hanging his head.

"Well, can't be helped, then. We'll take it slow."

Lindley looked at his watch. It was six o'clock. He heard a high-up, fluttering sound. They looked at the sky. Coming down was a large, round, glowing object throwing off sparks in all directions. It was curved with points, like the thing in the crater at the Atkinson place. A long, thin trail of smoke from the back end hung in the air behind it.

They watched in awe as it sailed down. It went into the horizon to the north of Pachuco City.

"One," said one of the kids in the wagon, "two, three—"

Silently they took up the count. At twenty-seven there was a roaring boom, just like the night before.

"Five and a half miles," said the sheriff. "That puts it eight miles from the other one. Leo said the ones in London came down twenty-four hours apart, regular as clockwork."

They started off as fast as they could under the circumstances.

There were flashes of light beyond the Atkinson place in the near dusk. The lights moved off toward the north where the other thing had plowed in.

It was the time of evening when your eyes can fool you. Sheriff Lindley thought he saw something that shouldn't have been there sticking above the horizon. It glinted like metal in the dim light. He thought it moved, but it might have been the motion of the wagon as they lurched down a gully. When they came up, it was gone.

Skip was gone. His rifle was still there. It wasn't melted but had been crushed, as had the three-foot-thick tree trunk in front of it. All the caps and cartridges were gone.

There was a monstrous series of footprints leading from the crater down to the tree, then off into the distance to the north where Lindley thought he had seen something. There were three footprints in each series.

Sweets' hat had been mashed along with Skip's gun. Clanging and banging still came from the crater.

The four of them made their plans. Lindley had his shotgun and pistol, which Luke had brought out with him that morning, though he was still wearing his burnt suit and his untouched Stetson.

He tied together the fifteen sweatiest sticks of dynamite he could fine.

They crept up, then rushed the crater.

*　　*　　*

"Hurry up!" yelled the sheriff to the men at the courthouse. "Get that cannon up those stairs!"

"He's still coming this way!" yelled Luke from up above.

They had been watching the giant machine from the courthouse since it had come up out of the Atkinson place, before the sheriff and Elmer and his boys made it into town after their sortie.

It had come across to the north, gone to the site of the second crash, and stood motionless there for quite a while. When it got dark, the deputies brought out the night binoculars. Everybody in town saw the flash of dynamite from the Atkinson place.

A few moments after that, the machine had moved back toward there. It looked like a giant water tower with three legs. It had a thing like a teacher's desk bell on top of it, and something that looked like a Kodak roll-film camera in front of that. As the moon rose, they saw the thing had tentacles like thick wires hanging from between the three giant legs.

The sheriff, Elmer, and his boys made it to town just as the machine found the destruction they had caused at the first landing site. It had turned toward town and was coming at a pace of twenty miles an hour.

"Hurry the hell up!" yelled Luke. "Oh, shit—!" he ducked. There was a flash of light overhead. The building shook. "That heat gun comes out of the box on the front!" he said. "Look out!" The building glared and shook again. Something down the street caught fire.

"Load that sonofabitch," said Lindley. "Bob! Some of you men make sure everybody's in the cyclone cellars or where they won't burn. Cut out all the damn lights!"

"Hell, Sheriff. They know we're here!" yelled a deputy.

Lindley hit him with his hat, then followed the cannon up to the top of the clock-tower steps.

Luke was cramming powder into the cannon muzzle. Sweets ran back down the stairs. Other people carried cannonballs up the steps to the tower one at a time.

Leo came up. "What did you find, Sheriff, when you went back?"

There was a cool breeze for a few seconds in the courthouse tower. Lindley breathed a few deep breaths, remembering. "Pretty rough. There was some of them still working after that thing had gone. They were building another one just like it." He pointed toward the machine, which was firing up houses to the northeast side of town, swinging the ray back and forth. They could hear its hum. Homes and chicken coops burst into flames. A mooing cow was stilled.

"We threw in the dynamite and blew most of them up. One was in a machine like a steam tractor. We shot up what was left while they was hootin' and a-hollerin'. There was some other things in there, live things maybe, but they was too blowed up to put back together to be sure what they looked like, all bleached out and pale. We fed everything there a diet of buckshot till there wasn't nothin' left. Then we hightailed it back here on horses, left the wagon sitting."

The machine came on toward the main street of town. Luke finished with the powder. There were so many men with guns on the building across the street it looked like a brick porcupine. It must have looked that way for the James Gang when they were shot up in Northfield, Minnesota.

The courthouse was made of stone. Most of the wooden buildings in town were scorched or already afire. When the heat gun came this way, it blew bricks to dust, played flame over everything. The air above the whole town heated up.

They had put out the lamps behind the clock faces. There was nothing but moonlight glinting off the three-legged machine, flames of burning buildings, the faraway glows of prairie fires. It looked like Pachuco City was on the outskirts of Hell.

"Get ready, Luke," said the sheriff. The machine stepped between two burning stores, its tentacles pulling out smoldering horse tack, chains, kegs of nails, then heaving them this way and that. Someone at the end of the street fired off a round. There was a high, thin ricochet off the machine.

Sweets ran upstairs, something in his arms. It was a curtain from one of the judge's windows. He'd ripped it down and tied it to the end of one of the janitor's long window brushes.

On it he had lettered in tempera paint COME AND TAKE IT.

There was a ragged, nervous cheer from the men on the building as they read it by the light of the flames.

"Cute, Sweets," said Lindley, "too cute."

The machine turned down Main Street. A line of fire sprang up at the back side of town from the empty corrals.

"Oh, shit!" said Luke. "I forgot the wadding!"

Lindley took off his hat to hit him with. He looked at its beautiful felt in the mixed moonlight and firelight.

The thing turned toward them. The sheriff thought he saw eyes way up in the bell-thing atop the machine, eyes like a big cat's eyes seen through a dirty windowpane on a dark night.

"Gol Dang, Luke, it's my best hat, but I'll be damned if I let them cooters burn down my town!"

He stuffed the Stetson, crown first, into the cannon barrel. Luke shoved it in with the ramrod, threw in two thirty-five-pound cannon balls behind it, pushed them home, and swung the barrel out over Main Street.

The machine bent to tear up something.

"Okay, boys," yelled Lindley. "Attract its attention."

Rifle and shotgun fire winked on the rooftop. It glowed like a hot coal from the muzzle flashes. A great slather of ricochets flew off the giant machine.

It turned, pointing its heat gun at the building. It was fifty feet from the courthouse steps.

"Now," said the sheriff.

Luke touched off the powder with his cigarillo.

The whole north side of the courthouse bell tower flew off, and the roof collapsed. Two holes you could see the moon through appeared in the machine: one in the middle, one smashing through the dome atop it. Sheriff Lindley saw the lower cannonball come out and drop lazily toward the end of burning Main Street.

All six of the tentacles of the machine shot straight up into the air, and it took off like a man running with his arms above his head. It staggered, as fast as a freight train could go, through one side of a house and out the other, and ran partway up Park Street. One of its three legs went higher than its top. It hopped around like a crazy man on crutches before its feet got tangled in a horse-pasture fence, and it went over backward with a shudder. A great cloud of steam came out of it and hung in the air.

No one in the courthouse tower heard the sound of the steam. They were all deaf as posts from the explosion. The barrel of the cannon was burst all along the end. The men on the other roof were jumping up and down and clapping each other on the back. The COME AND TAKE IT sign on the courthouse had two holes in it, neater than you could have made with a biscuit-cutter.

First a high whine, then a dull roar, then something like normal hearing came back to the sheriff's left ear. The right one still felt like a kid had its fist in there.

"Dang it, Sweets!" he yelled. "How much powder did Luke use!"

"Huh?"

Luke was banging on his head with both his hands.

"How much powder did he use?"

"Two, two and a half cans," said Sweets.

"It only takes half a can a ball!" yelled the sheriff. He reached for his hat to hit Luke with, touched his bare head. "I feel naked," he said. "Come on, we're not through yet. We got fires to put out and some hash to settle."

Luke was still standing, shaking his head. The whole town was cheering.

*   *   *

It looked like a pot lid slowly boiling open, moving just a little. Every time the end unscrewed a little more, ashes and cinders fell off into the second pit. There was a piled ridge of them. The back turned again, moved a few inches, quit. Then it wobbled, there was a sound like a stove being jerked up a chimney, and the whole back end rolled open like a mad bank vault and fell off.

There were 184 men and 11 women all standing behind the open end of the thing, their guns pointing toward the interior. At the exact center were Sweets and Luke with the other courthouse cannon. This time there was one can of powder, but the barrel was filled to the end with everything from the blacksmith-shop floor—busted window glass, nails, horseshoes, bolts, stirrup buckles, and broken files and saws.

Eyes appeared in the dark interior.

"Remember the Alamo," said the sheriff.

Everybody, and the cannon, fired.

*   *   *

When the third meteor came in that evening, south of town at thirteen minutes past six, they knew something was wrong. It wobbled in flight, lost speed, and dropped like a long, heavy leaf.

They didn't have to wait for this one to cool and open. When the posse arrived, the thing was split in two and torn. Heat and steam came up from the inside.

One of the pale things was creeping forlornly across the ground with great difficulty. It looked like a thin gingerbread man made of glass with only a knob for a head.

"It's probably hurting from the gravity," said Leo.

"Fix it, Sweets," said Lindley.

"Sure thing, Sheriff."

There was a gunshot.

*　　*　　*

No fourth meteor fell, though they had scouts out for twenty miles in all directions, and the railroad tracks and telegraph wires were fixed again.

"I been doing some figuring," said Leo. "If there were ten explosions on Mars last month, and these things started landing in England last Thursday week, then we should have got the last three. There won't be any more."

"You been figurin', huh?"

"Sure have."

"Well, we'll see."

*　　*　　*

Sheriff Lindley stood on his porch. It was sundown on Sunday, three hours after another meteor should have fallen, had there been one.

Leo rode up. "I saw Sweets and Luke heading toward the Atkinson place with more dynamite. What are they doing?"

"They're blowing up every last remnant of them things—lock, stock and asshole."

"But," said Leo, "the professors from the University will be here tomorrow, to look at their ships and machines! You can't destroy them!"

"Shit on the University of Texas and the horse it rode in on," said the sheriff. "My jurisdiction runs from Deer Piss Creek to Buenos Frijoles, back to Olatunji, up the Little Clear Fork of the North Branch of Mud River, back to the Creek, and everything in between. If I say something gets blowed up, it's on its way to Kingdom Come."

He put his arms on Leo's shoulders. "Besides, what little grass grows in this county's supposed to be green, and what's growing around them things is red. I *really* don't like that."

"But, Sheriff! I've got to meet Professor Lowell in Waxahachie tomorrow morning . . ."

"Listen, Leo. I appreciate what you done. But I'm an old man. I been kept up by Martians for three nights, I lost my horse and my new hat, and they busted my favorite gargoyle off the courthouse. I'm going in and get some sleep, and I only want to be woke up for the Second Coming, by Jesus Christ Himself."

Leo jumped on his horse and rode for the Atkinson place.

Sheriff Lindley crawled into bed and went to sleep as soon as his head hit the pillow.

He had a dream. He was a king in Babylon, and he lay on a couch at the top of a ziggurat, just like the Tower of Babel in the Bible. He surveyed the city and the river. There were women all around him, and men with curly beards and golden headdresses. Occasionally someone would feed him a great big fig from a golden bowl.

His dreams were not interrupted by the sounds of dynamiting, first from one side of town, then another, and then another.

heck Out Receipt

esperia
60-552-6050
ttp://www.sbclib.org

;unday, July 31, 2022 4:11:32 PM
'illanueva, Lisbeth

[tem: 31483041403878
Title: The campfire collection : thrilling, chil
ling tales of alien encounters
Call no.: SF FIC
Material: Book
Due: 8/14/2022

Total items: 1

Please review your receipt carefully as the due
dates or fine amounts may vary.
Most SBCL materials can be checked out
for 2 weeks and renewed up to 9 times.
Any additional notices are courtesy.

574

PART III

ALIEN
ABDUCTIONS

THE WOMEN MEN DON'T SEE
BY JAMES TIPTREE JR.

I see her first while the Mexicana 727 is barreling down to Cozumel Island. I come out of the can and lurch into her seat, saying "Sorry," at a double female blur. The near blur nods quietly. The younger one in the window seat goes on looking out. I continue down the aisle, registering nothing. Zero. I never would have looked at them or thought of them again.

Cozumel airport is the usual mix of panicky Yanks dressed for the sand pile and calm Mexicans dressed for lunch at the Presidente. I am a used-up Yank dressed for serious fishing; I extract my rods and duffel from the riot and hike across the field to find my charter pilot. One Captain Estéban has contracted to deliver me to the bonefish flats of Belize three hundred kilometers down the coast.

Captain Estéban turns out to be four feet nine of mahogany Maya puro. He is also in a somber Maya snit. He tells me my Cessna is grounded somewhere and his Bonanza is booked to take a party to Chetumal.

Well, Chetumal is south; can he take me along and go on to Belize after he drops them? Gloomily he concedes the possibility—if the other party permits, and if there are not too many *equipajes*.

The Chetumal party approaches. It's the woman and her young companion—daughter?—neatly picking their way across the gravel and yucca apron. Their Ventura two-suiters, like themselves, are small, plain, and neutral-colored. No problem. When the captain asks if I may ride along, the mother says mildly, "Of course," without looking at me.

I think that's when my inner tilt-detector sends up its first faint click. How come this woman has already looked me over carefully enough to accept on her plane? I disregard it. Paranoia hasn't been useful in my business for years, but the habit is hard to break.

As we clamber into the Bonanza, I see the girl has what could be an attractive body if there was any spark at all. There isn't. Captain Estéban folds a serape to sit on so he can see over the cowling and runs a meticulous check-down. And then we're up and trundling over the turquoise Jell-O of the Caribbean into a stiff south wind.

The coast on our right is the territory of Quintana Roo. If you haven't seen Yucatán, imagine the world's biggest absolutely flat green-gray rug. An empty-looking land. We pass the white ruin of Tulum and the gash of the road to Chichén Itzá, a half-dozen coconut plantations, and then nothing but reef and low scrub jungle all the way to the horizon, just about the way the conquistadors saw it four centuries back.

Long strings of cumulus are racing at us, shadowing the coast. I have gathered that part of our pilot's gloom concerns the weather. A cold front is dying on the henequen fields of Mérida to the west, and the south wind has piled up a string of coastal storms: what they call *lloviznas*. Estéban detours methodically around a couple of small thunderheads. The Bonanza jinks, and I look back with a vague notion of reassuring the women. They are calmly intent on what can be seen of Yucatán. Well, they were offered the copilot's view, but they turned it down. Too shy?

Another *llovizna* puffs up ahead. Estéban takes the Bonanza upstairs, rising in his seat to sight his course. I relax for the first time in too long, savoring the latitudes between me and my desk, the week of fishing ahead. Our captain's classic Maya profile attracts my gaze: forehead sloping back from his predatory nose, lips and jaw stepping back below it. If his slant eyes had been any more crossed, he couldn't have made his license. That's a handsome combination, believe it or not. On the little Maya chicks in their minishifts with iridescent gloop on those cockeyes, it's also highly erotic. Nothing like the oriental doll thing; these people have stone bones. Captain Estéban's old grandmother could probably tow the Bonanza. . . .

I'm snapped awake by the cabin hitting my ear. Estéban is barking into his headset over a drumming racket of hail; the windows are dark gray.

One important noise is missing—the motor. I realize Estéban is fighting a dead plane. Thirty-six hundred; we've lost two thousand feet!

He slaps tank switches as the storm throws us around; I catch something about *gasolina* in a snarl that shows his big teeth. The Bonanza reels down. As he reaches for an overhead toggle, I see the fuel gauges are high. Maybe a clogged gravity feed line; I've heard of dirty gas down here. He drops the set; it's a million to one nobody can read us through the storm at this range anyway. Twenty-five hundred—going down.

His electric feed pump seems to have cut in: the motor explodes—quits—explodes—and quits again for good. We are suddenly out of the bottom of the clouds. Below us is a long white line almost hidden by rain: the reef. But there isn't any beach behind it, only a big meandering bay with a few mangrove flats—and it's coming up at us fast.

This is going to be bad, I tell myself with great unoriginality. The women behind me haven't made a sound. I look back and see they've braced down with their coats by their heads. With a stalling speed around eighty, all this isn't much use, but I wedge myself in.

Estéban yells some more into his set, flying a falling plane. He is doing one jesus job, too—as the water rushes up at us he dives into a hair-raising turn and hangs us into the wind—with a long pale ridge of sand-bar in front of our nose.

Where in hell he found it I never know. The Bonanza mushes down, and we belly-hit with a tremendous tearing crash—bounce—hit again—and everything slews wildly as we flat-spin into the mangroves at the end of the bar. Crash! Clang! The plane is wrapping itself into a mound of strangler fig with one wing up. The crashing quits with us all in one piece. And no fire. Fantastic.

Captain Estéban pries open his door, which is now in the roof. Behind me a woman is repeating quietly, "Mother. Mother." I climb up the floor and find the girl trying to free herself from her mother's embrace. The woman's eyes are closed. Then she opens them and suddenly lets go, sane as soap. Estéban starts hauling them out. I grab the Bonanza's aid kit and scramble out after them into brilliant sun and wind. The storm that hit us is already vanishing up the coast.

"Great landing, Captain."

"Oh, yes! It was beautiful." The women are shaky, but no hysteria. Estéban is surveying the scenery with the expression his ancestors used on the Spaniards.

If you've been in one of those things, you know the slow-motion inanity that goes on. Euphoria, first. We straggle down the fig tree and out onto the sandbar in the roaring hot wind, noting without alarm that there's nothing but miles of crystalline water on all sides. It's only a foot or so deep, and the bottom is the olive color of silt. The distant shore around us is all flat mangrove swamp, totally uninhabitable.

"Bahía Espíritu Santo." Estéban confirms my guess that we're down in that huge water wilderness. I always wanted to fish it.

"What's all that smoke?" The girl is pointing at the plumes blowing around the horizon.

"Alligator hunters," says Estéban. Maya poachers have left burn-offs in the swamps. It occurs to me that any signal fires we make aren't going to be too conspicuous. And I now note that our plane is well buried in the mound of fig. Hard to see it from the air.

Just as the question of how the hell we get out of here surfaces in my mind, the older woman asks composedly, "If they didn't hear you, Captain, when will they start looking for us? Tomorrow?"

"Correct," Estéban agrees dourly. I recall that air-sea rescue is fairly informal here. Like, keep an eye open for Mario, his mother says he hasn't been home all week.

It dawns on me we may be here quite some while.

Furthermore, the diesel-truck noise on our left is the Caribbean piling back into the mouth of the bay. The wind is pushing it at us, and the bare bottoms on the mangroves show that our bar is covered at high tide. I recall seeing a full moon this morning in—believe it, St. Louis—which means maximal tides. Well, we can climb up in the plane. But what about drinking water?

There's a small splat! behind me. The older woman has sampled the bay. She shakes her head, smiling ruefully. It's the first real expression on either of them; I take it as the signal for introductions. When I say I'm Don Fenton from St. Louis, she tells me their name is Parsons, from Bethesda, Maryland. She says it so nicely I don't at first notice we aren't being given first names. We all compliment Captain Estéban again.

His left eye is swelled shut, an inconvenience beneath his attention as a Maya, but Mrs. Parsons spots the way he's bracing his elbow in his ribs.

"You're hurt, Captain."

"*Roto*—I think is broken." He's embarrassed at being in pain. We get him to peel off his Jaime shirt, revealing a nasty bruise in his superb dark-bay torso.

"Is there tape in that kit, Mr. Fenton? I've had a little first-aid training."

She begins to deal competently and very impersonally with the tape. Miss Parsons and I wander to the end of the bar and have a conversation which I am later to recall acutely.

"Roseate spoonbills," I tell her as three pink birds flap away.

"They're beautiful," she says in her tiny voice. They both have tiny voices. "He's a Mayan Indian, isn't he? The pilot, I mean."

"Right. The real thing, straight out of the Bonampak murals. Have you seen Chichén and Uxmal?"

"Yes. We were in Mérida. We're going to Tikal in Guatemala. . . . I mean, we were."

"You'll get there." It occurs to me the girl needs cheering up. "Have they told you that Maya mothers used to tie a board on the infant's forehead to get that slant? They also hung a ball of tallow over its nose to make the eyes cross. It was considered aristocratic."

She smiles and takes another peek at Estéban. "People seem different in Yucatán," she says thoughtfully. "Not like the Indians around Mexico City. More, I don't know, independent."

"Comes from never having been conquered. Mayas got massacred and chased a lot, but nobody ever really flattened them. I bet you didn't know that the last Mexican-Maya war ended with a negotiated truce in nineteen thirty-five?"

"No!" Then she says seriously, "I like that."

"So do I."

"The water is really rising very fast," says Mrs. Parsons gently from behind us.

It is, and so is another llovizna. We climb back into the Bonanza. I try to rig my parka for a rain catcher, which blows loose as the storm hit fast and furious. We sort a couple of malt bars and my bottle of Jack Daniel's out of the jumble in the cabin and make ourselves reasonably comfortable. The Parsons take a sip of whiskey each, Estéban and I considerably more. The Bonanza begins to bump soggily. Estéban makes an ancient one-eyed Mayan face at the water seeping into his cabin and goes to sleep. We all nap.

When the water goes down, the euphoria has gone with it, and we're very, very thirsty. It's also damn near sunset. I get to work with a bait-casting rod and some treble hooks and manage to foul-hook four small mullets. Estéban and the women tie the Bonanza's midget life raft out in the mangroves to catch rain. The wind is parching hot. No planes go by.

Finally another shower comes over and yields us six ounces of water apiece. When the sunset envelops the world in golden smoke, we squat on the sandbar to eat wet raw mullet and Instant Breakfast crumbs. The women are now in shorts, neat but definitely not sexy.

"I never realized how refreshing raw fish is," Mrs. Parsons says pleasantly. Her daughter chuckles, also pleasantly. She's on Mamma's far side away from Estéban and me. I have Mrs. Parsons figured now; Mother Hen protecting only chick from male predators. That's all right with me. I came here to fish.

But something is irritating me. The damn women haven't complained once, you understand. Not a peep, not a quaver, no personal manifestations whatever. They're like something out of a manual.

"You really seem at home in the wilderness, Mrs. Parsons. You do much camping?"

"Oh, goodness no." Diffident laugh. "Not since my Girl Scout days. Oh, look—are those man-of-war birds?"

Answer a question with a question. I wait while the frigate birds sail nobly into the sunset.

"Bethesda . . . Would I be wrong in guessing you work for Uncle Sam?"

"Why, yes. You must be very familiar with Washington, Mr. Fenton. Does your work bring you there often?"

Anywhere but on our sandbar the little ploy would have worked. My hunter's gene twitches.

"Which agency are you with?"

She gives up gracefully. "Oh, just GSA records. I'm a librarian."

Of course. I know her now, all the Mrs. Parsonses in records divisions, accounting sections, research branches, personnel and administration offices. Tell Mrs. Parsons we need a recap on the external service contracts for fiscal '73. So Yucatán is on the tours now? Pity . . . I offer her the tired little joke. "You know where the bodies are buried."

She smiles deprecatingly and stands up. "It does get dark quickly, doesn't it?

Time to get back into the plane.

A flock of ibis are circling us, evidently accustomed to roosting in our fig tree. Estéban produces a machete and a Mayan string hammock. He proceeds to sling it between tree and plane, refusing help. His machete stroke is noticeably tentative.

The Parsons are taking a pee behind the tail vane. I hear one of them slip and squeal faintly. When they come back over the hull, Mrs. Parsons asks, "Might we sleep in the hammock, Captain?"

Estéban splits an unbelieving grin. I protest about rain and mosquitoes.

"Oh, we have insect repellent and we do enjoy fresh air."

The air is rushing by about force five and colder by the minute.

"We have our raincoats," the girl adds cheerfully.

Well, okay, ladies. We dangerous males retire inside the damp cabin. Through the wind I hear the women laugh softly now and then, apparently cozy in their chilly ibis roost. A private insanity, I decide. I know myself for the least threatening of men; my noncharisma has been in fact an asset job-wise, over the years. Are they having fantasies about Estéban? Or maybe they really are fresh-air nuts. . . . Sleep comes for me in invisible diesels roaring by on the reef outside . . .

We emerge dry-mouthed into a vast windy salmon sunrise. A diamond chip of sun breaks out of the sea and promptly submerges in cloud. I go to work with the rod and some mullet bait while two showers detour around us. Breakfast is a strip of wet barracuda apiece.

The Parsons continue stoic and helpful. Under Estéban's direction they set up a section of cowling for a gasoline flare in case we hear a plane, but nothing goes over except one unseen jet droning toward Panama. The wind howls, hot and dry and full of coral dust. So are we.

"They look first in sea," Estéban remarks. His aristocratic frontal slope is beaded with sweat; Mrs. Parsons watches him concernedly. I watch the cloud blanket tearing by above, getting higher and dryer and thicker. While that lasts nobody is going to find us, and the water business is now unfunny.

Finally I borrow Estéban's machete and hack a long light pole. "There's a stream coming in back there, I saw it from the plane. Can't be more than two, three miles."

"I'm afraid the raft's torn." Mrs. Parsons shows me the cracks in the orange plastic; irritatingly, it's a Delaware label.

"All right," I hear myself announce. "The tide's going down. If we cut the good end off that air tube, I can haul water back in it. I've waded flats before."

Even to me it sounds crazy.

"Stay by plane," Estéban says. He's right, of course. He's also clearly running a fever. I look at the overcast and taste grit and old barracuda. The hell with the manual.

When I start cutting up the raft, Estéban tells me to take the serape. "You stay one night." He's right about that, too; I'll have to wait out the tide.

"I'll come with you," says Mrs. Parsons calmly.

I simply stare at her. What new madness has got into Mother Hen? Does she imagine Estéban is too battered to be functional? While I'm being astounded, my eyes take in the fact that Mrs. Parsons is now quite rosy around the knees, with her hair loose and a sunburn starting on her nose. A trim, in fact a very neat, shading-forty.

"Look, that stuff is horrible going. Mud up to your ears and water over your head."

"I'm really quite fit and I swim a great deal. I'll try to keep up. Two would be much safer, Mr. Fenton, and we can bring more water."

She's serious. Well, I'm about as fit as a marshmallow at this time of winter, and I can't pretend I'm depressed by the idea of company. So be it.

"Let me show Miss Parsons how to work this rod."

Miss Parsons is even rosier and more windblown, and she's not clumsy with my tackle. A good girl, Miss Parsons, in her nothing way. We cut another staff and get some gear together. At the last minute Estéban shows how sick he feels: he offers me the machete. I thank him, but no; I'm used to my Wirkkala knife. We tie some air into the plastic tube for a float and set out along the sandiest-looking line.

Estéban raises one dark palm. "*Buen viaje.*" Miss Parsons has hugged her mother and gone to cast from the mangrove. She waves. We wave.

An hour later we're barely out of waving distance. The going is purely god-awful. The sand keeps dissolving into silt you can't walk on or swim through, and the bottom is spiked with dead mangrove spears. We flounder from one pothole to the next, scaring up rays and turtles and hoping to god we don't kick a moray eel. Where we're not soaked in slime, we're desiccated, and we smell like the Old Cretaceous.

Mrs. Parsons keeps up doggedly. I only have to pull her out once. When I do so, I notice the sandbar is now out of sight.

Finally we reach the gap in the mangrove line I thought was the creek. It turns out to open into another arm of the bay, with more mangroves ahead. And the tide is coming in.

"I've had the world's lousiest idea."

Mrs. Parsons only says mildly, "It's so different from the view from the plane."

I revise my opinion of the Girl Scouts, and we plow on past the mangroves toward the smoky haze that has to be shore. The sun is setting in our faces, making it hard to see. Ibis and herons fly up around us, and once a big hermit spooks ahead, his fin cutting a rooster tail. We fall into more potholes. The flashlights get soaked. I am having fantasies of the mangrove as universal obstacle; it's hard to recall I ever walked down a street, for instance, without stumbling over or under or through mangrove roots. And the sun is dropping down, down.

Suddenly we hit a ledge and fall over it into a cold flow.

"The stream! It's fresh water!"

We guzzle and garble and douse our heads; it's the best drink I remember. "Oh my, oh my—!" Mrs. Parsons is laughing right out loud.

"That dark place over to the right looks like real land."

We flounder across the flow and follow a hard shelf, which turns into solid bank and rises over our heads. Shortly there's a break beside a clump of spiny bromels, and we scramble up and flop down at the top, dripping and stinking. Out of sheer reflex my arm goes around my companion's shoulder—but Mrs. Parsons isn't there; she's up on her knees peering at the burnt-over plain around us.

"It's so good to see land one can walk on!" The tone is too innocent. *Noli me tangere.*

"Don't try it." I'm exasperated; the muddy little woman, what does she think? "That ground out there is a crush of ashes over muck, and it's full of stubs. You can go in over your knees."

"It seems firm here."

"We're in an alligator nursery. That was the slide we came up. Don't worry, by now the old lady's doubtless on her way to be made into handbags."

"What a shame."

"I better set a line down in the stream while I can still see."

I slide back down and rig a string of hooks that may get us breakfast. When I get back Mrs. Parsons is wringing muck out of the serape.

"I'm glad you warned me, Mr. Fenton. It is treacherous."

"Yeah." I'm over my irritation; god knows I don't want to *tangere* Mrs. Parsons, even if I weren't beat down to mush. "In its quiet way, Yucatán is a tough place to get around in. You can see why the Mayas built roads. Speaking of which—look!"

The last of the sunset is silhouetting a small square shape a couple of kilometers inland; a Maya *ruina* with a fig tree growing out of it.

"Lot of those around. People think they were guard towers."

"What a deserted-feeling land."

"Let's hope it's deserted by mosquitoes."

We slump down in the 'gator nursery and share the last malt bar, watching the stars slide in and out of the blowing clouds. The bugs aren't too bad; maybe the burn did them in. And it isn't hot anymore, either—in fact, it's not even warm, wet as we are. Mrs. Parsons continues tranquilly interested in Yucatán and unmistakably uninterested in togetherness.

Just as I'm beginning to get aggressive notions about how we're going to spend the night if she expects me to give her the serape, she stands up, scuffs at a couple of hummocks, and says, "I expect this is as good a place as any, isn't it, Mr. Fenton?"

With which she spreads out the raft bag for a pillow and lies down on her side in the dirt with exactly half the serape over her and the other corner folded neatly open. Her small back toward me.

The demonstration is so convincing that I'm halfway under my share of serape before the preposterousness of it stops me.

"By the way. My name is Don."

"Oh, of course." Her voice is graciousness itself. "I'm Ruth."

I get in not quite touching her, and we lie there like two fish on a plate, exposed to the stars and smelling the smoke in the wind and feeling things underneath us. It is absolutely the most intimately awkward moment I've had in years.

The woman doesn't mean one thing to me, but the obtrusive recessiveness of her, the defiance of her little rump eight inches from my fly—for two pesos I'd have those shorts down and introduce myself. If I were twenty years younger. If I wasn't so bushed . . . But the twenty years and the exhaustion are there, and it comes to me wryly that Mrs. Ruth Parsons has judged things to a nicety. If I *were* twenty years younger, she wouldn't be here. Like the butterfish that float around a sated barracuda, only to vanish away the instant his intent changes, Mrs. Parsons knows her little shorts are safe. Those firmly filled little shorts, so close . . .

A warm nerve stirs in my groin—and just as it does I become aware of a silent emptiness beside me. Mrs. Parsons is imperceptibly inching away. Did my breathing change? Whatever, I'm perfectly sure that if my hand reached, she'd be elsewhere—probably announcing her intention to take a dip. The twenty years bring a chuckle to my throat, and I relax.

"Good night, Ruth."

"Good night, Don."

And believe it or not, we sleep, while the armadas of the wind roar overhead. . . .

Light wakes me—a cold white glare.

My first thought is 'gator hunters. Best to manifest ourselves as *turistas* as fast as possible. I scramble up, noting that Ruth has dived under the bromel clump.

"*Quién estás? Al socorro! Help, Señores!*"

No answer except the light goes out, leaving me blind.

I yell some more in a couple of languages. It stays dark. There's a vague scrabbling, whistling sound somewhere in the burn-off. Liking everything less by the minute, I try a speech about our plane having crashed and we need help.

A very narrow pencil of light flicks over us and snaps off.

"Eh-ep," says a blurry voice, and something metallic twitters. They for sure aren't locals. I'm getting unpleasant ideas.

"Yes, help!"

Something goes *crackle-crackle whish-whish*, and all sounds fade away.

"What the holy hell!" I stumble toward where they were.

"Look." Ruth whispers behind me. "Over by the ruin."

I look and catch a multiple flicker which winks out fast.

"A camp?"

And I take two more blind strides. My leg goes down through the crust, and a spike spears me just where you stick the knife in to unjoint a drumstick. By the pain that goes through my bladder I recognize that my trick kneecap has caught it.

For instant basket-case you can't beat kneecaps. First you discover your knee doesn't bend anymore, so you try putting some weight on it, and a bayonet goes up your spine and unhinges your jaw. Little grains of gristle have got into the sensitive bearing surface. The knee tries to buckle and can't, and mercifully you fall down.

Ruth helps me back to the serape.

"What a fool, what a god-forgotten imbecile—"

"Not at all, Don. It was perfectly natural." We strike matches; her fingers push mine aside, exploring. "I think it's in place, but it's swelling fast. I'll lay a wet handkerchief on it. We'll have to wait for morning to check the cut. Were they poachers, do you think?"

"Probably," I lie. What I think they were is smugglers.

She comes back with a soaked bandanna and drapes it on. "We must have frightened them. That light . . . seemed so bright."

"Some hunting party. People do crazy things around here."

"Perhaps they'll come back in the morning."

"Could be."

Ruth pulls up the wet serape, and we say good-night again. Neither of us is mentioning how we're going to get back to the plane without help.

I lie staring south where Alpha Centauri is blinking in and out of the overcast and cursing myself for the sweet mess I've made. My first idea is giving way to an even less pleasing one.

Smuggling, around here, is a couple of guys in an outboard meeting a shrimp boat by the reef. They don't light up the sky or have some kind of swamp buggy that goes whoosh. Plus a big camp . . . paramilitary-type equipment?

I've seen a report of Guévarista infiltrators operating on the British Honduran border, which is about a hundred kilometers—sixty miles— south of here. Right under those clouds. If that's what looked us over, I'll be more than happy if they don't come back. . . .

I wake up in pelting rain, alone. My first move confirms that my leg is as expected—a giant misplaced erection bulging out of my shorts. I raise up painfully to see Ruth standing by the bromels, looking over the bay. Solid wet nimbus is pouring out of the south.

"No planes today."

"Oh, good morning, Don. Should we look at that cut now?"

"It's minimal." In fact the skin is hardly broken, and no deep puncture. Totally out of proportion to the havoc inside.

"Well, they have water to drink," Ruth says tranquilly. "Maybe those hunters will come back. I'll go see if we have a fish—that is, can I help you in any way, Don?"

Very tactful. I emit an ungracious negative, and she goes off about her private concerns.

They certainly are private, too; when I recover from my own sanitary efforts, she's still away. Finally I hear splashing.

"It's a big fish!" More splashing. Then she climbs up the band with a three-pound mangrove snapper—and something else.

It isn't until after the messy work of filleting the fish that I begin to notice.

She's making a smudge of chaff and twigs to singe the fillets, small hands very quick, tension in that female upper lip. The rain has eased off for the moment; we're sluicing wet but warm enough. Ruth brings me my fish on a mangrove skewer and sits back on her heels with an odd breathy sigh.

"Aren't you joining me?"

"Oh, of course." She gets a strip and picks at it, saying quickly, "We either have too much salt or too little, don't we? I should fetch some brine." Her eyes are roving from nothing to no place.

"Good thought." I hear another sigh and decide the Girl Scouts need an assist. "Your daughter mentioned you've come from Mérida. Have you seen much of Mexico?"

"Not really. Last year we went to Mazatlán and Cuernavaca. . . ." She puts the fish down, frowning.

"And you're going to see Tikal. Going to Bonampak too?"

"No." Suddenly she jumps up brushing rain off her face. "I'll bring you some water, Don."

She ducks down the slide, and after a fair while comes back with a full bromel stalk.

"Thanks." She's standing above me, staring restlessly round the horizon.

"Ruth, I hate to say it, but those guys are not coming back and it's probably just as well. Whatever they were up to, we looked like trouble. The most they'll do is tell someone we're here. That'll take a day or two to get around, we'll be back at the plane by then."

"I'm sure you're right, Don." She wanders over to the smudge fire.

"And quit fretting about you daughter. She's a big girl."

"Oh, I'm sure Althea's all right. . . . They have plenty of water now." Her fingers drum on her thigh. It's raining again.

"Come on, Ruth. Sit down. Tell me about Althea. Is she still in college?"

She gives that sighing little laugh and sits. "Althea got her degree last year. She's in computer programming."

"Good for her. And what about you, what do you do in GSA records?"

"I'm in Foreign Procurement Archives." She smiles mechanically, but her breathing is shallow. "It's very interesting."

"I know a Jack Wittig in Contracts, maybe you know him?"

It sounds pretty absurd, there in the 'gator slide.

"Oh, I've met Mr. Wittig. I'm sure he wouldn't remember me."

"Why not?"

"I'm not very memorable."

Her voice is factual. She's perfectly right, of course. Who was that woman, Mrs. Jannings, Janny, who coped with my per diem for years? Competent, agreeable, impersonal. She had a sick father or something. But dammit, Ruth is a lot younger and better looking. Comparatively speaking.

"Maybe Mrs. Parsons doesn't want to be memorable."

She makes a vague sound, and I suddenly realize Ruth isn't listening to me at all. Her hands are clenched around her knees, she's staring inland at the ruin.

"Ruth, I tell you our friends with the light are in the next country by now. Forget it, we don't need them."

Her eyes come back to me as if she'd forgotten I was there, and she nods slowly. It seems to be too much effort to speak. Suddenly she cocks her head and jumps up again.

"I'll go look at the line, Don. I thought I heard something—" She's gone like a rabbit.

While she's away I try getting up onto my good leg and the staff. The pain is sickening; knees seem to have some kind of hot line to the stomach. I take a couple of hops to test whether the Demerol I have in my belt would get me walking. As I do so, Ruth comes up the back with a fish flapping in her hands.

"Oh, no, Don! No!" She actually clasps the snapper to her breast.

"The water will take some of my weight. I'd like to give it a try."

"You mustn't!" Ruth says quite violently and instantly modulates down. "Look at the bay, Don. One can't see a thing."

I teeter there, tasting bile and looking at the mingled curtains of sun and rain driving across the water. She's right, thank god. Even with two legs we could get into trouble out there.

"I guess one more night won't kill us."

I let her collapse me back onto the gritty plastic, and she positively bustles around, finding me a chunk to lean on, stretching the serape on both staffs to keep rain off me, bringing another drink, grubbing for dry tinder.

"I'll make us a real bonfire as soon as it lets up, Don. They'll see our smoke, they'll know we're all right. We just have to wait." Cheery smile. "Is there any way we can make you more comfortable?"

Holy Saint Sterculius: playing house in a mud puddle. For a fatuous moment I wonder if Mrs. Parsons has designs on me. And then she lets out another sigh and sinks back onto her heels with that listening look. Unconsciously her rump wiggles a little. My ear picks up the operative word: wait.

Ruth Parsons is waiting. In fact, she acts as if she's waiting so hard it's killing her. For what? For someone to get us out of here, what else? . . . But why was she so horrified when I got up to try to leave? Why all this tension?

My paranoia stirs. I grab it by the collar and start idly checking back. Up to when whoever it was showed up last night, Mrs. Parsons was, I guess, normal. Calm and sensible, anyway. Now she's humming like a high wire. And she seems to want to stay here and wait. Just as an intellectual pastime, why?

Could she have intended to come here? No way. Where she planned to be was Chetumal, which is on the border. Come to think, Chetumal is an odd way round to Tikal. Let's say the scenario was that she's meeting somebody in Chetumal. Somebody who's part of an organization. So now her contact in Chetumal knows she's overdue. And when those types appeared last night, something suggests to her that they're part of the same organization. And she hopes they'll put one and one together and come back for her?

"May I have the knife, Don? I'll clean the fish."

Rather slowly I pass the knife, kicking my subconscious. Such a decent ordinary little woman, a good Girl Scout. My trouble is that I've bumped into too many professional agilities under the careful stereotypes. I'm not very memorable. . . .

What's in Foreign Procurement Archives? Wittig handles classified contracts. Lots of money stuff; foreign currency negotiations, commodity price schedules, some industrial technology. Or—just as a hypothesis—it could be as simple as a wad of bills back in that modest beige Ventura, to be exchanged for a packet from, say, Costa Rica. If she were a courier, they'd want to get at the plane. And than what about me and maybe Estéban? Even hypothetically, not good.

I watch her hacking at the fish, forehead knotted with effort, teeth in her lip. Mrs. Ruth Parsons of Bethesda, this thrumming, private woman. How crazy can I get? *They'll see our smoke.* . . .

"Here's your knife, Don. I washed it. Does the leg hurt very badly?"

I blink away the fantasies and see a scared little woman in a mangrove swamp.

"Sit down, rest. You've been going all out."

She sits obediently, like a kid in a dentist chair.

"You're stewing about Althea. And she's probably worried about you. Well get back tomorrow under our own steam, Ruth."

"Honestly I'm not worried at all, Don." The smile fades; she nibbles her lip, frowning out at the bay.

"You know, Ruth, you surprised me when you offered to come along. Not that I don't appreciate it. But I rather thought you'd be concerned about leaving Althea alone with our good pilot. Or was it only me?"

This gets her attention at last.

"I believe Captain Estéban is a very fine type of man."

The words surprise me a little. Isn't the correct line more like "I trust Althea," or even, indignantly, "Althea is a good girl"?

"He's a man. Althea seemed to think he was interesting."

She goes on staring at the bay. And then I notice her tongue flick out and lick that prehensile upper lip. There's a flush that isn't sunburn around her ears and throat too, and one hand is gently rubbing her thigh. What's she seeing, out there in the flats?

Oho.

Captain Estéban's mahogany arms clasping Miss Althea Parsons's pearly body.

Captain Estéban's archaic nostrils snuffling in Miss Parsons's tender neck.

Captain's Estéban's copper buttocks pumping into Althea's creamy upturned bottom. . . . The hammock, very bouncy. Mayas know all about it.

Well, well. So Mother Hen has her little quirks.

I feel fairly silly and more than a little irritated. Now I find out. . . . But even vicarious lust has much to recommend it, here in the mud and rain. I settle back, recalling that Miss Althea the computer programmer had waved good-bye very composedly. Was she sending her mother to flounder across the bay with me so she can get programmed in Maya? The memory of Honduran mahogany logs drifting in and out of the opalescent sand comes to me. Just as I am about to suggest that Mrs. Parsons might care to share my rain shelter, she remarks serenely, "The Mayas seem to be a very fine type of people. I believe you said so to Althea."

The implications fall on me with the rain. *Type*. As in breeding, bloodline, sire. Am I supposed to have certified Estéban not only as a stud but as a genetic donor?

"Ruth, are you telling me you're prepared to accept a half-Indian grandchild?"

"Why, Don, that's up to Althea, you know."

Looking at the mother, I guess it is. Oh, for mahogany gonads.

Ruth has gone back to listening to the wind, but I'm not about to let her off that easy. Not after all that *noli me tangere* jazz.

"What will Althea's father think?"

Her face snaps around at me, genuinely startled.

"Althea's father?" Complicated semi-smile. "He won't mind."

"He'll accept it too, eh?" I see her shake her head as if a fly were bothering her, and add with a cripple's malice: "Your husband must be a very fine type of man."

Ruth looks at me, pushing her wet hair back abruptly. I have the impression that mousy Mrs. Parsons is roaring out of control, but her voice is quiet.

"There isn't any Mr. Parsons, Don. There never was. Althea's father was a Danish medical student. . . . I believe he has gained considerable prominence."

"Oh." Something warns me not to say I'm sorry. "You mean he doesn't know about Althea?"

"No." She smiles, her eyes bright and cuckoo.

"Seems like rather a rough deal for her."

"I grew up quite happily under the same circumstances."

Bang, I'm dead. Well, well, well. A mad image blooms in my mind: generations of solitary Parsons women selecting sires, making impregnation trips. Well, I hear the world is moving their way.

"I better look at the fish line."

She leaves. The glow fades. No. Just no, no contact. Good-bye, Captain Estéban. My leg is very uncomfortable. The hell with Mrs. Parsons' long-distance orgasm.

We don't talk much after that, which seems to suit Ruth. The odd day drags by. Squall after squall blows over us. Ruth singes up some more fillets, but the rain drowns her smudge; it seems to pour hardest just as the sun's about to show.

Finally she comes to sit under my sagging serape, but there's no warmth there. I doze, aware of her getting up now and then to look around. My subconscious notes that she's still twitchy. I tell my subconscious to knock it off.

Presently I wake up to find her penciling on the water-soaked pages of a little notepad.

"What's that, a shopping list for alligators?"

Automatic polite laugh. "Oh, just an address. In case we—I'm being silly, Don."

"Hey," I sit up, wincing. "Ruth, quit fretting. I mean it. We'll all be out of this soon. You'll have a great story to tell."

She doesn't look up. "Yes . . . I guess we will."

"Come on, we're doing fine. There isn't any real danger here, you know. Unless you're allergic to fish?"

Another good-little-girl laugh, but there's a shiver in it.

"Sometimes I think I'd like to go . . . really far away."

To keep her talking I say the first thing in my head.

"Tell me, Ruth. I'm curious why you would settle for that kind of lonely life, there in Washington? I mean, a woman like you—"

"Should get married?" She gives a shaky sign, pushing the notebook back in her wet pocket.

"Why not? It's the normal source of companionship. Don't tell me you're trying to be some kind of professional man-hater."

"Lesbian, you mean?" Her laugh sounds better. "With my security rating? No, I'm not."

"Well, then. Whatever trauma you went through, these things don't last forever. You can't hate all men."

The smile is back. "Oh, there wasn't any trauma, Don, and I don't hate men. That would be as silly as—as hating the weather." She glances wryly at the blowing rain.

"I think you have a grudge. You're even spooky of me."

Smooth as mouse bite she says, "I'd love to hear about your family, Don?"

Touché. I give her the edited version of how I don't have one anymore, and she says she's sorry, how sad. And we chat about what a good life a single person really has, and how she and her friends enjoy plays and concerts and travel, and one of them is head cashier for Ringling Brothers, how about that?

But it's coming out jerkier and jerkier like a bad tape, with her eyes going round the horizon in the pauses and her face listening for something that isn't my voice. What's wrong with her? Well, what's wrong with any furtively unconventional middle-aged woman with an empty bed? And a security clearance. An old habit of mind remarks unkindly that Mrs. Parsons represents what is known as the classic penetration target.

"—so much more opportunity now." Her voice trails off.

"Hurrah for women's lib, eh?"

"The lib?" Impatiently she leans forward and tugs the serape straight. "Oh, that's doomed."

The apocalyptic words jar my attention.

"What do you mean, doomed?"

She glances at me as if I weren't hanging straight either and says vaguely, "Oh . . ."

"Come on, why doomed? Didn't they get that equal rights bill?"

Long hesitation. When she speaks again her voice is different.

"Women have no rights, Don, except what men allow us. Men are more aggressive and powerful, and they run the world. When the next real crisis upsets them, our so-called rights will vanish like—like that smoke. We'll be back where we always were: property. And whatever has gone wrong will be blamed on our freedom, like the fall of Rome was. You'll see."

Now all this is delivered in a gray tone of total conviction. The last time I heard that tone, the speaker was explaining why he had to keep his file drawers full of dead pigeons.

"Oh, come on. You and your friends are the backbone of the system; if you quit, the country would come to a screeching halt before lunch."

No answering smile.

"That's fantasy." Her voice is still quiet. "Women don't work that way. We're a—a toothless world." She looks around as if she wanted to stop talking. "What women do is survive. We live by ones and twos in the chinks of your world-machine."

"Sounds like a guerrilla operation." I'm not really joking, here in the 'gator den. In fact, I'm wondering if I spent too much thought on mahogany logs.

"Guerrillas have something to hope for." Suddenly she switches on a jolly smile. "Think of us as opossums, Don. Did you know there are opossums living all over? Even in New York City."

I smile back with my neck prickling. I thought I was the paranoid one.

"Men and women aren't different species, Ruth. Women do every-thing men do."

"Do they?" Our eyes meet, but she seems to be seeing ghosts between us in the rain. She mutters something that could be "My Lai" and looks away. "All the endless wars . . ." Her voice is a whisper. "All the huge author-itarian organizations for doing unreal things. Men live to struggle against each other; we're just part of the battlefield. It'll never change unless you change the whole world. I dream sometimes of—of going away—" She checks and abruptly changes voice. "Forgive me, Don, it's so stupid saying all this."

"Men hate wars too, Ruth," I say as gently as I can.

"I know." She shrugs and climbs to her feet. "But that's your problem, isn't it?"

End of communication. Mrs. Ruth Parsons isn't even living in the same world with me.

I watch her move around restlessly, head turning toward the ruins. Alienation like that can add up to dead pigeons, which would be GSA's problem. It could also lead to believing some joker who's promising to change the whole world. Which could just probably be my problem if one of them was over in that camp last night, where she keeps looking. *Guerrillas have something to hope for?* . . .

Nonsense. I try another position and see that the sky seems to be clearing as the sun sets. The wind is quieting down at last too. Insane to think this little woman is acting out some fantasy in this swamp. But that equipment last night was no fantasy; if those lads have some connection with her, I'll be in the way. You couldn't find a handier spot to dispose of the body. . . . Maybe some Guévarista is a fine type of man?

Absurd. Sure . . . The only thing more absurd would be to come through the wars and get myself terminated by a mad librarian's boyfriend on a fishing trip.

A fish flops in the stream below us. Ruth spins around so fast she hits the serape. "I better start the fire," she says, her eyes still on the plain and her head cocked, listening.

All right, let's test.

"Expecting company?"

It rocks her. She freezes, and her eyes come swiveling around to me like a film take captioned FRIGHT. I can see her decide to smile.

"Oh, one never can tell!" She laughs weirdly, the eyes not changed. "I'll get the—the kindling." She fairly scuttles into the brush.

Nobody, paranoid or not, could call *that* a normal reaction.

Ruth Parsons is either psycho or she's expecting something to happen—and it has nothing to do with me: I scared her pissless.

Well, she could be nuts. And I could be wrong, but there are some mistakes you only make once.

Reluctantly I unzip my body belt, telling myself that if I think what I think, my only course is to take something for my leg and get as far as possible from Mrs. Ruth Parsons before whoever she's waiting for arrives.

In my belt also is a .32-caliber asset Ruth doesn't know about—and it's going to stay there. My longevity program leaves the shoot-outs to TV and stresses being somewhere else when the roof falls in. I can spend a perfectly safe and also perfectly horrible night out in one of those mangrove flats. . . . Am I insane?

At this moment Ruth stands up and stares blatantly inland with her hand shading her eyes. Then she tucks something into her pocket, buttons up, and tightens her belt.

That does it.

I dry-swallow two 100-mg tabs, which should get me ambulatory and still leave me wits to hide. Give it a few minutes. I make sure my compass and some hooks are in my own pocket and sit waiting while Ruth fusses with her smudge fire, sneaking looks away when she thinks I'm not watching.

The flat world around us is turning into an unearthly amber and violet light show as the first numbness sweeps into my leg. Ruth has crawled under the bromels for more dry stuff; I can see her foot. Okay. I reach for my staff.

Suddenly the foot jerks, and Ruth yells—or rather, her throat makes the Uh-uh-hhh that means pure horror. The foot disappears in a rattle of bromel stalks.

I lunge upright on the crutch and look over the bank at a frozen scene.

Ruth is crouching sideways on the ledge, clutching her stomach. They are about a yard below, floating on the river in a skiff. While I was making up my stupid mind, her friends have glided right under my ass. There are three of them.

They are tall and white. I try to see them as men in some kind of white jumpsuits. The one nearest the bank is stretching out a long white arm toward Ruth. She jerks and scuttles farther away.

The arm stretches after her. It stretches and stretches. It stretches two yards and stays hanging in the air. Small black things are wiggling from its tip.

I look where their faces should be and see black hollow dishes with vertical stripes. The stripes move slowly. . . .

There is no more possibility of their being human—or anything else I've ever seen. What has Ruth conjured up?

The scene is totally silent. I blink, blink—this cannot be real. The two in the far end of the skiff are writhing those arms around an apparatus on a tripod. A weapon? Suddenly I hear the same blurry voice I heard in the night.

"Guh-give," it groans. "G-give . . . "

Dear god, it's real, whatever it is. I'm terrified. My mind is trying not to form a word.

And Ruth—Jesus, of course—Ruth is terrified too; she's edging along the bank away from them, gaping at the monsters in the skiff, who are obviously nobody's friends. She's hugging something to her body. Why doesn't she get over the bank and circle back behind me?

"G-g-give." That wheeze is coming from the tripod. "Pee-eeze give." The skiff is moving upstream below Ruth, following her. The arm undulates out at her again, its black digits looping. Ruth scrambles to the top of the bank.

"Ruth!" My voice cracks. "Ruth, get over here behind me!"

She doesn't look at me, only keeps sidling farther away. My terror detonates into anger.

"Come back here!" With my free hand I'm working the .32 out of my belt. The sun has gone down.

She doesn't turn but straightens up warily, still hugging the thing. I see her mouth working. Is she actually trying to *talk* to them?

"Please . . ." She swallows. "Please speak to me. I need your help."

"RUTH!"

At this moment the nearest white monster whips into a great S-curve and sails right onto the bank at her, eight feet of snowy rippling horror.

And I shoot Ruth.

I don't know that for a minute—I've yanked the gun up so fast that my staff slips and dumps me as I fire. I stagger up, hearing Ruth scream, "No! No! No!"

The creature is back down by his boat, and Ruth is still farther away, clutching herself. Blood is running down her elbow.

"Stop it, Don! They aren't attacking you!"

"For god's sake! Don't be a fool, I can't help you if you won't get away from them!"

No reply. Nobody moves. No sound except the drone of a jet passing far above. In the darkening stream below me the three white figures shift uneasily; I get the impression of radar dishes focusing. The word spells itself in my head: *Aliens*.

Extraterrestrials.

What do I do, call the President? Capture them single-handed with my peashooter? . . . I'm alone in the arse end of nowhere with one leg and my brain cuddled in meperidine hydrochloride.

"Prrr-eese," their machine blurs again. "Wa-wat hep . . ."

"Our plane fell down," Ruth says in a very distinct, eerie voice. She points up at the jet, out toward the bay. "My—my child is there. Please take us there in your boat."

Dear god. While she's gesturing, I get a look at the thing she's hugging in her wounded arm. It's metallic, like a big glimmering distributor head. What—?

Wait a minute. This morning: when she was gone so long, she could have found that thing. Something they left behind. Or dropped. And she hid it, not telling me. That's why she kept going under that bromel clump—she was peeking at it. Waiting. And the owners came back and caught her. They want it. She's trying to bargain, by god.

"—Water," Ruth is pointing again. "Take us. Me. And him."

The black faces turn toward me, blind and horrible. Later on I may be grateful for the "us." Not now.

"Throw your gun away, Don. They'll take us back." Her voice is weak.

"Like hell I will. You—who are you? What are you doing here?"

"Oh, god, does it matter? He's frightened," she cries to them. "Can you understand?"

She's as alien as they, there in the twilight. The beings in the skiff are twittering among themselves. Their box starts to moan.

"Ss-stu-dens," I make out. "S-stu-ding . . . not—huh-arm-ing . . . w-we . . . buh . . ." It fades into garble and then says, "G-give . . . wee . . . g-go. . . ."

Peace-loving cultural-exchange students—on the interstellar level now. Oh, no.

"Bring that thing here, Ruth—right now!"

But she's starting down the bank toward them saying, "Take me."

"Wait! You need a tourniquet on that arm."

"I know. Please put the gun down, Don."

She's actually at the skiff, right by them. They aren't moving.

"Jesus Christ." Slowly, reluctantly, I drop the .32. When I start down the slide, I find I'm floating; adrenaline and Demerol are a bad mix.

The skiff comes gliding toward me, Ruth in the bow clutching the thing and her arm. The aliens stay in the stern behind their tripod, away from me. I note the skiff is camouflaged tan and green. The world around us is deep shadowy blue.

"Don, bring the water bag!"

As I'm dragging down the plastic bag, it occurs to me that Ruth really is cracking up, the water isn't needed now. But my own brain seems to have gone into overload. All I can focus on is a long white rubbery arm with black worms clutching the far end of the orange tube, helping me fill it. This isn't happening.

"Can you get in, Don?" As I hoist my numb legs up, two long white pipes reach for me. *No, you don't.* I kick and tumble in beside Ruth. She moves away.

A creaky hum starts up, it's coming from a wedge in the center of the skiff. And we're in motion, sliding toward dark mangrove files.

I stare mindlessly at the wedge. Alien technological secrets? I can't see any, the power source is under that triangular cover, about two feet long. The gadgets on the tripod are equally cryptic, except that one has a big lens. Their light?

As we hit the open bay, the hum rises and we start planing faster and faster still. Thirty knots? Hard to judge in the dark. Their hull seems to be a modified trihedral much like ours, with a remarkable absence of slap. Say twenty-two feet. Schemes of capturing it swirl in my mind. I'll need Estéban.

Suddenly a huge flood of white light fans out over us from the tripod, blotting out the aliens in the stern. I see Ruth pulling at a belt around her arm, still hugging the gizmo.

"I'll tie that for you."

"It's all right."

The alien device is twinkling or phosphorescing slightly. I lean over to look, whispering, "Give that to me, I'll pass it to Estéban."

"No!" She scoots away, almost over the side. "It's theirs, they need it!"

"What? Are you crazy?" I'm so taken aback by this idiocy I literally stammer. "We have to, we—"

"They haven't hurt us. I'm sure they could." Her eyes are watching me with feral intensity; in the light her face has a lunatic look. Numb as I am, I realize that the wretched woman is poised to throw herself over the side if I move. With the alien thing.

"I think they're gentle," she mutters.

"For Christ's sake, Ruth, they're *aliens!*"

"I'm used to it," she says absently. "There's the island! Stop! Stop here!"

The skiff slows, turning. A mound of foliage is tiny in the light. Metal glints—the plane.

"Althea! Althea! Are you all right?"

Yells, movement on the plane. The water is high, we're floating over the bar. The aliens are keeping us in the lead with the light hiding them. I see one pale figure splashing toward us and a dark one behind, coming more slowly. Estéban must be puzzled by that light.

"Mr. Fenton is hurt, Althea. These people brought us back with the water. Are you all right?"

"A-okay." Althea flounders up, peering excitedly. "You all right? Whew, that light!" Automatically I start handing her the idiotic water bag.

"Leave that for the captain," Ruth says sharply. "Althea, can you climb in the boat? Quickly, it's important."

"Coming."

"No, no!" I protest, but the skiff tilts as Althea swarms in. The aliens twitter, and their voice box starts groaning. "Gu-give . . . now . . . give . . ."

"*Qué llega?*" Estéban's face appears beside me, squinting fiercely into the light.

"Grab it, get it from her—that thing she has—" but Ruth's voice rides over mine. "Captain, lift Mr. Fenton out of the boat. He's hurt his leg. Hurry, please."

"Goddamn it, wait!" I shout, but an arm has grabbed my middle. When a Maya boosts you, you go. I hear Althea saying, "Mother, your arm!" and fall onto Estéban. We stagger around in the water up to my waist; I can't feel my feet at all.

When I get steady, the boat is yards away. The two women are head-to-head, murmuring.

"Get them!" I tug loose from Estéban and flounder forward. Ruth stands up in the boat facing the invisible aliens.

"Take us with you. Please. We want to go with you, away from here."

"Ruth! Estéban, get that boat!" I lunge and lose my feet again. The aliens are chirruping madly behind their light.

"Please take us. We don't mind what your planet is like; we'll learn—we'll do anything! We won't cause any trouble. Please. Oh, *please*." The skiff is drifting farther away.

"Ruth! Althea! Are you crazy? Wait—" But I can only shuffle nightmare-like in the ooze, hearing that damn voice box wheeze, "N-not come . . . more . . . not come . . . " Althea's face turns to it, openmouthed grin.

"Yes, we understand," Ruth cries. "We don't want to come back.` Please take us with you!"

I shout and Estéban splashes past me shouting too, something about radio.

"Yess-s-s," groans the voice.

Ruth sits down suddenly, clutching Althea. At that moment Estéban grabs the edge of the skiff beside her.

"Hold them, Estéban! Don't let her go."

He gives me one slit-eyed glance over his shoulder, and I recognize his total uninvolvement. He's had a good look at that camouflage paint and the absence of fishing gear. I make a desperate rush and slip again. When I come up Ruth is saying, "We're going with these people, Captain. Please take your money out of my purse, it's in the plane. And give this to Mr. Fenton."

She passes him something small; the notebook. He takes it slowly.

"Estéban! No!"

He has released the skiff.

"Thank you so much," Ruth says as they float apart. Her voice is shaky; she raises it. "There won't be any trouble, Don. Please send this cable. It's to a friend of mine, she'll take care of everything." Then she adds the craziest touch of the entire night. "She's a grand person; she's director of nursing training at N.I.H."

As the skiff drifts, I hear Althea add something that sounds like "Right on."

Sweet Jesus . . . Next minute the humming has started; the light is receding fast. The last I see of Mrs. Ruth Parsons and Miss Althea Parsons is two small shadows against that light, like two opossums. The light snaps off, the hum deepens—and they're going, going, gone away.

In the dark water beside me Estéban is instructing everybody in general to *chingarse* themselves.

"Friends, or something," I tell him lamely. "She seemed to want to go with them."

He is pointedly silent, hauling me back to the plane. He knows what could be around here better than I do, and Mayas have their own longevity program. His condition seems improved. As we get in I notice the hammock has been repositioned.

In the night—of which I remember little—the wind changes. And at seven-thirty the next morning a Cessna buzzes the sandbar under cloudless skies.

By noon we're back in Cozumel. Captain Estéban accepts his fees and departs laconically for his insurance wars. I leave the Parsons' bags with the Caribe agent, who couldn't care less. The cable goes to a Mrs. Priscilla Hayes Smith, also of Bethesda. I take myself to a medico and by three P.M. I'm sitting on the Cabañas terrace with a fat leg and a double margarita, trying to believe the whole thing.

The cable said, *Althea and I taking extraordinary opportunity for travel. Gone several years. Please take charge our affairs. Love, Ruth.*

She'd written it that afternoon, you understand.

I order another double, wishing to hell I'd gotten a good look at that gizmo. Did it have a label, Made by Betelgeusians? No matter how weird it was, *how* could a person be crazy enough to imagine—?

Not only that but to hope, to plan? If I could only go away. . . . That's what she was doing, all day. Waiting, hoping, figuring how to get Althea. To go sight unseen to an alien world . . .

With the third margarita I try a joke about alienated women, but my heart's not in it. And I'm certain there won't be any bother, any trouble at all. Two human women, one of them possibly pregnant, have departed for, I guess, the stars; and the fabric of society will never show a ripple. I brood: do all Mrs. Parsons' friends hold themselves in readiness for any eventuality, including leaving Earth? And will Mrs. Parsons somehow one day contrive to send for Mrs. Priscilla Hayes Smith, that grand person?

I can only send for another cold one, musing on Althea. What suns will Captain Estéban's sloe-eyed offspring, if any, look upon? "Get in, Althea, we're taking off for Orion." "A-okay, Mother." Is that some system of upbringing? *We survive by ones and twos in the chinks of your world-machine.... I'm used to aliens....* She'd meant every word. Insane. How could a woman choose to live among unknown monsters, to say good-bye to her home, her world?

As the margaritas take hold, the whole mad scenario melts down to the image of those two small shapes sitting side by side in the receding alien glare.

Two of our opossums are missing.

SAUL
BY PETER SCHWEIGHOFER

Paul Donegal's house was a typical ranch in a normal suburban neighborhood development. It sat in its numbered lot, guarded from the rest of its neighbors by tidy front and back yards. On a good day there was just enough space between the houses to afford a bit of privacy, if not independence. Their owners displayed expensive cars and prim minivans in front of two-car garages. And on this autumn Saturday, some of the houses' inhabitants could be found in their driveways performing their biweekly car-washing rituals.

Nobody, however, was actually washing the cars in Donegal's driveway. Paul's wife sat in the minivan, the windows rolled down a bit. The radio was loud enough to drown the television sounds leaking from the house. She was lost in some trashy romance novel, her attention diverted only occasionally by the soda in the minivan's cup holder.

A cracked concrete walkway led from the cars to the front door. Several feeble flowerbeds guarded the house's perimeter nearby. Paul's wife planted them in her copious spare time while the kids were in school all week. The weeds festering there were about as well-behaved as his children and untidy as the home's interior.

Inside, the house would have looked friendly if not for the chaotic bits of clutter everywhere. Boots, shoes, and designer sneakers lived permanently near the front door, sheltered beneath a few fall jackets ordered from catalogs. A mountain of laundry, fancy logos leering at odd angles, sat on the couch like an uninvited guest. An aura of cigarette smoke hung over everything, haunting the air, upholstery, and plush carpet.

Paul sat amidst it all, a fallen suburban emperor on his leather recliner throne. He waved his beer at the blaring television as if his shouted decrees for victory would matter. Nothing was going to come between him, a few beers, and this game. ·It wasn't his fault Beth had made bridge plans for this afternoon, and he'd told her so that morning. She should know what this meant to him. Hell, she did know, she was just trying to kiss up to the neighbor: a busybody housewife who called incessantly and babbled about who just bought which luxury car and which island they were visiting for the holidays. Paul didn't even like bridge. And besides, he had a bit of money riding on this one, an impulsive bet made with Reynolds from Marketing during their late meeting last Thursday, a bet which he was now in danger of losing.

His team was losing, but they had a few more seconds in the final quarter. If they could just tie the score, the game could go into overtime. Paul wondered for a moment how that would affect his schedule. He didn't want to miss his other game which started in only twenty minutes. The clock ticked down. Commentators' voices blared from the speakers over the cheering crowds. Paul sat forward in the recliner, tightening the grip on his beer. "Come on," he grumbled through lips pressed around a cigarette. His glance flitted from the players to the timer on the screen. "Come on," he growled. "Make the pass. Get out of there . . . "

"R'aahhrrgg!" The roar came from the girls' bedroom. "Space monster eat dollhouse family! Mmmm. Dolly brains yummy for space monster."

One of the kids screamed, another started name-calling. The two younger girls buzzed into the living room, running the short-strided thumping way little kids use to shake the entire house. "Daddy, Jimmy tore off our doll's head!" they cried, pulling at his sleeve. "He's wrecking our dollhouse."

Paul's eyes were still transfixed by the game's ticking clock. He swatted casually at the girls. "Tell your brother to play nice, or I'll send him to his room."

"He won't listen to us," they whined, trying to climb into his lap.

Paul pushed the girls from the easy chair, turning toward the bedrooms. "Hey! Stop bothering your sisters!" he yelled. "Don't make me come in there!"

"I'm not doing anything," the boy called. Paul thought he heard a doll's head drop on the floor.

"Can't you see I'm trying to watch the game?" When he turned back, it was over. His team had lost in the final seconds, and he'd missed it. Paul finished his beer, then looked at the two girls staring at him. "If your brother's giving you trouble, go tell your mother. And while you're at it, let her know I'm going down to Richie's Sports Bar to catch the next game. At least they have peace and quiet there." He stormed out of the house, ignoring his wife reading in the minivan just as he was sure she was ignoring him. His Mercedes roared to life and tore out of the driveway.

*   *   *

Paul left Richie's Sports Bar near midnight. He was lost in the euphoria of beer, a good game, and his buddies' companionship. Paul should have spent all day there. His kids and wife were always nagging him at home, distracting him from his special time to himself. They interrupted every game with their problems. His drinking friends knew the sanctity of the game, could revel with him in victory, and comfort him in defeat. Paul could be himself among them.

He maneuvered the Mercedes around curves leading home, taking a few too tight thanks to a few beers, but he only occasionally cut into the opposite lane. The car's illuminated clock read 11:49 P.M. He grimaced at the thought of his wife squawking at him when he got home. She'd want to know where he'd been and why he hadn't called, why he couldn't spend more time with her or the kids. His inner grumblings consumed his mind, fueled the dread of going home to a disarranged life.

Paul slipped a cigarette into his lips, then fumbled for the car lighter while his other hand jockeyed the steering wheel sharply around another curve. He didn't really see the truck ahead, with its massive banks of square headlights blinding him. Even shielding his eyes Paul couldn't see the truck's bulk behind the brightness.

To his consciousness, the car disappeared around him. In those lights he saw his children growing up, acting in school plays, going on dates and to dances, graduating college, marrying their sweethearts, enjoying their lives. Happy lives suddenly without him.

Paul jerked the wheel to avoid the headlights and hit the brakes. The car skidded off the road. In the blurred and spinning trees he saw family and acquaintances standing rigidly at his grave, the children clinging to his sobbing wife. Tires spinning on gravel and grass sounding like dirt falling on his coffin.

Time slowed. The car careened over turf. Paul whipped the steering wheel one way, then another, trying to gain control. The ancient maple loomed ahead, a tall specter of death waiting to embrace him. Paul saw it disappear in the final spin. The car slammed into the tree, the driver's side taking the full impact.

The last thing Paul noticed as he slipped into the long darkness was the car's luminescent clock insistently blinking 12:00 A.M.

*   *   *

Paul wasn't even sure he was awake. He couldn't tell if his eyes were open, but everything was dark. He felt buoyant, as if floating on a cloud. His nose wrinkled as he smelled freshly cut grass tinged with the sting of ammonia. Voices wafted around him, angelic choirs whispering in harmonious conversation. Given the circumstances, Paul assumed this was the afterlife.

Light began forming in his blurred vision, a fuzzy glow which shimmered around the edges. He felt his body's weight gliding along. Someone was pushing his prone corpse down a corridor. A warm, comforting hand held his. Although Paul couldn't see who it was, her touch conveyed concern and love for him. Another hand gently brushed the hair from his eyes. Among the voices drifting around him, he thought he heard someone say everything was going to be all right, he was safe now. The sounds soothed him even if he only faintly understood the words.

Paul's vision cleared. The faces peering down at him were neither angelic nor human. The bulbous heads glimmered with pearly luminescence. They stared at him with large almond-shaped eyes, unblinking with shiny blackness. Paul could find no traces of ears, nose, or mouth, though he still heard them talking in that soft choir-voice. Their spindly bodies glowed, too, filling the atmosphere with gauzy light. Behind them rose shimmering auras, fluttering in folds of muted color. He had never before cared about all those alien autopsy commercials, tabloid headlines, silly abduction movies, or conspiracy theory television shows. Now their images flooded his mind: probes, cranial implants, painfully extracted tissue samples, needles, lasers drilling into his teeth, torturous experiments.

He tried escaping—breathing uncontrollably, jerking muscles, screaming in silence—but some invisible force held him in place. Struggling only tightened the unseen, restraining grip, and brought blank stares from the aliens around him. Paul felt naked, though he could see his clothes through the gauzy haze. He couldn't feel most of his body, but sensed someone was holding his hand. One of the aliens had its glowing, four-digit hand wrapped around his, still a calming caress amid the frightening uncertainty.

Paul watched the corridor pass. Above him the ceiling rushed past the luminescent alien heads. Panels of dark metal alternated with arches illuminated by glowing glyphs: letters, sensor readouts, computer controls, Paul wasn't sure. The spaceship smelled antiseptic, but the alien bodies exuded a flowery odor, not too sweet, but green. Somewhere below, he felt a low-pitched throbbing, like some engine buried deep within the hull. The pounding hum surged slowly as the aliens whisked him along the corridor.

The passageway opened into an enormous chamber. Columns of dark metal climbed to form a dome. The spaces between glowed with symbols strung together in what Paul assumed were sentences. Their light shone through the haze and obscured his vision. Three luminous aliens hovered along one wall, their shimmering auras brighter than those of the aliens surrounding Paul. His escort stopped, looked away from him, and bowed toward the three alien commanders enthroned in the dome. They spoke a short greeting, like several choirs singing in unison. The crowd parted so the leaders could gaze on Paul's helpless form. He struggled, moving numbed lips and speaking silence, trying to plead for release. Through the foggy air he caught bits of their conversation, a responsive duet between his escort's choir-speech and the lead alien's sonorous voice. As it spoke, the glyphs covering the wall pulsed brighter with each phrase. Paul cried for mercy, promising to change his life if spared the unknown experiments awaiting him, but the words only echoed in his mind. The creature holding his hand did not concern itself with the exchange. It caressed Paul's hand and gazed at him with watery obsidian eyes. Unlike the others, this alien's eyes transformed from almond shapes to inverted tear-drop pools. It seemed more concerned for Paul than what was going on around it. He wasn't sure who this creature was: protector, guide, kindred soul?

The center leader raised a bent-fingered hand. When he lowered it, he pointed to the center of the chamber like a judge pronouncing a death sentence. His last words sounded the final chords of a tragic symphony. Paul's alien escort brought him to the spot where their leader had pointed, then swiveled him almost upright. A horrorific machine leered at him, like some sinister doll-mangling device his son might make from blocks. A flurry of fingers and arms attached suckers to his head and chest, a clear plastic hose extending from each suction node. The tubes felt like living leeches, tentacles waiting to smother him and drag him off to some hideous death.

The hoses fed into a black-metal canister, part of a larger array of capacitors, pipes, coolant ventilators, and control panels. One of his alien guards pressed glowing buttons and glyphs on the main command console, and the apparatus began humming. Somewhere below the pulsing space-ship's engines pounded faster in Paul's ears. A massive conduit led from the main machine to a crystalline tank reinforced by a metal cage. The aliens had situated Paul directly in front of this containment tank. It was empty for now, but he had a queasy feeling he was soon going to see his innards extracted into that oversized specimen bottle.

He had long ceased struggling against his unseen bonds, but Paul still tried taming the fear fogging his brain. He couldn't close his eyes to shut out the menacing machine's glare, so he rolled his eyes up and thought of anything comforting: his recliner's embrace, his children climbing on him, his wife cuddling with him on the sofa in front of the fire. The calm in his mind seemed to subdue the chamber.

The aliens now milled about as if they really didn't want to use the contraption. Some checked the components slowly, but most hovered nearby with no sense of purpose. Paul sensed they were reluctant to carry out their duties. Had they read his thoughts and seen his wife and children? A stern chorus from the alien commander and his two lieutenants above roused them from their melancholy. Backs straightened, they took their stations at various places around the device.

The alien holding Paul's hand released it. The luminescent fingers gently touched his face as Paul watched his reflection in its obsidian eyes. He felt an urge to lift his own hand to stroke the face, as if it were his wife's. At the thought, Paul's forearm was released. He reached up and gently touched the face, feeling warmth and compassion. For a moment he thought he saw lips mouthing words: "I am here for you." This alien was somehow special to him, though Paul didn't know why. He knew he should be afraid, for himself and for what was about to happen, but this alien seemed to absorb his fear, replacing it with comfort.

The creature stepped away from the crowd and presented itself to the three leaders above. Its face wore that same sad gaze, as if it were pleading for Paul's life. Or was it offering itself up in his stead? The alien commanders bowed to it. Looking around, Paul realized all the alien heads were lowered, their black almond eyes averted from their fellow. They clearly revered this single creature who showed sympathy for him, but he sensed it was doomed for this same reason.

The lead commander once again raised a bent-fingered hand, then pointed at the crystal containment tank. The lone alien nodded, then turned and bowed to Paul. Why was it honoring him with this solemn gesture? The creature faced the glass cage. Two of its fellows opened a reinforced panel, through which the single alien crawled. It sat hunched and cramped in the tank while others closed and sealed the panel with a pressurized hiss. The creature's bright skin lit the crystal like a glowing diamond. Its eyes stared blankly at Paul. He knew their fates were linked by that contraption. His stomach churned like it had on his first date, his wedding night, the days his kids were born, his last argument with his wife. He worried the machine would save one of them and destroy the other.

The alien at the control panel pressed a series of symbols. The deep throbbing in the ship's bowels raced through Paul's ears. The machinery groaned, and the hoses came to life. The tubes sucked at his brain, heart, and gut. Spasms ripped through Paul's body. He resisted, tightening his muscles and trying to calm his manic breathing. Images of his children and wife, their warm hands, helped him regain some peace. His eyes glanced at the suction nodes attached to his chest. Gooey black tar slithered out in globs which too often stuck to the tube's insides. He wasn't sure what it was—innards, blood, his life's essence—but it was painfully drawn from him. Paul struggled again and cried out in silence. His body seemed feather light, insubstantial, almost transparent. He could feel his mind fighting itself, uncertain whether to resist and stay conscious or surrender and faint. And when it finally decided that merciful unconsciousness was best, something outside his mind kept him awake.

The apparatus converted the slime sucked from him into something it pumped into the crystal containment unit. Paul couldn't see anything in the heavy conduit leading from the machine to the tank, but it was infecting the alien inside. The creature pressed its face and hands to the glass, wailing a mournful chorus to its indifferent comrades. Already its luminescent glow had dimmed. Its skin faded from translucent white to murky gray. The feathery aura arcing from its shoulders withered into burned leaves. Its skin shriveled into black cinder scales, no longer supple, but dry and crumbly. The creature banged its fists against the crystal tank until its spindly fingers broke off, parched and blackened by whatever the machine absorbed from Paul. It continued thumping the stumps in a vain effort to escape.

When the machine cycled down, all that was left in the tank was a charred husk of an alien. It was still alive, hissing, biting, throwing itself at the crystal wall. Each impact tore more seared flesh from its lanky bones. Paul stared at this monster, his own pain and fear momentarily forgotten. His frantic thoughts about what the machine had done to him evaporated. The alien in the tank once held his hand, offered comfort, and shown compassion. Now it was a savage beast, infected with something which tore it apart from within. Paul didn't know what he had done to cause this punishment to be inflicted on this formerly innocent creature.

The alien at the control panel turned and peered up at the three illuminated beings with saddened eyes. Paul saw similar expressions on the others. Whether they bowed their heads in sorrow or shame he could not tell. The one alien's smooth brow crinkled, as if pleading with the three commanders for mercy. After a moment he bowed to his superiors, then turned solemnly to the tank containing his comrade. His hands reached for the control panel, hesitated, then lightly touched the glowing tiles. He halted once more. His elongated finger hovered over a final, red glyph. Paul held his breath, too. The alien's chest swelled and released one final breath—a sigh?—and he pressed the button.

A capacitor unit atop the crystal tank sparked to life. It throbbed and glowed until it seemed the device would overload and destroy everything. At the last moment, it discharged a wave of crackling red energy into the tank. The monster inside squealed, raising its stump-arms to shield its face from the fire. Paul felt part of himself incinerated in that tank. The wave traveled down the crystal in an agonizing instant, vaporizing stumps, arms, head, and body with arcs of red light. It was finished.

Paul's muscles relaxed. The frenzied hysteria clouding his mind cleared, and he breathed cool, deep air. His ears searched for the throbbing spaceship engine, but he could only discern an airy whispering, a soft, spring morning breeze rustling budding branches. Paul could no longer see the machine. Everything was bathed in light. He peered down at his own body. The suction units had fallen from his head, chest and stomach, leaving no traces.

But something pulled at his gut. Why did they kill one of their own and let him live? They were luminescent aliens with advanced technology and culture. He was just a miserable human with a crummy marriage and unruly kids. Paul didn't deserve this, and wondered if they were saving him for a fate worse than what he had just witnessed.

He breathed deeply, the smell of freshly cut grass wafting to his nose again. The dark alien eyes hovered before him in the haze. Four fingers brushed his face from forehead to lips, closing Paul's eyes. He felt his consciousness ebb away, though he did not struggle. Paul slipped into the calm sleep of a child after a long day of innocent play.

＊　　＊　　＊

He was moving again, voices floating around him, lights flashing above, though he could not see. A warm hand held his own. The gentle touch assured him everything would be okay, he was going to be fine now. Her caress soothed him with love and concern.

Ammonia and rubbing alcohol wrinkled his nose. "Mr. Donegal! Do you know where you are?"

"Yes," he answered wearily, amazed he could speak. "I'm . . . I'm alive, aren't I?"

The doctor chuckled. "Yes, Mr. Donegal, you're going to make it. We need to evaluate your injuries. You were in a car accident. Do you remember that, Mr. Donegal?"

"There was a large truck, I think. I saw a tree."

"Your car slammed into a tree, Mr. Donegal. You were thrown clear of the wreckage. You're very lucky to be alive."

"I can't see anything."

"We're working on that. Just stay with us, Mr. Donegal. Mr. Donegal, can you hear me? Stay with us here!"

The voices wafted away as Paul drifted into a dream of angels and doctors, truck headlights, slow-motion spinning across grass, ghosts pulling him from the car. The burned face cried to him, banging charred stumps against the crystal tank. Paul struggled, but the angels eased the image from his mind, calming him. Voices like choirs and orchestras reminded him he was alive, even if something else was dead.

Someone caressed his hair, brushing it from his face as she prayed and sobbed softly nearby, pleading for his life. Warm lips breathed life into his own. He could feel the radiance of her hand and face near his. "Paul, can you hear me?"

His vision cleared. Morning sunlight illuminated a halo of golden hair framing a warm face. Beth hovered over him, tears streaking down her cheeks. "Oh, Paul," she cried, hugging him. "We thought you were dead."

"My God, I'm so glad to see you, hon." He wrapped his arms around her and wept. "Where are the kids?"

"Annie and Steve are watching them," Beth explained. "The children were upset, but I didn't want to tell them anything until I spoke to the doctors." Paul creased his brow, but quickly recalled that Annie and Steve were their friends, and remembered his children, Brian, Alison, and Nancy. "Everyone's concerned for you."

"Yes, I know, I can feel it." Paul could sense the warm, reassuring emotions within him, that he was loved and needed by others. He knew they had always been there for him, but he truly hadn't felt them until now.

"I brought your cigarettes," Beth said, pulling a pack from her purse. "I'm not sure the doctor will let you smoke in here, though."

Paul almost instinctively reached for them. Inside his mind winced. The burned visage stared back at him with pleading obsidian eyes, its charred stumps banging against crystal as fire consumed its body. The vision flashed before his eyes and disappeared just as quickly. "No," he said, settling down and breathing deeply and clearly. "Throw those things way, would you?"

A doctor entered the hospital room. "Good to see you're awake," he said, checking the chart. "How do you feel?"

Paul breathed deeply, trying to evaluate the strong emotions within. "Uh, I'm a bit confused, but okay."

"Disorientation under these circumstances is normal. Just sit back and get some rest. Mrs. Donegal, could I speak with you for a moment?" Beth gave Paul a hopeful smile, then followed the doctor just outside the door. Paul could still hear their conversation clearly, watching through the hallway window to his room. "I can't explain it, other than to say your husband is extremely lucky. He sustained a few minor cuts and bruises, and that's it. There were no traces of alcohol in his blood, no internal bleeding as we suspected, definitely not the blunt trauma we'd see from an accident of this magnitude. We'd like to keep him a few more hours for observation, then he can go home."

Paul saw his wife hug the doctor through the hall window. Relief and almost desire flooded through him as she turned and slipped through the doorway. "You had a close call," Beth said, bringing Paul's hand to wipe the tears from her face. "I'm so lucky I didn't lose you."

"We're lucky," Paul said. "For a moment there, I thought I was dead." He almost told her about the strange visions he'd had, but Paul wasn't certain it was a dream. Was he really saved by aliens, or was it some strange reaction to trauma, like his life flashing before him as the car spun out of control? He didn't understand the mind, or how his subconscious might have tried protecting him from the harsh truth that he might die. Paul only knew he was alive through some inexplicable miracle.

"Hon, could you call the kids on the phone?" he asked, pointing to the nearby table. "I want them to hear me, to know I'm okay." The anticipation of his children's voices, the comfort of his wife's arms around him, both flooded his heart with a joy he hadn't felt in a long time.

A RUSTLE OF OWLS' WINGS
BY THOMAS SMITH

I hear them mostly at night. Mostly when I sleep.

Sleeping.

Waking.

Sometimes I'm not sure which is which.

But I know I hear them.

The owls.

I hear them mostly at night.

I first heard them when I was a child. I dreamed about the owls. The owls with the big eyes. Staring. Probing. Watching me. Evaluating. Questioning. Talking without making a sound. Never a sound.

I remember how I used to sit in the dark, afraid to go to sleep. That's when I would hear them. Them and their rustling blue-gray wings. They were all blue gray. The owls who spoke without speaking.

I remember I used to sit in the dark and wait for the sunlight. I prayed for the sunlight, but there was only darkness. Always too much darkness, and the big-eyed, soundless owls.

They asked me questions. Big questions. Questions I didn't understand then and don't fully understand now. Questions about where I came from and how I got here. I'm from here and I've always been here. I don't understand what they mean.

I've always been here.

And the owls have always been here. They have sailed the silver-black skies as long as there has been a sky to sail. Theirs is the whole universe, and they take wing at will and span time and space.

They say they are somewhat like us.

But they don't understand.

The first time I saw the owls clearly I was six. I had caught glimpses of them, seen them through the haze before that, but the Christmas I was six was the first time I really saw them.

We were at my grandma's house, had spent Christmas eve there; and though I loved Grandma Templeton better than almost anybody in the world, I couldn't help wondering how Santa Claus would ever find me. I hadn't told him in my letter that I was going to be gone. And once I realized my mistake I was afraid he would either leave all my toys at our house (and I would have to wait three days to see them), or find no one at home and just take them all back to the North Pole until next year.

But Mama said he would be able to find me. Santa has ways, she said. He always knows how to find you, wherever you are.

Somehow that thought didn't comfort me.

But Christmas eve turned into Christmas day, and he did indeed find me. Then Christmas day turned into Christmas night. And the house, so recently filled with light and the sound of carols, the smell of cider and evergreen boughs, turned dark and still and cold.

And they found me. They have their ways.

At first I sensed them more than saw them. I was asleep in the attic room of Grandma Templeton's big Victorian house. Over the years that huge room had been the lookout tower of a great castle, a rocket to the moon, Superman's Fortress of Solitude, and the site of a hundred other little boy fantasies. But that night those fantasies were lost forever. That night I felt something that shouldn't have been there—something that shouldn't be period—and shuddered myself awake from a sound sleep.

I rubbed my eyes and looked around the room. The forms around me took vague shape in the dim light of the moon. I saw the rocking chair in one corner and the faint image of the small Christmas tree against the far wall. I saw the dresser and the toy box, right where they had been for years. Everything exactly as it should be, exactly as it had always been, but nothing was right. The night was wrong. The lights were wrong. The light of the moon and the dust motes that swam down its lunar stream were wrong.

As I lay there listening with every nerve in my body wide open to the slightest sound, straining to catch even the most minute change in the air, the chair in the corner started to rock. Slowly at first, then faster. Back and forth and back and forth. *Creee, thumpa. Creee, thumpa.* Faster and faster and back and forth until I knew it just had to tumble over and slide across the room. And all the time the chair—possessed with a manic life of its own— was rocking, the lights on the tree began to glow. Not all at once, but gradually. Like some unseen hand was slowly turning up a rheostat.

Without warning, the electric train began to travel around the base of the Christmas tree. Smoke poured from the stack, the headlight flashed, pistons advanced and retreated while the wheels clattered on the track at breakneck speed. *Clackity, clackity, clackity, clack, clack. Clackity, clackity, clackity, clack, clack.* Train and tree, carefully unplugged hours before, glowed and clattered while the rocker in the corner continued its frenzied dance.

I wanted to scream. To call out for help. But I couldn't. I couldn't speak. I couldn't move. I could only watch in a combination of mute fascination and abject terror as the other occupants of the room, inanimate until a moment earlier, mutinied against the laws of science and sense.

Clackity, clackity, clackity, clack, clack. Creee, thumpa. Creee, thumpa. Clackity, clackity, clackity, thumpa. Clackity, clackity, creee, thumpa.

I wondered why nobody heard. Wondered why my rescuers weren't already running up the stairs, rushing to pull me from the confines of my animated prison and rush me to safety. I looked down and willed my legs to move, to kick away the covers and carry me to safety, but they wouldn't move. They were as useless as if I had been paralyzed since birth.

My chest and throat burned with the effort of trying to make myself heard. A great internal pressure pushed against my rib cage, and I felt my lungs would burst any second.

You have nothing to fear from us.

The voice came from all around me.

You are safe.

More a thought than an actual voice. I didn't hear it so much as I was aware of it. Like someone else was thinking my thoughts for me. I tried my legs again without success.

Why do you struggle?

Even then the grand absurdity of the question was laughable, not that I felt the least bit like laughing then, or now. How could they not know I was terrified? Couldn't they understand I was just a little boy? And even though I tried to make the questions come out, tried to make them go away, the sensual onslaught continued.

The questions continued as did the reassurances. But I didn't want reassurance. I wanted them out of my room and out of my head. I wanted to wake up and find the train still, the tree dark, and the rocker sitting quietly in its place. But the train still whizzed around the track, teetering and smoking on every curve, the tree flashed in time to the thrumming of the train, and the already frenzied chair had increased its tempo.

Then, as quickly as it started, it stopped. Train, chair, and tree all ceased their macabre rondelet and went back to their previous inanimate existence as if nothing out of the ordinary had happened. In less than an instant they went from whirling dervish to deadly still.

Why are you afraid?

The large black eyes of the one speaking—I don't know how I knew that was the one, I just knew—were the last thing I saw before I passed out. The pressure in my lungs and the pressure in my mind needed a safety valve and unconsciousness was blissful release.

The rest of my memory of that night comes in bits and pieces. Flashes of coherence in the midst of insanity. I can remember a large gray room with a table or stretcher or some such thing in the middle of it. The owls were all standing around the table. Standing and staring. Watching. And the walls; the walls seemed to be moving in and out ever so slightly. I felt like I was inside something alive. Something breathing. In and out. In and out. Rippling and flexing. In and out.

All the while there were voices. The whole time I drifted between consciousness and oblivion, there were the constant voices. Voices that made no sound.

What are you?

. . . walls moving . . . breathing.

We must see . . .

eyes . . .

is in place and intact . . .

voices with no sound, pain. I need . . .

It is time to return . . .

The next morning found me in bed, Roy Rogers pajamas and bed covers rumpled, but no more than usual. I didn't remember anything beyond the time I first crawled into bed. I was nauseous until about noon and didn't have much to say—too much excitement had been Grandma Templeton's diagnosis—but there was no memory of anything other than going to sleep. Mama and Daddy packed up the car, and I packed up my memories. Buried them deep.

Thirty years deep.

I know I have seen the owls since then. I remember bits and pieces. I remember seeing the lights. And though I've never been to Texas, I can tell you what the Corpus Christi skyline looks like reflected in the water.

I remember vast expanses of black dotted with silver-white light.

I've been studying the owls. Learning what I can without having too many people look at me like I have a third eye.

I used to be afraid of the owls. Afraid of what they might do to me . . .

the pain

Afraid of what they have to say. But I'm not so afraid any more. Not so much. Because I've found others like me. Others who have seen things. Others who have feelings they can't explain and time for which they can't account. They haven't all seen owls—some can't remember just what it was they have seen—but they remember the eyes.

And together we remember bits and pieces. Some have seen the room with the table, and some have seen other things.

But we all remember the eyes.

And we all remember what it was like trying to explain to everybody we care about that our lives didn't seem to be our own anymore. We remember the eyes of our wives and husbands; the faces of our children. That's another memory we'd like to forget.

But even those things don't seem so important any more. Not now. Because for some reason the memories of the owls have been coming in larger bits and pieces. And when I wake up fast enough, or write my thoughts down quick enough, I can make out more of what the owls were saying. Are saying. Not all of it, but more than before.

I've always been here. And they've always been here. The owls with the big black eyes. Eyes that watch and probe. Eyes as black as a bottomless pit.

But I've started to remember. And I've seen their pitch-black eyes up close. Their empty, haunting eyes. Empty, but not vacant. Not by a long shot. The owls know things. There is the wisdom of the ages in those eyes.

They have always been here. They have always been everywhere. This universe is their domain.

Every universe their domain.

And they are coming back. Soon. I don't know how I know, but I know it as sure as I know my own name. And this time when they come, I am going to remember it all. The sights, the sounds, the smells. I'm going to remember every last detail.

They have been back many times, but I wasn't ready. They said so. They told me in my head and in my heart. But this time I am ready.

And I know they're coming back.

The sun is setting. Night is falling. And before long, they'll come for me. The blue-gray owls who speak without speaking.

I am going to sail the boundless reaches of time and space. The universe will be mine.

And just before we make the last transition and I stand poised on the edge of infinity, I am going to look back on who and what I was before the owls came. I am going to watch as the memory fades into the distance, and listen with a new understanding. And I am going to sail the silver-black sky as long as there is a sky to sail.

I will not be back.

AUTHOR BIOGRAPHIES

J. G. BALLARD is a novelist, essayist, and short story writer. He is the author of numerous books, including *Empire of the Sun*, the underground classic *Crash*, and *The Kindness of Women*. Revered as one of the most important fiction writers to address the consequences of twentieth-century technology, his books have won the Guardian Fiction Prize, the James Tait Black Memorial Prize, and the Commonwealth Writers Prize, and have been short-listed for the Booker Prize for Fiction and the Whitbread Novel Award. His latest novel is *Millennium People*. He lives in Middlesex, England.

PHILIP K. DICK (1928–1982) was born in Chicago and lived most of his life in California. He briefly attended the University of California, Berkeley, but dropped out before completing any classes. In 1952, he began writing professionally, going on to publish forty-four novels, including *Martian Time-Slip*, *A Scanner Darkly*, and *Ubik*, and fourteen short story collections. He won the 1963 Hugo Award for Best Novel for *The Man in the High Castle* and the 1975 John W. Campbell Memorial Award for Best Novel of the Year for *Flow My Tears, the Policeman Said*. Many blockbuster Hollywood films have been based on his works, among them *The Minority Report*, *Total Recall*, and *Blade Runner*.

NINA KIRIKI HOFFMAN has published more than two hundred short stories, as well as novels, juvenile series, and media tie-in books. She is the recipient of the Bram Stoker Award and has been a finalist for the Nebula, the World Fantasy, the Surgeon, and the Endeavor awards. Her novels include The Thread That Binds the Bones, The Silent Strength of Stones, A Red Heart of Memories, Past the Size of Dreaming, and A Fistful of Sky. Her most recent books include a young adult fantasy novel, A Stir of Bones, and her third short story collection, Time Travelers, Ghosts, and Other Visitors. She lives in Eugene, Oregon.

STEPHEN KING was born in Portland, Maine, in 1947. He made his first professional short story sale in 1967 to Startling Mystery Stories. In the fall of 1973, he began teaching high school English classes at Hampden Academy, the public high school in Hampden, Maine. Writing in the evenings and on the weekends, he continued to produce short stories and to work on novels. In the spring of 1973, Doubleday & Co. accepted the novel Carrie for publication, providing him the means to leave teaching and write full-time. He has since published over forty books and has become one of the world's most successful writers. Mr. King lives in Maine and Florida with his wife, novelist Tabitha King.

DAMON KNIGHT (1922–2002) was an esteemed critic, writer, and anthology editor. A science fiction fan from an early age, in his teens he traveled from his home in Oregon to New York, where he became part of the Futurians, a group of writers that included, among others, the young Frederik Pohl and Isaac Asimov. During the 1950s and 1960s he wrote many short stories, including "To Serve Man," which was memorably adapted for the Twilight Zone television series. His novels include A for Anything and Humpty Dumpty: An Oval. Mr. Knight won a Pilgrim Award from the Science Fiction Research Association in 1975 and a Grand Master Award from the Science Fiction Writers of America in 1995.

KATHERINE MACLEAN was one of the first published female science fiction writers. Her first story, "Defense Mechanism," appeared in *Astounding Science Fiction* in 1949. Ms. MacLean's short stories have been collected in *The Diploids* and *The Trouble with You Earth People*. Her novels include *Cosmic Checkmate*, *Missing Man*, and *Dark Wing*. In 2002, the Science Fiction and Fantasy Writers of America honored her as Author Emeritus at their annual Nebula Awards banquet. She lives in Maine.

RAY NELSON is a science fiction author and cartoonist, well known for his artwork from the Golden Age of Science Fiction in the 1940s and 1950s, up until the present day. In addition to having written nine novels and numerous short stories, Mr. Nelson is the inventor of the propeller beanie. His short story "Eight O'Clock in the Morning" was made into the cult movie classic *They Live*, directed by John Carpenter. He lives in Northern California.

KRISTINE KATHRYN RUSCH writes novels under many names (including her own), but her first love is short stories. In 2004, she was nominated for mystery's prestigious Edgar Award for Best Short Story of the Year. Her science fiction stories have won the Hugo, the Locus Award, the Asimov's Readers Choice Award, and many others. She has a short story in two recent "year's best" volumes: *The Year's Best Science Fiction 2004*, edited by Gardner Dozois, and *The Year's Best Crime and Suspense Stories 2004*, edited by Ed Gorman. She was also one of twenty-six authors chosen for the anthology *One Hundred Years of Crime Stories by Women*, edited by Elizabeth George. Ms. Rusch's most recent science fiction novel is *Buried Deep*. Her three short fiction collections are still in print as well. She lives on the Oregon Coast.

PETER SCHWEIGHOFER lives in Northern Virginia, where he works as a freelance writer, editor, and game designer. He has written material for adventure role-playing games, published several science fiction and historical fantasy stories, edited two *Star Wars* short story anthologies for Bantam Spectra, and reported for a newspaper in Connecticut.

THOMAS SMITH is a short story writer, playwright, reporter, essayist, and television producer. He has also worked as a professional magician and written jokes for comedian Joan Rivers. His writing has appeared in many books, magazines, and anthologies, including *Gothic Ghosts, Horrors! 365 Scary Stories, Haunts* magazine, and *Quietly Now: A Tribute to Charles L. Grant*. He divides his time between Raleigh and Topsail Island, North Carolina.

WILLIAM TENN is the pen name of Philip Klass, who was born in London in 1920. He began writing in 1945 after being discharged from the Army, and his first story, "Alexander the Bait," was published a year later. His stories and articles have been widely anthologized, a number of them in "year's best" collections. In 1999, the Science Fiction and Fantasy Writers of America honored him as Author Emeritus at their annual Nebula Awards banquet. Mr. Tenn's short fiction was recently collected by NESFA Press and published in two volumes as *Immodest Proposals* and *Here Comes Civilization*. He lives in Pennsylvania.

JAMES TIPTREE JR. (1915–1987) was the pseudonym of Nebula and Hugo award–winning science fiction author Alice Sheldon. Celebrated for breaking down the barriers between perceived "male writing" and "female writing" (it was not publicly known until 1976 that she was a woman), her short story collections include *Her Smoke Rose Up Forever, Ten Thousand Light Years from Home, Warm Worlds and Otherwise*, and *Star Songs of an Old Primate*. Since 1991, an award in Tiptree's name has honored science fiction and fantasy writing that explores and expands gender roles.

HOWARD WALDROP was born in Mississippi and has lived most of his life in Texas. His iconoclastic fiction has won both the World Fantasy Award and the Nebula Award and has been nominated for the Hugo multiple times. He is the author of several story collections, including *Howard Who?, All About Strange Monsters of the Recent Past*, and *Night of the Cooters*, as well as the novels *The Texas-Israeli War* (in collaboration with Jake Saunders), *Them Bones*, and *A Dozen Tough Jobs*. Subterranean Press published his most recent story collection, *Heart of Whiteness*, as a limited edition in 2004.

ACKNOWLEDGMENTS

Thanks to Dave Barrett, Jodi Davis, Megan Flautt, Amy Rennert, Gordon Van Gelder, and to the denizens of Borderlands Books, The Other Change of Hobbit Science Fiction and Fantasy Bookstore, and Readerville.com for their kind assistance and support. Grateful acknowledgment is made for permission to reprint from the following material: "I Am the Doorway" by Stephen King. First appeared in *Cavalier*, March 1971. Reprinted with permission of the author. "Project: Earth" by Philip K. Dick. First appeared in *Imagination*, December 1953. Now appears in *Volume Two: The Collected Works of Philip K. Dick*, Underwood-Miller, 1987. Copyright © renewed 1987 by The Estate of Philip K. Dick. Reprinted by permission of the author's estate and the estate's agents, Scovil Chichak Galen Literary Agency, Inc. "Radiance" by Nina Kiriki Hoffman. Copyright © 1999 by Nina Kiriki Hoffman. First published in *Whitley Strieber's Aliens*, Pocket Star Books, 1999. Reprinted with permission of the author. "The Venus Hunters" by J. G. Ballard. Copyright © 1967, 1995 by J. G. Ballard. Reprinted with permission of the author and the author's agent, Robin Straus Agency, Inc. "The One That Got Away" by Kristine Kathryn Rusch. Copyright © 1998 by Kristine Kathryn Rusch. First published in *The UFO Files*, DAW Books, 1998. Reprinted with the permission of the author. "To Serve Man" by Damon Knight. Copyright © 1950 by Galaxy Publishing Corporation. Reprinted with permission of Kate Wilhelm.